THE ART OF THE DEVIL

Only one man stands in the way of a plot to murder President Eisenhower in this riveting historical thriller.

In 1955, one woman holds the key to America's future: a ruthless and beautiful ex-Nazi assassin, posing as a maid inside President Eisenhower's isolated Gettysburg estate. One man stands in her way: a disgraced Secret Service agent, driven from active duty by battle fatigue, now the unlikely inheritor of a slim chance to avert disaster.

THE ART OF THE DEVIL

John Altman

Severn House Large Print
London & New York

This first large print edition published 2014
in Great Britain and the USA by
SEVERN HOUSE PUBLISHERS LTD of
19 Cedar Road, Sutton, Surrey, England, SM2 5DA.
First world regular print edition published 2014 by
Severn House Publishers Ltd., London and New York.

British Library Cataloguing in Publication Data

Altman, John, 1969- author.
  The art of the devil.
  1. Female assassins--Fiction. 2. United States--Politics
  and government--1953-1961--Fiction. 3. Eisenhower, Dwight
  D. (Dwight David), 1890-1969--Fiction. 4. Suspense
  fiction. 5. Large type books.
  I. Title
  813.6-dc23

  ISBN-13: 9780727897541

Severn House Publishers support the Forest Stewardship Council™
[FSC™], the leading international forest certification organisation. All
our titles that are printed on FSC certified paper carry the FSC logo.

Printed and bound in Great Britain by
T J International, Padstow, Cornwall.

To Sima

ACKNOWLEDGEMENTS

Thanks to Robert Altman, Richard Curtis, Leslie Silbert, Steve Sims, and Kate Lyall Grant and Rachel Simpson Hutchens at Severn House.

PROLOGUE

COLUMBIA ISLAND, WASHINGTON DC:
NOVEMBER 11, 1955
The sniper faced south.

To his left, the Potomac sparkled cheerfully beneath the midday sun. To his right, a low hill provided shelter from a gentle breeze. Wide fragrant pines cast deep shadows. Dense tangles of brush and bramble concealed his prone six-foot four-inch frame from head to toe.

Clear weather. Soft wind. Range of just one hundred yards. He had made tougher shots hung over and half-asleep. Thickly wooded slopes rolled away in every direction; the trees would offer cover for his escape. The nearest hiking path was fifty yards downhill and clearly within view. He would see anyone approaching before they saw him. The first effort, six weeks ago, had failed ... but this time, he thought, success was guaranteed.

He checked his wristwatch. The last round of security before the moment of truth was past due. Thirty seconds later, he saw them: two men of about the sniper's own age, wearing charcoal suits and navy ties, hatless, striding up the hiking path in lockstep. He covered the rifle's barrel with his black-clad body, pulled a dark watchcap lower around his ears, hunched down behind a parapet of low rocks. Averting his eyes to hide the whites, he counted mechanically to thirty. When he looked up again, the patrol had passed.

Moving the gun into position, he lowered his eye to the scope. Segmented by cross hairs, the stretch of George Washington Memorial Parkway he had chosen swam into focus. Already calm and regular, his breathing became even deeper, even slower. His left hand steadied the forestock of the M1903A4 Springfield rifle. His right index finger worked lightly against the trigger, guaranteeing free movement. Cheek touched thumb, making his body into a tripod that would absorb recoil. If the first cold shot failed, he would have time for a second, perhaps even a third. This same rifle had served him well during the Battle of Anzio; through its scope, he had targeted many a jackbooted Nazi commander. Now, ironically, he would use the gun against the very man who had ultimately dealt Hitler's minions a death blow.

He went through a final checklist. Escape routes and line of fire remained unobstructed. A yellow leaf tumbling straight down confirmed that the breeze remained negligible. This time, he thought again, success was guaranteed.

In the next instant, the hum of approaching engines reached his ears.

The leading edge of the motorcade eased into view. Sunlight heliographed off polished fenders and white helmets. Out front rode an unmarked pilot vehicle, followed by a phalanx of motorcycles with sidecars. The sniper moved the cross

10

hairs down the line, seeking his target. He felt extraordinarily calm.

A Chrysler sedan followed the motorcycles: glistening black, covered by a bullet-proofed dark bubble-top. Fluttering American flags and a presidential seal on the front grille identified this as Eisenhower's vehicle – but Ike had never before ridden in a covered car.

The sniper's calm faltered, dissolved.

Beneath his breath, he cursed bitterly. What had happened to the brave soldier who had been chosen over Marshall, against all odds, to serve as the architect of D-Day? That man would never have cringed in a closed car as he made his triumphant return to Washington after a hospital stay in Denver. Ike the Soldier, insisting on projecting strength, health, and authority, would have shown himself to the cheering crowd of civilians and servicemen awaiting him just over the bridge. But this was the President's vehicle, beyond doubt; Ike's jovial, balding countenance was visible through a sliver of open window. Thanks to the sniper's elevation, however, the shot was impossible.

Cursing again, he took his eye from the scope.

Seconds later, the pilot car achieved Arlington Memorial Bridge. Scowling, the sniper gained his feet. Taking a plaid handkerchief from a pocket, he wiped his lips compulsively. Already his frustration was fading, replaced by prickly apprehension. Did the bubble-top indicate that the previous failure had put Eisenhower on his guard?

Grimly, he spent a last moment gazing down at

11

the parkway. Then he used a foot to scatter some brush, covering the traces he'd left in the fallen pine needles. He turned, strapping the rifle over one shoulder, and vanished into the trees, leaving only a vague depression hidden beneath the bramble to show that he had ever been there at all.

PART ONE

Whatever America hopes to bring to pass in the world must first come to pass in the heart of America.

Dwight D. Eisenhower

ONE

THE TREASURY BUILDING,
WASHINGTON DC: NOVEMBER 11
Approaching the checkpoint, Francis Isherwood
scanned for a familiar face.

The lobby bustled with men wearing charcoal
suits and navy ties – but he recognized nobody.
Nor, after his long absence from Treasury, did
the guards recognize him. He was not spared a
thorough and humiliating search. As rude hands
patted down his inseams, hips, and ribcage,
noses wrinkled disapprovingly at the smell of
whiskey. Straightening with shabby pride, Isherwood made no apology.

Waved through, he was left to readjust his
clothes and his dignity by himself. The office he
was seeking was farther back on the first floor,
behind a brass plaque reading EMIL SPOONER,
CHIEF OF THE SECRET SERVICE. Reaching
for the knob, Isherwood caught a flash of his
own hazy reflection in the brass plaque. The unexpected glimpse made him flinch. *How the
mighty have fallen.*

He entered a grand reception area elegantly
appointed with cream-colored wallpaper and
antique furniture. Porticoed windows faced west,
affording a picture-postcard view of the White

15

House. Seated behind a desk, the Chief's personal secretary – a hulking man with broad shoulders, flat-top haircut, and affable blue eyes – said, without looking up, 'Be right with you.'

'Take your time, Max.'

Raising his eyes, Max Whitman grinned. Although he had occupied this post for as long as Isherwood could remember, Whitman never seemed to age. 'Ish. Lookin' good.'

Isherwood tipped his hat smartly. 'The Chief's expecting me...?'

'Sure. Go on in.'

The Chief's office was drab and faded, and more modest than the reception area, reflecting Emil Spooner's lack of concern for appearances. Muted oil portraits of his predecessors lined the walls. The sole personal touch was an autographed photograph mounted behind the desk, depicting Joe DiMaggio with one arm slung companionably around the Chief's shoulders.

Cadaverously thin, five-feet six-inches tall, gray of hair and pallor, Chief Emil Spooner appeared significantly older than his personal secretary, although in fact the men had grown up together, graduating from the same high school class. Half-rising from his chair, he gestured Isherwood into a seat. Settling down again, he spent a moment regarding his visitor. A complex mixture of expressions played across his face: curiosity, concern, pity ... and something else, which Isherwood couldn't quite put his finger on.

'Thanks for coming,' Spooner said at last. 'How's Evy?'

'Hanging in there.' No need to get into the gory details.

'Please send her my love.'

'Sure thing. How's Claire?'

'Little bit at loose ends, with the kids out of the house. But making do.'

'Give her my best.'

'She'll appreciate that.'

A pause ensued, during which Isherwood absorbed the office more thoroughly. Everything seemed the same, down to the stale odor of cigarette smoke ground into the carpet and worn curtains. At length he returned his attention to Spooner. He was starting to think that the man had gotten lost wool-gathering when the Chief suddenly said, 'Our conversation today doesn't leave this office, Ish. All right?'

Cautiously, Isherwood nodded.

'Couple hours ago, a call came in. I probably wouldn't have given it a second thought – you know how many cranks we get – but this was a more reputable source than usual, a professional newsman. But *still*, I wouldn't have given it a second thought ... if I hadn't already been thinking.'

Another pause, longer than the first. The silence drew out conspicuously. From his desk the Chief produced a pack of Winstons, which he set down unopened.

'Thinking,' Isherwood prodded at last.

The elder man furrowed his brow. 'Six weeks ago, as you may recall, the President suffered a heart attack.'

Isherwood grunted. Eisenhower had experienced chest pains while playing golf in Colorado. Admitted by his personal physician to Fitzsimons Army Hospital in Denver, the President had languished in bed for a month and a half as the nation held its collective breath. At last he had been pronounced well enough to be moved, and just that morning had flown back east, to complete his recuperation at his Gettysburg farm after a brief stopover in Washington.

'Does it strike you as strange?' From another drawer the Chief took out a crystal ashtray, which he set on the desk beside the pack of cigarettes. 'Dwight D. Eisenhower – the poster boy for military fitness – hit in his prime by a heart attack, without a single warning sign?'

Isherwood only shrugged.

A shadow of disapprobation crossed the Chief's face. 'Well,' he said after a moment, 'it struck *me* as strange. So I had a private conversation with Howard Snyder. He threw me a lot of medical jargon—' He glanced down at a notepad on the blotter. 'The President suffered a "coronary thrombosis, diagnosis confirmed by electrocardiograph showing QS deformity with marked RS-T segment elevation", et cetera, and so on. But the upshot's simple enough: the heart attack came out of nowhere. Sometimes, of course, that's how heart disease works. But get this: Ike has slightly elevated blood pressure, monitored daily. In fact, Doc Snyder took readings the very day of the heart attack. What do think he found?'

'A healthy man,' Isherwood ventured.

'Bingo. The President's pulse was sixty beats per minute, his blood pressure one-forty over

18

eighty. And yet just a few hours later, on the eighth hole at the Cherry Hills Country Club, *bam*, a massive coronary.' Spooner lit a cigarette and deposited the match carefully in the ashtray. 'When I pressed for details, everything followed the same lines. There were no warning signs, no evidence of heart disease, and no family history. Ike watches his diet, quit smoking years ago, and takes regular exercise ... and yet, out of left field...' He raised one eyebrow suggestively.

'Where did he eat that day?'

'Ah! Great minds think alike, old buddy. The President's breakfast that day was taken at Mamie's childhood home, on Lafayette Street in Denver. His lunch was taken at the golf club: a hamburger with Bermuda onions. In my opinion – and I might sound paranoid, but that's an occupational hazard – it's as likely that he ingested something toxic with that hamburger, which may have *looked* like a heart attack, as this "coronary thrombosis" out of nowhere. No lack of poisons, you know, that mimic the symptoms. And many denature quickly enough to leave no trace.'

Isherwood nodded again.

'So I did a little more digging. Pulled a file, and found out that an underchef in that golf club was considered a potential security risk ... a known sodomite, open to blackmail. Days when Eisenhower visited the club, this fellow wasn't allowed to work. But he worked the day *before* Eisenhower's heart attack. And the day after, he disappeared into thin air. Puff, no more poof.' Spooner ground out his cigarette, barely smoked. 'I've got an all-points out, but so far, nothing. So

19

I was already thinking something smelled rotten, you can see, when we got this call couple hours ago. This NBC cameraman – Charlie Morgan is the name – was riding in the motorcade today behind Ike. And he thought he saw a glint on a rise above the George Washington Memorial Parkway. Now, here's the interesting thing about that: the President was supposed to be riding in an open car during the parade. Which would have meant easy pickings for a sniper. But thanks to doctor's orders, he was switched at the last second to a bubble-topped Chrysler.'

'I see where you're heading.'

'Sure. Let's say, just for the sake of argument, that the "heart attack" was actually an attempt on the President's life. If that failed, what would his enemies do next? I'll tell you what *I* would do: place a gunman on that very ridge. Take out the President during his homecoming parade. Between National Airport and Arlington Memorial Bridge, a sniper has a clear shot from short range, concealing cover from the trees, and escape routes in every direction. But Ike, against expectations, was riding in a closed car – second chance down the drain.'

'Mm.'

'Hell, Ish, I'll go you one better. If there *was* a sniper up in those hills, then he knew the exact time and route of the motorcade, and probably patrol schedules too – so we're talking about someone with connections on the inside. Someone who could have, say, blackmailed our sodomite at the golf club into forgetting to lock a back door the day before Eisenhower showed up.'

All at once, then, Isherwood understood why the Chief had called on him, of all people. Whatever else Francis Isherwood might be these days, he certainly wasn't on the inside.

'Go talk with the NBC cameraman,' the Chief urged. 'Check out the rise above the Parkway. Strictly on the QT, old buddy. Let me know what you find, and I'll take it from there – and I'll owe you one.'

Slowly, Isherwood nodded again.

CHARLOTTESVILLE, VIRGINIA

One hundred miles south-west of Washington, set far back from the road, protected by thickets of trees still holding on to the last of their leaves, the mansion seemed a relic of a bygone era – pre-war, and not either of the World Wars – with a granite colonnade framing an asymmetrical porch.

Passing through a tall gate, the Buick pulled up before the porch in the failing afternoon light. Unlimbering his six-foot four-inch frame from the car, Richard Hart handed his keys to a valet and then closed the distance to the mansion on foot. As he climbed the stairs, dark-suited body-guards lining the porch avoided his gaze, staring solemnly straight ahead.

Crossing the porch, Hart found himself re-membering from nowhere a long-ago fairground from his native Saint Clairsville, Ohio. The sum-mer air had smelled of corn dogs, cotton candy, and popcorn. An old gypsy fortune-teller had examined Hart's palm, *tsk*ed beneath her breath,

21

and predicted a short life. Hart hadn't thought about that for twenty years. But now he felt a whisper of foreboding, a clenching in his chest. The circumstances surrounding both failed attempts on the President had been beyond his control – but if the senator held him accountable, this might be the day that the prophecy finally came true. The fear was perverse – the senator would never discard him so carelessly – but undeniable, fluttering inside his sternum like a hummingbird.

Inside a vast foyer, he was met by a Negro butler wearing a crimson vest with buttons polished to a high shine. The butler led him down a hallway featuring tall arched windows, orchids in crystal vases, and alabaster busts on Grecian pediments: all clean, fluid lines, with every banister, door handle, and archway flowing sinuously into the next. At the end of the hall, French doors blocked by lush curtains opened into a study. The desk was an ocean-sized hunk of walnut, the fireplace brass-screened with instruments encased in platinum. Logs burning behind the screen hosted a small center of red-hot coal. The window, fashioned of stained glass, portrayed cubist kings, horses, and armored knights.

Upon Hart's entrance, Senator John Bolin stood from behind the desk. His silken white suit shimmered with the motion, rolling like water. Remote blue eyes flickered behind rimless spectacles. Thin lips fixed in a welcoming smile. The practiced smile and trustworthy spectacles belonged to a career politician. But the authoritative bearing and unmistakable air of power, thought Hart, belonged to a man more fundamentally born to lead: a general, a warlord, an emperor.

Bolin indicated a leather-upholstered chair before the fireplace. For a few moments, after Hart sat, the senator considered, stone-faced. Then he softened in a calculated way, designed to put company at ease – the same manner that had won him multiple terms of office and much fawning press.

'The President,' he said, 'has never before used a closed car. Our man on the inside should have given us warning. This was not your fault.'

The knot in Hart's chest loosened. The senator did not blame him; today would not be the day the fortune-teller's prediction came true, after all. 'What does it mean – the closed car?'

'Perhaps nothing.' Bolin adjusted his spectacles on the bridge of his aquiline nose. He put hands on hips, flaring out his white jacket, catching the faint firelight on a silver lining. His tendency to strike poses might make a cynic dismiss the man. But Hart knew better.

'The day was cold,' continued the senator after a moment. 'And his doctors believe he's recently suffered a heart attack. It may have been an ordinary precaution for his health.' He shrugged, took out a pack of Viceroys. For a moment before lighting a cigarette, he gazed broodingly into the middle distance. 'Or perhaps the effort in Denver has shown our hand. Have you ever read Emerson, Mister Hart?'

Richard Hart's formal education had ended

23

with high school. His real education had taken place in Salerno, and Lazio, and Anzio, and there had been no Emerson there. 'Sir?'

'"When you strike at a king, you must kill him."' Bolin lit his cigarette and then flicked the match negligently through the brass screen of the fireplace. 'But we have now struck twice without scoring a fatal blow. A wise man must realize that we are treading dangerous ground, indeed.'

'Yes, sir.'

'My associates will be within their rights, Mister Hart, to insist we try another approach.'

'Yes, sir.'

The senator turned to look out the window. In the expansive backyard an ashen moon was rising like a wraith above a forest of maple, elder, birch and walnut. 'Yet I think,' he said, 'that despite the setbacks, we still have reason for hope. *Bon courage*, Mister Hart. Get some rest. When I need you, I'll call.'

COLUMBIA ISLAND

Francis Isherwood stood on the shoulder of the George Washington Memorial Parkway, following the line of a man's arm.

He found himself looking at a thatch of pines perched on a hillside perhaps one hundred yards distant. A cool breeze moved the pine needles serenely. On his right, the Potomac stirred in time with the trees. On the road between park and river, vehicles whizzed past at reckless speeds.

'That rise yonder.' The NBC camera operator named Charlie Morgan was of average height and above-average weight, with thinning sandy hair, watchful green eyes, and a nascent double-chin. 'That's where I saw the glint. A sniper's scope,' he said with conviction. 'No doubt in my mind. I'm just glad you guys took me seriously enough to send someone out here.'

Isherwood didn't have the heart to tell the man that he had no real authority. Instead he said, 'No offense, friend. But what makes you think you can recognize a sniper's scope at one hundred yards?'

Charlie Morgan bristled. 'Eighty-two days in Okinawa,' he said. 'That's what, *friend*, thank you very much.'

Following a rough path up into the park, Isherwood encountered a few colorful autumn leaves and a handful of late-migrating birds; but for the most part, he saw only skeletal branches, deepening shadows, and bristling evergreens.

To reach the area indicated by Charlie Morgan, he had to go off-trail. Almost immediately, brambles scratched his hands, and a singlet of perspiration sprung up beneath his trench coat and threadbare blue suit. Emerging onto another crude path, he paused to wipe sour sweat from beneath his hat brim and fortify himself with a jolt from his flask.

Achieving the rise at last, he turned to look back at the vista spreading beneath him. The French called it *coup d'oeil*: the ability to take in a battlefield with a glance. After absorbing the lay of the land beneath the rising moon, he paced off a few wide circles, scowling down at a bed of

25

fallen pine needles and a low parapet of rocks. For several minutes he used a foot to shove aside dense tangles of brush, uncovering at length a roughly human-sized depression, which had kept its shape thanks to a gentle rise serving as a windbreak.

Lighting a cigarette with shaky hands, he kept looking around, seeking something innocent – a discarded bottle, a bracelet dropped by a couple of necking teenagers, a lost lipstick tube – to explain the glint reported by the newsman. The darkening night complicated his search. Using the flame of his Zippo, however, he pressed on until satisfied: there was nothing here except pine needles and dead leaves.

Knitting his brow, he brought the nub of the cigarette to his lips with trembling fingers.

Back in the Chief's office, sitting beneath the soft glow of an electric chandelier, he explained his findings. Overall, he concluded, the site would indeed have been ideal for a sniper whose target was traveling in a motorcade below, and in his opinion Charlie Morgan constituted a reliable witness. While the evidence was far from irrefutable, his mind had hardly been set at ease.

A brief, reflective quiet followed. Isherwood itched to reach for his flask; instead he reached for another cigarette, trying to steady his hands.

'Drinking much?' the Chief asked after a moment.

Isherwood started guiltily. He attempted – unsuccessfully – to cover his discomfort by snap-

ping open the Zippo. 'Here and there,' he allowed.

'Some men can handle drink.' The Chief's
gaze was direct and pitiless. 'But Ish: you're not
one of them.'

Blinking owlishly, Isherwood said nothing.

'Ike's scheduled to spend the next month and a
half at Gettysburg. If I get you onto that property,
can you stay sober – and keep an eye out –
quietly?'

'Yes, sir.'

'Don't answer so fast.' The Chief produced his
own cigarette, which he lit with damnably steady
hands. 'I can't afford to have a drunk stumbling
around out there. We're under specific orders
from the doctors not to rile the President during
his convalescence. He needs not only rest, but
relaxation: everything sunshine and roses. Moreover, we can't afford to stir up the hornet's nest.
If there *is* someone on the inside gunning for Ike,
we need information before we show our hand.
Keep a low profile and you can blend in with all
the other tag-alongs ... but not reeking of whiskey.'

'Yes, sir.'

'Go home, Ish. Dry out. Talk it over with the
little woman. If you still think you're the man for
the job, come back in the morning and we'll
talk.'

Isherwood was looking at a framed, gilt-edged
photograph on the desk. In the photograph, the
Chief's wife wore a wide-brimmed sun hat and a
huge smile. Isherwood could not remember the
last time his own wife had smiled so broadly – if

27

she ever had.

'Do right by this,' the Chief was saying, 'and it may be your ticket back to active duty. You're a good man. And everyone deserves a second chance now and then. Get it?'

Isherwood jerked his chin up and down. 'Got it,' he said, in a voice not quite steady, and reached for his fedora on the desk.

TWO

ANACOSTIA, WASHINGTON DC

Later that night Francis Isherwood sat in his study, stroking a tortoiseshell cat and restlessly quartering the bookcase with his gaze: Shakespeare, Milton, Mommsen, Housman; Shakespeare, Milton, Mommsen, Housman.

The stillness was palpable. For as long as Evy had been in the house, the constant babble of the TV from the parlor had put his nerves on edge – but the absence of sound proved even worse. His gaze ticked to a calendar on the desk. The day was Friday, the eleventh of November, 1955. Veteran's Day. Had Evy been here, he would have been trying to tune out the sound of Jack Bailey hamming it up with good-natured contestants on *Truth or Consequences*. Instead, he tried to tune out silence.

Eventually, he pushed out of his chair. Moving

closer to the bookcase, paced by cats winding between his ankles – with six cats in the house, four seemed to be underfoot at any given time – he ran his eyes along a line of photographs on a high shelf. Here was young Francis Isherwood, graduating from the University of Washington with a degree in criminal justice, his face shockingly boyish beneath a black mortar board. Here a slightly older Francis Isherwood posed as a state trooper, crisply outfitted in blue, half-sneering, proud to a fault. Here a still more mature variety wore a sober charcoal suit and navy tie, with a lugubrious expression to match. Appearances to the contrary, he thought, that had been the best year. He and Evy had been getting along like gangbusters, and at the tender age of twenty-seven, after less than eighteen months chasing counterfeiters, he had been assigned the plum role of presidential protection, safeguarding FDR himself.

His gaze ended up in a window, from which his reflection gazed stonily back. And here was Francis Isherwood at rock bottom: jobless, wifeless, and lacking now even the comfort of the bottle.

He returned to the desk, opened a drawer, removed a flask of Jack Daniels, and twisted off the cap.

In a fit of sudden fury, he flung the open flask across the room, whipsawing streams of whiskey onto ceiling and floor, sending cats scattering.

The flask landed on edge, pulsing liquor out onto the carpet. In a flash Isherwood was on his knees, cradling it like a wounded child. Too late;

the contents had emptied with devastating speed. But there were other hoards, of course – in the living room and the glove compartment of his Studebaker, and beneath their marriage bed and inside the toilet tank, and in the package store or the bar just down the block. And if all else failed, there was always Sterno beneath the sink, waiting patiently between cobwebbed bottles of Lysol and Gold Dust.

His hands were shaking worse than ever. God damn Evelyn, he thought. If he weakened and took a drink, the fault would be hers. He had done his best, but if his goddamned wife insisted on undermining him, his best would not be enough. Earlier that night he had placed a long-distance call to Boca Raton – damn the expense – where Evy was staying with her sister as she 'figured things out'. He'd heard the desperate note in his own voice as he'd told her about Spooner's call, begging her to come home and cover his back as he seized the long-awaited chance to redeem himself.

Would it have killed her to play along? He needed her faith, now more than ever. Yet faithless, worthless, nit-picking Evelyn had questioned him just when she should be reinforcing him. She had dared suggest that perhaps he *wouldn't* be able to stay dry—

Isherwood snorted aloud with enough vehemence to startle a nearby cat. He lit a cigarette which tasted like shit, dropped it into the puddle of whiskey on the carpet. After a moment he reached for another cigarette, which he snapped in two in the process of bringing to his mouth.

30

Cats spooling between his feet, he stumbled to the basement. Somehow he managed to descend the creaky steps in darkness without breaking his neck. At the flick of a switch, a single bare light-bulb mounted in the ceiling stuttered to life. The cellar was filled with accumulated junk, boxes and Mason jars, old magazines, dusty books, pottery and flowerpots and piping. After a momentary hesitation, he pressed forward. Silt and cobwebs smothered the clutter; his nose tickled, his eyes watered.

It took almost twenty minutes to find the box he was seeking. One by one, then, he removed photograph albums from the carton, considering them querulously in the dim light. Finding the album he wanted, he prevaricated briefly before opening it. Good memories could be the most painful of all. But this was why he was here. He wanted to remember.

Evy in her youth had been slim and dark and striking. In snapshots taken with a Kodak Brownie, the earliest days of their courtship played out: Evy posing before the Jefferson Memorial during the Cherry Blossom Festival, kicking up one playful heel; Evy sipping a root beer at the A&W in the Palisades. Then a trip to New York: Evy boarding the Cyclone at Coney Island, looking nervous (she had called it a death trap); Evy standing beside Isherwood, holding his hand, before the Statue of Liberty. He remembered kissing her, that evening, hard enough to feel the shape of her jaw. Everything had been perfect, or as close to perfect as real life allowed. And then had come the war...

31

After VE Day he had come home to a nation – and a woman – eager to throw a victory parade, award a medal, and move blithely ahead into a stainless-steel future. His wife's head had been filled with Doris Day and Pat Boone, Norman Rockwell and *Father Knows Best*. She had proudly showed him her new Frigidaire, stocked with iceberg lettuce which could last for weeks without spoiling. She had exhibited even less interest in hearing about the war than he had shown in telling about it ... and that was saying something.

Falling back onto his haunches, he sighed.

After a few moments, he stood; his knees popped like gunshots. Loading the memorabilia back into the box, he closed the flaps and then pushed the carton all the way into a corner, beneath cobwebs, into shadow.

EAST OF GUILFORD, PENNSYLVANIA: NOVEMBER 12

The train rocked gently across a landscape dotted with ponds, barns, tumbledown fences and weathered silos.

Inside a passenger car, Barbara Cameron sat ignoring the book in her lap, stealing glances at the girl sitting just across the aisle. The girl held a copy of *Confidential* magazine – the September issue, which had been one for the history books, revealing 'The Real Reason for Marilyn Monroe's Divorce' and 'The Astor Testimony The Judge Suppressed' and, juiciest of all, 'The LowDown on That 'Disorderly Conduct' Charge Against Tab Hunter'.

Of course, respectable people only read gossip rags behind closed doors. But this girl was perusing the magazine quite openly, without shame. Stealing another look, Barbara decided that *girl* wasn't quite the right word. This was a young woman, several years older than Barbara herself, wearing a stylish sapphire angora and an air of self-possession. Her blonde hairstyle was a fashionable beauty parlor wave – no home Toni perm here – which framed a pale, pretty, tranquil face.

After a few moments, Barbara summoned her courage and scooted a few inches closer to the aisle. 'That's a good article,' she said. 'I read it a million times. I practically memorized it.'

Looking up, the blonde smiled politely.

'"It all started with a vice cop who was drifting in and out of Hollywood's queer bars on the afternoon of October fourteenth,"' Barbara recited, '"looking and listening for tips on the newest notions of the limp-wristed lads. The deputy struck up a conversation with a couple of lispers who happily prattled that they were set for a big binge that very evening..."'

The blonde laughed. 'You've got some memory.'

Barbara shrugged. 'It's funny: if you're interested in something, I find, you can learn it without even trying. But math? Forget it. My name's Barbara Cameron, by the way.' After allowing a tiny pause, during which the young woman might have volunteered her own name, Barbara charged on. 'Where are you heading? I'm going to visit my sister in Guilford. I go every Saturday: my day off.'

'Isn't that funny! I'm going to Guilford, too.'

'Really! What for?'

'My husband's a pastor. They've offered him a position with the church. He asked me to come take a look around – you know, see what's what.'

'Well, you'll absolutely love it. Guilford's charming.'

'Oh, I hope so.'

'I know so.' The blare of the train's whistle broke the morning quiet. 'You can see for yourself; we're here.'

Together they rose, holding onto seat backs as a conductor passed through the car. Moments later, they stepped out onto a deserted platform. On this sleepy Saturday morning, the small town sprawling on the other side of a parking lot beneath a still-kindly November sun appeared uninhabited, with only the church steeple visible above the trees. The wind gusted, carrying scents of compost and distant burning leaves. Moving down the platform they passed a sign announcing GUILFORD: POPULATION 320.

The whistle blew again; doors closed, steam vented, and gears engaged. As the train pulled away, Barbara led the way off the platform, down a shallow staircase. 'Say, would you care to join us for lunch? I'm sure my sister would love a chance to tell you about the town. She's Guilford to the core: born and raised.'

'Oh, I wouldn't want to put her out.'

'No trouble at all, I'm sure.'

'That's so sweet of you. If you're really sure it's no trouble...' Crossing the empty parking lot, the blonde suddenly stopped, taking a pack of Luckies from her purse. 'Would you happen to have a light?'

Barbara stopped beside her, reached into her own Bakelite handbag.

'I don't know where my mind is,' the blonde added apologetically. 'I have plenty of cigarettes, but no matches.'

'Well, I know just how it is.' Absorbed in her handbag, Barbara paid no attention as the blonde stole behind her. 'Sometimes I can't even—'

The garrote slipped over her throat and drew taut.

A truncated gasp; the Bakelite handbag tumbled to the parking lot. Elisabeth threw her weight back, pulling. For the better part of a minute the two figures remained almost motionless, straining against each other as two pairs of hands clutched at the garrote.

At last Barbara Cameron went limp. But Elisabeth kept up the pressure for another full minute, just to be certain. Finally satisfied, she lowered the body onto the macadam, breathing hard. Forearms trembling, she checked for a pulse. Then she got her hands beneath the dead girl's arms and dragged the corpse toward a nearby shaded side street, where a two-door Ford sedan was parked with gardening implements waiting in the trunk.

THE TREASURY BUILDING

Behind his desk, the Chief no longer bothered to half-rise upon Isherwood's entrance; only his brow climbed.

35

For a long moment, he surveyed his agent in silence. Then he said, 'Sit down, Ish.'

Isherwood obeyed. A shaft of mid-morning sunlight streaming through the window made him wince. His brain throbbed; his joints felt filled with crushed glass. He could not bring himself to meet the Chief's eyes. Yet somehow he got a cigarette into his mouth without breaking it, and then held still enough to let the Chief light it for him.

'Dry?' the Chief asked.

'As a bone.'

'Can you keep it up?'

Isherwood grinned rakishly. 'No sweat.'

'Listen.' The Chief set his elbows on the desk, faced Isherwood directly. 'You're a good man, Ish. Otherwise we wouldn't be having this conversation. But that doesn't mean you won't be held accountable. If I had my druthers, you'd stay dry for a month before we try this. But we don't have that luxury.'

Isherwood said nothing.

'Agents at Gettysburg won't know your real reason for being there – we'll imply I'm just testing the waters before returning you to active duty – but they can still report back to me. If you take a drink, I'll hear about it.' A calculated pause. 'Also: you'll meet with Max in person, couple times a week, to keep me apprised of your progress.'

Isherwood managed not to stiffen. He nodded brusquely.

'One more thing.' The Chief pooched out his lips, choosing his words carefully. 'There's no lack of men in this country today sitting just where you are now – dying for a drink and trying to get the hell past whatever happened over there. There's no shame in it.'

Silence.

For a final moment, the Chief seemed to weigh something. Then he gave a tepid smile. Opening a drawer, he produced a holstered gun and a black billfold. 'Consider yourself back in service, Mister Isherwood – on a provisional basis. I'll call ahead; they'll make room for you on the farm. Anyone gives you trouble, tell them to talk to me. Keep your eyes open and poke around a little. But remember: Ike's not to be riled, and the hornet's nest's not to be stirred.'

For the first time since entering the office, Isherwood met the man's gaze. 'You won't be sorry,' he said.

'I hope not.' The Chief's smile turned wry. 'Half of me thinks this is a waste of time. But watch the President, Ish. And watch his watchmen even closer. If you suspect anybody – even if all you've got is a feeling – tell Max.'

'Got it.'

'Run along, then. As of now, you're back on the clock.'

On his way out, Isherwood passed Max Whitman at his desk. 'How'd it go?' Max asked.

'Not bad. You'll be seeing more of me, from now on.'

Max's affable blue eyes sparkled. 'Good deal, Ish. We missed you.'

Isherwood grunted, and let himself out.

* * *

He packed light, gave the liquor cabinet one last wistful glance, and tried Evy in Florida – no answer.

By late morning he was behind the wheel, with head pounding and temper short. City outskirts soon gave way to quaint towns – Main Streets, Woolworths, and penny candy shops – which gave way in turn to the foothills of the Alleghenies. A cup of coffee from a roadside stand helped clear his head for a moment; then the need for a drink returned, stronger than ever. Working down two aspirin, he pressed on. Tuning the dashboard radio, he found only static and the buzzing tone of a CONELRAD emergency broadcast test. He snapped off the radio.

During the years since he'd last driven out west, much had changed. Fields and mountains which recently had been unspoiled were now dotted with hotels and motor courts and rooming houses. On freshly-blacktopped highways, Corvairs and Oldsmobiles and Fords and Pontiacs all jockeyed ruthlessly for position, despite the perilously twisting mountain roads. Everyone seemed to be of the same mindset, moving into the future at top possible speed.

By three o'clock he was back on flatlands, nearing Gettysburg. He saw tar-papered cabins and gap-slatted privies, smelled sewage and acrid chickenshit. Only the immense natural beauty of the surrounding forest lightened the oppressive cloud of poverty. As he drew closer to town proper, however, the situation improved; he passed package stores and roadside stands, rooming houses and old factories, and eventually

38

Antebellums and Victorians and Cape Cods, cobblestones and white picket fences. The hamlet itself was small and charming, arranged around a central pavilion lined by restaurants and boutique shops.

Four miles west of town, he found the Eisenhower farm. Turning into the long driveway, he stepped out of the car at a gate, submitted to a search, relinquished his snub-nosed Colt – easy come, easy go – and watched as they picked over the bullet nose. After passing through two more guard posts, he turned at a fork and parked in a lot adjacent to the long, low Secret Service headquarters. Compared to glistening Packards and Chevrolets, his four-door Studebaker sedan seemed painfully humble. But the old trooper had served him well, although her looks were beginning to go, and he fully expected a few more years of good performance. He only hoped the same could be said of himself.

After using a clip to tame his twill necktie, he reached from habit for a hip flask which was no longer there. Then he saw in his side-view mirror two men, both of whom he recognized, crossing the small parking lot to meet him.

First was Bill Brennan, tall and broad-shouldered, too handsome and dapper for a cop, wearing a catty smirk beneath a pencil mustache. Next came Brennan's perpetual sidekick, a small, mean man named Bob Skinnerton. The duo had happened to be guarding Harry S. Truman during the assassination attempt of November first, 1950, when two Puerto Rican nationalists had descended with guns blazing on

39

Blair House, where Truman had been staying at the time. When the smoke had cleared, one would-be assassin and one Secret Service agent lay dead. Brennan and Skinnerton had been credited with keeping the President safe. From agents on the scene, however, Isherwood knew that their participation had been limited to waving Truman away from a window after the shooting had already finished. Nevertheless, both men had received wholly undeserved pro-motions. Meanwhile, Isherwood could think of half a dozen better men, just off the top of his head, who had not been so lucky, who toiled still in the lower reaches of the Service, warming desks or guarding foreign embassies.

'Look what the cat dragged in,' drawled Bren-nan as Isherwood stepped out into pale afternoon sunshine. 'Thought you got yourself decommis-sioned, soldier.'

'Consider me recommissioned,' Isherwood answered shortly. 'Chief said he'd call ahead.'

'He called.' Stout, florid, and balding, Skinner-ton offered a diminutive Jeff to his associate's Mutt. 'Said we should give you room to snoop around.'

Isherwood said nothing.

'Rapier wit, here,' said Brennan ironically. 'Skin, show him where he's staying. You'll notice you're next door, my friend. Not quite in the center of the action. Not like the old days, huh?'

Snickering, Agent Bob Skinnerton tried to lead Isherwood down a path leading toward a screen of Norway spruce – but Isherwood didn't follow.

Instead he put hands on hips, drew in a deep breath of fresh country air, and took in his surroundings methodically. The most effective way to apprehend a criminal, he had learned way back in Criminal Justice 101, was to put oneself as much as possible in the criminal's place...

Any incursion onto the property seemed doomed to failure. Three checkpoints interrupted the long driveway, tall fences surrounded the perimeter on all sides, and security details moved in circles within circles around rolling land interrupted only by a few buildings, some stables and corn cribs and chicken coops, and a single priapic grain silo. The Cherry Hills Country Club in Denver, where the President had eaten a possibly-tainted hamburger before suffering his heart attack, would have been considerably less secure – Isherwood could picture any number of people in that kitchen gaining momentary access to Ike's food – but here, the President had the home field advantage.

Briefly, he considered an armed sortie into the camp, from one of the roads or perhaps from the air, before rejecting the idea. Out here in the countryside, no unauthorized aircraft could reach the farm while retaining any element of surprise. And while an attack from the roads, with enough brute force behind it, might conceivably penetrate the fence and even the first perimeter, a dozen experienced agents bearing firearms would quickly swarm, neutralizing the intruder long before he could get near the President.

A stone's throw from the parking lot stood a modified Georgian farmhouse, white brick and fieldstone beneath a slate roof. North of the farmhouse was a helicopter landing pad. South, alongside the driveway, a low barn with tractors parked outside. East, a putting green, garden, greenhouse, small structure with Orientalist peaked roof – a tea house? – and the screen of Norway spruce. West, the long, low Secret Service headquarters, a small guest house, and farther out a skeet range, bare-treed orchard, equipment shed, and stable with attached horse pen. Then more rolling fields, terminating far away in a high fence. A public road passed within visible distance of the property on that side – but just barely; from there, range would be prohibitive for shooting.

'Who's in charge?' Isherwood asked Brennan.

'That would be me, pal.'

'Clue me in, then. Where does the President stay?'

He could see a drama play out in a twisting knot on Brennan's brow: the urge to withhold information fighting with the need to follow the Chief's orders. At last, with obvious reluctance, the agent indicated the Georgian farmhouse.

'Right here,' he said. 'This is Farm One. Over there, where you'll be staying, is Farm Two. That's the working part of the concern, with farmhands, domestic staff and such. But here on Farm One, personnel are strictly limited: just the President, the First Lady, her maid Rose, and the President's personal valet – Sergeant John Mooney. And in the guest house, six Secret Service agents, including Skin and myself, and Doctor Snyder. Nobody else. Mamie is determined to keep the place from becoming an office.'

'Who handles the President's food?'

'Don't worry your pretty little head, Ish. We've got everything under control.'

'Sure you do. But Chief told me you'd play along. Should we give him a call?'

Brennan sighed, shot Skinnerton a look. 'The President's food,' he answered wearily, 'is prepared by Sergeant Mooney – although sometimes Ike likes to make breakfast himself. Mamie's pretty much limited to warming up frozen dinners; you know, the kind in TV trays. Whatever touches the President's lips, though, Snyder supervises. He's prescribed a strict diet.'

'What's Eisenhower's daily schedule look like?'

'In a word, light. In Denver they didn't even let him out of bed. Here he's allowed to move around indoors, so long as he doesn't overdo it. The instant he shows the first sign of fatigue, they truck him right off to rest. He spends most of his time on the sun porch, answering correspondence and working on his paintings.'

'Where's this sun porch?'

Brennan waved toward the east side of the house. As Isherwood struck out, Brennan fell into step on his left, Skinnerton on his right. Hassled every step of the way by Tweedledee and Tweedledum, Isherwood thought he might have trouble working effectively. But one of these boys, he reminded himself, might even be the leak suspected by the Chief ... although personally, he didn't credit either with that much imagination.

Coming around the side of the house, he saw two men standing on a screened-in sun porch. With a small jolt of surprise, he recognized one as the President himself. Somewhat to his disappointment, the dashing figure that had become a familiar presence during the war appeared diminished by age and illness; the still-lean body, only a few pounds heavier than the day Ike had graduated from West Point, stood faintly stooped. The President wore a decidedly unflattering red bathrobe and used a golf club as a cane. Even from a small distance, however, the youthful gleam of humor and sardonic intelligence in the azure eyes was unmistakable.

After a heartbeat, Isherwood placed the other man as Major General Howard Snyder, Ike's long-time personal physician and friend. Although famed cardiologist Paul White had been the public face of the President's health care during the recent hospitalization – White, who liked the camera, had eagerly appeared before the press to discuss Eisenhower's diet, sleep habits, and bowel movements – it seemed that Snyder was actually overseeing the President's rehabilitation.

Stopping within earshot of the porch, Isherwood lit a cigarette and then looked off over rolling fields, listening.

'—pure stupidity,' the President was saying. His accent was as flat as the small Kansas town in which he had been raised. 'Staying locked up inside this damned house isn't going to make me better, goddamn it; it's going to make me worse.'

'Mister President,' Snyder answered patiently. 'We've got to err on the side of caution.'

'Is a short stroll really going to kill me?' The President's voice lowered. 'Mamie's driving me nuts. She's got a mouth like a motor boat. Just a few minutes out of the house by myself...'

'Next week,' Snyder promised. 'Don't get me in trouble here, Mister President. Doctor White, you know, believes strongly that we should still have you on a regimen of total bed rest.'

'Foolishness. I've never felt better.'

'Treat it as a vacation,' said Snyder lightly. 'Answer some letters; play some autobridge. We can get together a hand with the ladies if you like—'

'Dear Lord, anything but that.'

'—just take her slow, Ike. Ease back into the activity. By next week – week after at the latest – you'll be shooting skeet and playing golf. All right?'

'Not a bit, Howie. Not a goddamn bit. But doctor's orders, I suppose.'

'That they are.'

Brennan took Isherwood's arm, dragging him back around the corner of the house. 'Listen,' he said *sotto voce*. 'Chief said we should let you poke around. But help us out, for Christ's sake, and keep your head down.'

For a moment, Isherwood considered. Then he nodded. Pinching out his cigarette, he headed for the nearest door of the farmhouse. Brennan and Skinnerton tagged along as he stepped over the threshold – the screen door was unlocked, but another agent stood just inside – and into a back entry hall. From there they moved into a spotless kitchen which boasted an automatic dishwasher, a Crosley Shelvador refrigerator with chilled water dispenser built into the door, and counter-top appliances including a Veg-O-Matic and a Sunbeam mixer. The room was cozily small, surprisingly unostentatious, and mellowly lit by a slanting rafter of sun poking through gauze curtains.

With escorts sticking close, Isherwood inspected the pantry and then opened the refrigerator, glancing at one of the pre-packaged meals ('TV Brand Frozen Dinner', according to the label) stacked inside the freezer. With enough foresight, he supposed, one of these packaged dinners might be tampered with – but one could not know which meal the chief executive would be served.

From the kitchen he moved into a pink-and-green dining room, which felt unused. A formal plate setting on the table had acquired a thin layer of dust. After inspecting a tea service on a sideboard, he walked on to the house's main entrance hall, where a middle-aged woman wearing a black-and-white uniform – the First Lady's personal maid – glanced up from a curio cabinet she was wiping down. With a tip of his hat, Isherwood continued into the living room. A board game with the peculiar brand name *Scrabble* lay open atop a black-lacquered, mother-of-pearl inlaid coffee table. On a Norelco hi-fi sat a cigarette box; tipping up the lid, he found a cache of Pall Malls. Hanging near the window was an intimidating portrait of a dowager who, with dark bangs and sparkling blue eyes, bore more than a passing resemblance to Mamie Eisenhower.

The lady of the house herself was standing between living room and sun porch. Facing away from Isherwood and his escorts, she seemed either to be eavesdropping on the President's continuing parlay with Snyder, or standing guard, or perhaps both. This fit with the impression Isherwood held of Mamie Eisenhower – fiercely protective and unquestionably devoted to her husband, despite persistent rumors of his infidelity during the war, and relentless in a way that her down-home image never quite masked.

Turning away, he retraced his steps, briefly peeking in at Eisenhower's first-floor den – brick fireplace, oak beams, fishing-fly-covered lamp, Civil War pike and musket hanging on the wall – before climbing the stairs to the second floor. Brennan and Skinnerton followed all the while, coldly silent. Stepping off the top riser, Isherwood turned toward a door on his left which hung ajar, but Brennan stopped him with a hand on his shoulder. 'The master bedroom. Off-limits. No exceptions.'

Isherwood didn't argue. He contented himself with a glimpse through the open door: a room done in pink and peach, featuring a fireplace and television set. Although an assassin might feasibly scale down the chimney to access the bedroom through the fireplace, that would involve reaching the roof in the first place, no easy feat. And a figure atop the roof, in the midst of all this farmland, would be clearly silhouetted against the sky, presenting an easy target for armed guards.

Down the hall he discovered a small maid's room and two more guest bedrooms, one done in Provençal yellow, the other in gaudy red. Several mediocre landscapes – the President's own handiwork, if Isherwood wasn't mistaken – adorned the wall, representing simple farm scenes from outside. Like Winston Churchill, his comrade-in-arms during the war, Eisenhower possessed more ambition than talent.

'Satisfied?' Brennan asked.

Isherwood deliberated. 'For now,' he said. 'You boys wanted to show me to my room?'

THREE

U.S. ROUTE 15, CULPEPER, VIRGINIA

As the gloaming darkened toward night, Max Whitman glanced over and saw the ghost of a pretty chestnut-haired girl sitting in the passenger seat of his Dodge Coronet.

You're so handsome, Max. One of her slim white hands reached out to lovingly caress tension from his knotted shoulder. She wore a blue-and-white plaid dress, kohl pencil around her eyes, and an expression of distracted munificence. *I must be the luckiest girl in the world, to be driving here with you tonight...*

48

But then a ridge of concern crimped her brow; the hand massaging his shoulder turned tentative. *Max*, she said, troubled. *Are you sure you know what you're doing?*

The question irritated him – not least, he supposed, because he *didn't* know just what he was doing. But even as he grappled for a response, the revenant in the passenger seat seemed to forget her question. Combing absent fingers through long auburn hair, she turned to look vacantly out the window at the passing countryside. Even in fantasies, he could not sustain her interest.

In the next moment, she was gone altogether. But of course this girl existed, now, only in Max Whitman's imagination. In reality, Betsy Martin had long since grown into a mature woman. Last he'd heard she was married to a haberdasher somewhere in Connecticut, with three children of her own.

He refocused on the road unspooling steadily before his headlights. By the time he reached Charlottesville, full night had fallen; the Milky Way sprawled overhead in a confectionery spill. He stopped at one of Ma Bell's ubiquitous payphones to call ahead, and thus expected to be waved through the gates of the asymmetrical mansion without interference. When the guards insisted on searching him, his annoyance increased a notch. Fingers explored his shoes, poked up beneath his cuffs, flicked under the collar of his shirt, pushing and prodding, this way and that.

He glared. But on some deeper level, he understood: it was not a time to take chances. As if eager to rectify the insult, the colored butler hustled him directly to the study without making him wait, and Senator Bolin received him immediately. As Whitman gave his report, the senator listened somberly, his face cold and carefully blank, offering nothing.

After the account was done, the older man tarried for a few pensive moments. Whitman waited uncertainly, wondering if Bolin faulted him for Ike's use of a closed car during the motorcade. Mentally, he prepared his defense: It had been a last-minute decision by the doctors, and Whitman could not possibly have gotten word to the senator in time.

Then Bolin reached for his Viceroys, shook one into his mouth. He warmed: a half-smile, a relaxing of body language, a slight lowering of shoulders. 'How seriously,' he asked, 'does Spooner take the threat to Eisenhower?'

Whitman shrugged. 'If he knew anything for sure, he wouldn't trust this to Isherwood. But if he didn't have a gut feeling, he would have stayed within official channels.'

'Is this Isherwood likely to make trouble for us at Gettysburg?'

'Hard to say. He's a drunk – that's how he got in the glue in the first place. But he's not stupid. Before the war derailed him, he was on the fast track.' Whitman grinned wolfishly. 'But the Chief only trusts him so far. He's making Ish drive out to some pumpkin patch in Pennsylvania, twice a week, to let me smell his breath.'

Bolin absorbed this information. After a moment, he struck a match – his white suit flowed, glistened – and then tossed the match into the fireplace. Moving to the sideboard, he poured two glasses of Madeira. 'We cannot afford to let this man interfere with our operative. Yet removing him, it seems to me, might confirm Spooner's apprehensions.'

'That depends, Senator, on how you play it.'

Handing over a glass, Bolin raised an interrogative eyebrow.

'It's no secret that Frank Isherwood's his own worst enemy. Those mountain roads...' Whitman shrugged again. 'Nobody would think twice if he got liquored up before coming to meet me one night and had an accident.'

'But then another agent would replace him. Perhaps a less compromised one.'

'Another agent from where?' Avoiding a floating fragment of cork, Whitman sipped his wine: very sweet, but still light, and much fancier than anything he could afford himself. 'The Chief's got nowhere else to turn. He doesn't know who to trust inside the Service. And if he trusted anyone *outside*, Isherwood would still be cooling his heels on leave. The way Spooner sees it, Hoover's dirty enough to be in on it, and the CIA's only good overseas. And even if he wanted to try the Company, you've got to understand: me and the Chief grew up poor as church mice. Oh-So-Social just isn't our style. He'd rather go with an old friend from inside his Service, risks and all.'

Bolin thinned his lips and nodded.

'Get rid of Isherwood,' continued Whitman,

51

'and you buy some time. And you won't need much. Your agent's inside the gates. I did like you said: told the house matron that I ran into you on the Hill, and passed along your personal recommendation. Interview's in the morning.'

With eyes half-shut behind rimless spectacles, Bolin gazed thoughtfully into the brass-screened fireplace. He nodded again, as if to himself.

Outside, the wind rose, complaining.

GETTYSBURG, PENNSYLVANIA:
NOVEMBER 13
In Miss Dunbarton's opinion, the girl on the other side of the desk was entirely too pretty.

There she sat: young and blonde and pert, twenty-four or twenty-five, wearing a sapphire angora and an expectant half-smile. On the surface, the smile was polite and charming. But something about the young housemaid suggested a sense of entitlement, Miss Dunbarton thought, which would not have existed had she not been here on a senator's personal recommendation. The girl almost gave the sense that she considered Miss Dunbarton to be the lucky one, to be sitting here enjoying the honor of her presence.

Frowning, Miss Dunbarton cleared her throat. 'Well,' she said briskly, looking up from the letter in her hands. 'Three years in Senator Bolin's service, and only the highest praise ... One could hardly wish for a better letter of introduction.'

A modest dip of the head.

'Still, we're looking only for the most qualified help, here. So you won't mind if I ask a few follow-up questions.'

'Of course, ma'am.'

'Where are you from originally, Miss Grant?'

'Born in Maryland, ma'am.'

'How did you find your way to Charlottes-ville?'

'My mother found me the job with the senator. She and Mrs Bolin, bless her soul, were friendly growing up.'

'Can you read?'

'Yes, ma'am.'

'Write?'

A see-sawed hand.

'How do you feel about the prospect of coming to Gettysburg?'

'Excited, ma'am. A president is more important than a senator.'

'Friends you're sorry to leave behind?'

A shrug; the girl's bell of blonde hair shimmer-ed. 'I make new friends easily.'

'Starting wages are two dollars per hour, Miss Grant.'

'Yes, ma'am.'

'I would like you to understand,' said Miss Dunbarton after a moment, 'that we are only hiring because circumstances have conspired to put us in desperate straits. But if Senator Bolin thinks you're trustworthy, my dear, that's good enough for me.' She let the corners of her mouth tug down disapprovingly, belying the words. 'All things considered, I haven't got much choice,' she added drily, just to drive the point home.

If young Elisabeth Grant recognized the

reminder of her station, she kept it from her face. The half-smile barely flickered. The eyes – pale turquoise flecked with hazel – remained warm and unguarded.

Leaning back in her chair, crossing thick arms before her ample bosom, Miss Dunbarton suppressed a sigh. Mamie Eisenhower was touchy about pretty young women being around her husband, particularly since his affair with his wartime chauffeur Kay Summersby – and Summersby, in the house matron's opinion, had been no special prize, at least not compared to this girl. But with Ike's six weeks of convalescence already under way, time with which to interview potential maids was short. Barbara Cameron had chosen the worst possible moment to leave them in the lurch.

Spilt milk, *et cetera*. The only sensible thing now was to make the best of the situation.

'Well, then.' Miss Dunbarton pushed back from her desk with new-found resolve. 'Let's take the tour, shall we?'

'We call this Farm Two. We keep twenty-five cattle here, along with six hundred chickens – but you needn't worry about that. Your job will be entirely confined to this house, traditionally called the herdsman's home. In addition to the usual farmhands and agents, we'll have quite a few special guests over the next few weeks. Truly amazing, how many people tag along wherever the President goes. The majority of his staff is lodged in town, four miles away. We'll get only the barest minimum here on the farm, and it will still be just about more than we can handle. But no matter what, standards must be maintained.'

Remaining two steps behind Miss Dunbarton as they moved through the drafty but well-renovated barn, Elisabeth Grant said nothing.

'The President and First Lady are staying on the next property – Farm One, we call it – along with their closest bodyguards and the President's personal valet. That's over there.' With a loose gesture through a window, in the direction of a thick-planted row of Norway spruce. The girl followed the gesture curiously, letting her gaze linger. 'They've got a nice set-up,' Miss Dunbarton confided. 'The President gave Mamie free reign when they first bought the place, and she did an absolutely bang-up job with the decor – oh, perhaps a little precious for my taste, with all that pink, but still lovely. Unfortunately, my dear, but you won't be seeing it from any closer than this. Even *I* won't set foot over there unless they need a last-minute hand in the kitchen, and I've been employed here for three years.'

The girl nodded.

'In any case, we'll have our hands full with the spillover, as I said: secretaries, backup Secret Service, and the like. When encountering a VIP, smile politely and carry on with your duties. Never speak unless spoken to. Over here – if you please; thank you – we've got the dining room. Your duties include food preparation, serving, and clean-up, as well as dusting, washing floors and windows, and whatever else we may require. After serving and clearing each meal, you can take your own, back in the kitchen, of course. You're expected to work from six each morning until your work is done each night. Curfew is at nine. Once per week you'll get a day off – perhaps both days of a weekend, every once in a while, if you can square it with the other girls – which is yours to spend as you like. Many of the girls head into town, to catch a matinee. Your first day off will be Tuesday; you'll be expected to use it to stock up on any provisions you find you need.'

The young woman nodded again.

'Now through here,' Miss Dunbarton said, 'we'll find the kitchen – the center of your workday. I hope this isn't sounding too onerous, my dear. We wouldn't want you complaining to the senator.'

Elisabeth Grant shook her head graciously and stepped aside to let Miss Dunbarton lead the way.

ROUTE 30: WEST OF LEWISVILLE, PENNSYLVANIA

By the time Richard Hart found the perfect place to stage his ambush, the last streaks of color were dissolving in the sky.

But the hours of searching had been well spent; the terrain was ideal for his purposes. Wooded hills lining the road offered myriad hiding places from which to shoot. The slope by the guard rail was steep and rocky, appropriately treacherous. A scenic overlook half a mile away would function as a fine staging area. Traffic was thin out here, which meant time in which to operate without witnesses.

Parking back at the scenic overlook, he moved through the woods on foot, avoiding the knurliest roots which threatened to trip him. After twenty minutes of blundering through dense foliage he was rewarded by the discovery of a copse of white birch which, perched above a sharp turn in the road, suited his needs to a T. A shot from this rise through the windshield at night, killing the driver, might be beyond his ability – the oncoming headlamps would blind him – but he could easily enough shoot out a tire. Disabled, the automobile would slew into the turn, hitting the guard rail. Perhaps it would go through of its own accord. If not, Hart would leave his hiding place, descend the hillside, and finish the job at close quarters. Perhaps he would throw an open bottle into the car, just to help investigators along.

Inside the Buick again, he turned back toward the setting sun. Isherwood's rendezvous with Max Whitman – and hence with Richard Hart, and hence with fate – was still three days away. Before then, Hart had business in Gettysburg.

He felt almost sorry for Agent Francis Isherwood, whom he had never met, and who would never know what hit him. The man was a fellow veteran. But war required sacrifices. And despite the lack of uniforms or conventional battlefields, this was definitely war. The theaters were not trenches or beaches but country clubs, like the one in which Eisenhower had ingested an insufficient quantity of succinylcholine (the doctor who had misestimated the dosage, now deceased, would not find the chance to repeat the mistake), and grassy rises overlooking presidential motorcades outside of Washington ... and rocky ridges above twisting, hazardous mountain roads.

FOUR

GETTYSBURG: NOVEMBER 14

Scowling, Isherwood closed the newspaper.

For a few moments, he looked emptily at nothing. No denying, he reflected: the simple small-town America in which he'd grown up was a quickly fading memory. Once upon a time, all a boy could ask for was a cool glass of lemonade, a jazz quartet on a bandstand, and a pretty girl in a flowered skirt. But now scientists had identified a new peril called 'smog'. Soviets were perfecting an improved hydrogen Bomb, capable of destroying the world two hundred times over. Doctors had found strontium-90 in children's baby teeth. Fallout shelters were being urged to stock cans of pineapple juice, for treatment of radiation burns; unrest roiled South America, the stock market had tumbled fourteen billion dollars in the wake of Ike's heart attack, and Formosa festered like an open wound. Khrushchev's saber rattled, Israel agitated for Gaza, and the Warsaw Pact challenged NATO...

He tried to push it all away. The coffee was hot and the week was new. He had seventy-plus hours of sobriety beneath his belt, and today he would try again to call his wife.

With a sigh, he let his eyes drift shut. Waiting in the darkness were the days leading up to Omaha: a bunch of wiry, scared kids, training and fooling around, with a slightly older man – Isherwood himself – supervising, cigarette burning jauntily between fingertips. He saw in a flash Dick Harrison, playing cards and grinning. And then another flash, quick as heat lightning at night: Dick Harrison three weeks later, gutshot on the beach, begging for water, bubbles of red frothing from the corners of his mouth. Here was Freddy Penworth, laughing with tears streaming down his face as he jammed a fresh clip into his Greaser. Here were Germans raking the gray sand with terribly organized parallel lines of Schwarzlose machine-gun fire; and Isherwood, tangled in barbed wire and soaked with the blood of his fellows, returning fire blindly, fruitlessly. Here were the survivors after the landing: grim, dark, ranks thinned, faces aged: Bosford, Carlson, Vasquez, Guerra, Wilson, Mahoney, all old before their time.

The landing had been only the beginning. Here was Francis Isherwood sixty hours later, in the dead of night, two klicks inland, sneaking up on a young Nazi standing guard over a makeshift supply depot. Isherwood grabbed a clump of hair with one hand, drawing his KA-BAR across the exposed throat with the other. A parabola of blood arced onto frozen grass. He dragged the body, with head barely connected, into a nearby hedgerow, and then pressed on without looking back.

And here was Evy, drenched in sunlight three years later, brightly singing Doris Day from the passenger seat of the Studebaker: 'My Dreams Are Getting Better All The Time'.

Groaning, he rubbed at his temples. Duty called. He must finish the task of familiarizing himself with every agent, farmhand, security patrol and square foot on the farm. A survey of town, concentrating on centers of gossip – drugstores, lunch counters, bars – would acquaint him with any suspicious characters lurking about. But applying himself to the task at hand could keep him distracted for only so long ... and he had passed those package stores, on the outskirts of town, beckoning...

After the briefest fillip of hesitation he opened his eyes, pushed back from the rectory table, folded the newspaper beneath one arm, and went to face the day.

Four miles away, over scrambled eggs and coffee, Richard Hart perused the same articles in the same newspaper.

In Buenos Aires, Provisional President Lonardi had been overthrown by General Pedro Aramburu. In Russia, the Soviets were working on a bigger Bomb, with a payload equal to one million tons of TNT. Closer to home, the stock market recovery was sluggish. And in Germany rearming had begun – atrocity of atrocities! – which the newspaper's editors downplayed. But of course they did. Eisenhower's America, as the senator said, was weak and irresolute, determined to coddle and circumvent the enemy rather than engage them full-on.

Had General Eisenhower only shown more backbone, thought Hart, they could have avoided this current geopolitical morass altogether. America could have beaten the Russians to Berlin. On April eleventh, 1945, following an advance of sixty miles in a single day, a spearhead of the US Ninth Army had reached the Elbe River, leaving only sixty miles more between themselves and the capital city of the Third Reich. But Eisenhower had hesitated, fearing that German armies might regroup to make a last stand in the Alpine mountains of southern Bavaria, where the impenetrable territory could extend the war indefinitely. And so, from that day forward, he had concentrated on preventing such a retreat, leaving the way open for the Russian advance and everything which had followed.

Turning from international news to national, Hart scanned for an article, as he had every day since returning from Denver, concerning a body part discovered in Colorado's South Platte River, or Chatfield or Cherry Creek Reservoirs. He found none. The story might not be big enough to make a national paper. Yet he kept looking anyway – from morbid curiosity, or from a lingering pang of guilt.

Pushing the newspaper away, he finished his coffee and then stepped out onto the sidewalk, buttoning his dark coat against the chill. The

61

rooming house had been chosen for its location: far enough from the center of town that he could avoid the worst of the crowds, but close enough that he could conveniently reach the bench before the Plaza Restaurant every day at noon.

Even on its outskirts, Gettysburg harbored a noticeably larger population than its infrastructure could comfortably support: a side effect of the President's sudden proximity. The faces crowding the sidewalk belonged to fox-like journalists or stern members of the Signals Corps, or to the administrative team of Chief of Staff Sherman Adams, who according to the papers had been installed above the post office where Ike could summon him at a moment's notice. All the extra eyes put Hart on edge; at six-foot-four, he was not exactly inconspicuous.

The day was windy but mild, with skies of dazzling blue. He drove west, toward the Eisenhower farm. Parking a safe mile away, well off the road, he screened his vehicle behind branches and foliage. From the glove compartment he removed a pair of binoculars and Peterson's third edition of *A Field Guide To The Birds*. Then he walked through the forest to within five hundred yards of the Eisenhower farm's main gate, where he concealed himself behind a wide oak, laid prone, brought binoculars to eyes, and waited.

During the war he had become accustomed to the stresses, both physical and mental, attending long-term surveillance. For the first hour, then, he barely felt the discomfort of remaining motionless in raw terrain, holding Bushnells to his eyes and focusing on the distant gate. Throughout that hour he saw minimal traffic into and out of the farm. A single delivery truck pulled up to the gate, unloaded its cargo, and turned around again. A single dark Chevrolet, driven by a slight bald man, exited in the direction of town. A pick-up truck carrying sightseers made several passes before giving up.

By the second hour, Hart felt the prone position catching up with him. In Italy he had been young, eager, and in peak physical condition. Now he carried a few extra pounds around his midsection, and his muscles were not quite as toned as they once had been. An ache began in his knees and elbows, radiated out to his other joints, and soon turned his entire back into a throbbing mass of bone and gristle. Changing position on the forest floor relieved the stress only for a moment. His nicotine center insisted that tobacco would alleviate his discomfort. But smoking might draw attention, which despite his birdwatching cover he hoped to avoid, and so he denied himself the cigarette, much to his body's displeasure.

By the third hour, he was deciding that he had become too soft for such work. Civilian life, advancing age, and the material benefits of association with the senator had weakened him ... but even as he was thinking it, luck favored him at last. The gate opened again, disgorging the second vehicle of the day: a Studebaker sedan.

Through the lens of the Bushnells, Hart found the driver behind the wheel. Francis Isherwood looked older than in the photographs Hart had been given – rounder in the face, rumpled and paunchy – but the resemblance was unmistakable, and the model of the car was right. He had found his target.

He waited until the sedan vanished from sight (Isherwood drove quickly, recklessly) and then stood, joints creaking. Brushing off his dark coat, he hurried back to the Buick. He would not catch the man before he reached town. But in a place the size of Gettysburg, the Studebaker should not be difficult to locate again, despite the crowds.

Indeed, forty minutes later Hart found the vehicle parked on the main drag outside a drugstore. Inside, Isherwood sat before a malted and a cheeseburger, chatting easily with a red-headed girl behind the counter as he ate. Parking across the street, Hart feigned reading the morning's newspaper while keeping an eye on his quarry.

Upon exiting the drugstore, Isherwood walked to a nearby phone booth. There he stood for another few minutes, feeding nickels into the coin slot, looking increasingly frustrated. Emerging at length, he glanced up and down the street before striking off on foot. Leaving the Buick, Hart paced him, maintaining a secure distance.

Five minutes later Isherwood stepped into a small bar-and-grill. Through a window Hart watched the man order a seltzer and then exchange words with the bartender. If a small town had a pulse, barkeeps and counter clerks were its arteries; Agent Isherwood had put his finger unerringly on Gettysburg's lifeblood. Hart didn't know what questions the man was asking, but he was proving himself a dangerous fellow to have sniffing around.

Leaving the bar, the agent stopped at a chemist's to buy a small gift-wrapped parcel. He then returned to his car and drove at an illegal speed to the outskirts of town. Parking in a gravel lot by a package store, he left the Studebaker again, carrying a brown paper bag. After depositing the bag in a dumpster, he climbed back into the bullet nose and continued west. Hart debated between following and checking the dumpster. Checking his watch, he saw that the hour of his rendezvous was almost nigh. He decided on the latter.

The contents of the paper bag turned out to be an ordinary, half-empty bottle of Jack Daniels.

Curious.

Hart drove back into town. At one minute before noon, he settled down onto the agreed-upon bench before the Plaza Restaurant ('LOUNGE STEAKS CHOPS SINCE 1863'). Smoking, he waited. On the walkway before him, a little girl wearing a bonnet threw a crying fit as her mother tugged hard on one arm. A motorcycle without a muffler circled the pavilion, revving its engine unnecessarily. Two teenagers sauntered past, each loudly laying claim to the title of pinball champion. When the wrought-iron clock in the center of the pavilion read 12:15, Hart stood again, pitching away the butt of his second cigarette. He would try again tomorrow.

He took his midday meal in the same bar-and-grill Isherwood had visited, in case a garrulous bartender revealed some insight into the man's purpose; but the shift had changed, and the barkeep was gone. Yet the day had been far from wasted. Hart had identified his target and some of the man's habits – most saliently a tendency to drive too fast – and confirmed the make of his automobile. When he encountered Agent Isherwood again on the dark mountain road, he would have no trouble finding his mark.

Polishing a pair of brass candlesticks in the dining room, Elisabeth became slowly aware of a gaze drilling into her back.

Turning, she saw a girl watching her. Pretty if chubby, the girl had skin the color of sandalwood, and lively eyes beneath smears of blue mascara. 'You replaced Babs, right?'

Elisabeth nodded.

'My name's Josette. What's yours?'

'Elisabeth.'

'Pleased to meet you, Elisabeth.'

Cautiously, Elisabeth nodded again.

'Dunbarton's taking a nap. Want to sneak a cigarette?'

Elisabeth hesitated only briefly. 'Why not?' she said lightly.

They went out through a side door and hid behind a venerable oak. Without warning the sky had turned the color of bruises, livid with thickening storm clouds. The air was frigid enough to make Josette shiver beneath her thin afternoon maid's uniform, although Elisabeth, accustomed to mountain climates, felt comfortable.

'How'd they find you so quick?' Lighting two cigarettes, Josette casually passed one over. 'Usually it takes a year for anyone to get hired here, with all the security precautions.'

'I had a good recommendation.' Elisabeth puffed her tobacco to evenness. 'I used to work for Senator Bolin.'

'Ooh – fancy.' Josette looked at her with naked interest. 'Well, I've been here almost two years already. If you've got any questions, just ask.'

'Thanks.'

For a few moments, both smoked in silence.

'So what do you think of Dunbarton?' Elisabeth asked.

'She's not bad. Although ... Well, I don't like to complain. You catch more flies with honey, right?'

'Just between us,' promised Elisabeth.

'She can be tough sometimes, that's all.'

'For example?'

'Well.' Leaning in closer, Josette lowered her voice conspiratorially. 'Last year I found a little sparrow, right over there, with a broken wing? So I brought it up to my room, in a shoebox lined with cotton. And I was nursing it back to health – fresh worms, water from an eye dropper, the whole nine yards – but when Dunbarton found out, she made me get rid of it.'

'She didn't!'

'She did. Even though everybody knows that once you've handled a bird, the mother won't take it back.'

'How heartless.'

'Well, I felt that way at the time. But looking back, I can see that maybe she was right. We're here to work, after all. That's why we don't get a TV, and radio's not allowed, although – just

between us? – I've got one hidden in my room.'
Josette shrugged, smoked. 'Dunbarton doesn't
have the easiest time of it herself. You know, she
drinks.'

'What!'

'Like a fish.'

'I never would have guessed.'

'Just goes to show, doesn't it? Walk a mile in
someone else's shoes. Even President Eisenhower struggles with demons, you know. The big
man himself.'

Elisabeth raised her eyebrows.

'He had that girlfriend during the war. Kay
Summersby. Everybody knows about it – that's
what drives the First Lady crazy. It's not as if she
actually minds the cheating. It's just the gossip
that bothers her. She likes to keep up appearances. But then Mamie isn't so perfect herself.
Dunbarton's not the only one around here who
likes to tip the bottle. But listen to me: Josie the
blabbermouth. It's one of my worst habits. Oh, I
really must do better.'

'Don't worry; I won't hold it against you.'

A first drop of rain fell. Josette gave a girlish
shriek. 'To be continued,' she promised. They
snuffed out their cigarettes half-smoked and ran
back inside.

Throughout the rest of that rainy afternoon,
Elisabeth kept her eyes peeled for a chance to
engage the girl again, to find out what else Josie
the blabbermouth might reveal.

But Miss Dunbarton, up from her nap, played
quite the taskmaster. During a brief pause, Elisa-

beth critically examined the calloused palms of her hands. The humiliation of lowly physical labor – a member of the master race, working as an equal alongside sub-humans – was galling. But it was toward a purpose, she reminded herself. The end would justify the means.

Following the hard labor came suffocating tedium: for two endless hours, assigned the task of polishing the demitasse, she charily ran a chamois cloth around the inside of tiny porcelain cups. By the time her chores were finished, the sun was down. Falling across her bed, she tried to find a hidden reserve of energy.

She was spared seeking out Josette, as it happened, because a moment later the younger girl knocked on her door. 'Hi,' Josette said, breezing in. 'Oh, you look beat. Tell me about it. My dogs are barking.'

Elisabeth sat up. 'Dunbarton has no mercy.'

'I told you, she can be tough. But remember what I said: walk a mile in her shoes.'

Josette proceeded to explore the quarters familiarly, fiddling with items on the bureau. All were innocent – but Elisabeth nonetheless felt the urge to thump a warning across the girl's snout. 'You ought to come by and listen to my Philco sometime,' said Josette as she snooped. 'Do you like music?'

'I love it.'

'Me too. I listen at night, after everyone's asleep. Mostly to Dick Biondi out of Chicago – he plays good stuff. My favorites right now are 'Rock Around The Clock' and 'Mr Sandman' and 'That's All Right' and 'Earth Angel'. Do you like rock and roll?'

'Do you have to ask?'

'What about movies? Do you like movies?'

'I love movies,' said Elisabeth seriously.

'Me too. One day I'm going to pack up and head out to Tinseltown and get discovered sitting at a soda fountain, just like Lana Turner.' She dropped down onto the edge of the bed beside Elisabeth; the springs creaked complainingly. 'A friend of mine – Babs, who you replaced – recently did just that. Dunbarton thinks she ran off with some guy. But I'm sure she went to Hollywood. We talked about it all the time.'

'Lucky girl.'

'Yeah. But ... well, not to sound mean, of course. But she's not too easy on the eyes, Babs. And she doesn't have much in the way of talent. And she's got lousy posture, to boot. I'm afraid she'll end up waiting tables, or worse.' Josette sighed. 'Personally, I hope to get a shot at something more. I was named after a French film star, you know. My mother says I've always had a flair for acting, and modeling, and telling stories. You know: drama.'

'Yes, I can see that about you.'

'One day I hope to star in a movie opposite Clark Gable or William Holden. That would just be the living end. When Clark took off his shirt in *It Happened One Night* and wasn't wearing anything underneath, I thought I had died and gone to heaven.'

'They're both dreamy.'

'Say, let's play a game. It's called "Truth". You answer one question honestly, and then I have to do the same.'

Elisabeth smiled. 'Okay,' she said.

'Swell. You can go first, if you like.'

Bluntness would be counterproductive; any valuable information would need to come indirectly. 'Who on the farm,' asked Elisabeth slowly, 'do you find most attractive?'

'Bill Brennan,' answered Josette promptly. 'He's a dead ringer for a young Clark Gable, if you ask me. Plus he's important; he's head of security. You probably haven't seen him around, because he spends most of his time on Farm One. But every once in a while he comes over to butter up Miss Dunbarton, so he can get extra coffee or bacon when he wants it, or toss back a few and sing some songs when she goes out. Next time, I'll point him out to you.'

'If he's really so handsome, I wish you would.'

'Maybe even later tonight,' said Josette cheerfully. 'Dunbarton's gone into town to see her sister – that's why she took a nap today – and a few of the guys might stop by. Now: my turn.' Elisabeth could see wheels turning in the girl's head. 'Have you ever ... you know?'

'What?'

'You know.' One corner of Josette's mouth rose suggestively.

'Josette! Of course not.'

'Well,' said Josette, adopting a sudden air of sophistication. 'That's a mistake, Libby, if you ask me. On your wedding night, you need to have some idea what you're doing. You can't just jump into the deep end of the pool if you've never had any practice swimming.'

'So you have?'

'Is that your question, officially?'

'Yes, officially: have you?'

'I have,' said Josette demurely. 'I'm no child, you know. In fact I've already been engaged to be married.'

'Did it hurt?'

'Being engaged?'

'Don't tease!'

'Well, technically it's my turn to ask a question, but, why not, I'll give you one for free: no, it didn't hurt one bit. But that may be because I grew up with brothers, playing ball and riding horses. Now, my turn – if you could go on a date with anyone in the world, who would it be?'

'Dirk Bogarde, I suppose.'

'You've got good taste, don't you?'

'I like to think so. My turn: have you ever, in all your time working here, seen the President up close?'

'Just once. He came over to inspect the steers. But that was last year. From what I hear he's not even allowed to leave the house any more, since the heart attack.'

'Never?'

'Not according to Caroline, who's friendly with Jane, who's friendly with Rose – that's Mrs Eisenhower's maid. These days the President spends all his time on the porch, from sunup to sundown. Now: my turn. I know you've only been here a few days, but – who do you dislike most?'

'Dunbarton, of course.'

'I should have guessed. That was a wasted

question. Give me another one?'

'My turn first! Okay, so – who actually lives on Farm One, and who gets to visit...?'

That night Josette and a group of Secret Service men took advantage of Dunbarton's absence to stay up past curfew, singing and drinking and strumming an out-of-tune guitar.

Despite a burgeoning friendship, Josette had not extended Elisabeth an invitation to join the party; she must not have wanted competition for the favor of the men. Still, through the thin walls Elisabeth could hear every tipsy word. If she paid close attention, there was valuable intelligence to be gained.

She counted four male voices. One apparently belonged to Bill Brennan, identified by Josette as the handsomest man on the farm, akin to a young Clark Gable – the one she had named as head of security. Another was called 'Skin', which sounded like a nickname. The remaining two were never addressed directly. None seemed bothered by Josette's mixed blood; they all flirted carelessly. But what else would one expect from men like these, probably half-mongrel themselves?

They bellowed out songs from West Point: 'I want to be, I want to be, I want to be away on furlough' to the tune of Dixie; 'There's a long long trail awinding, into the land of my dreams', with a maudlin lilt; 'Pack up your troubles in your old kit bag, and smile, smile, smile.' The fact that these overgrown children had won the war still felt unreal to Elisabeth, like a bad dream. But it had been only a matter of re-sources, she reminded herself, of America's great natural bounty, and not an indication of the relative quality of their nation's menfolk. Be-sides, the lion's share of damage to the Reich had been done by the Russians.

The tuneless guitar was played badly by Josette herself, as Elisabeth gathered from Bren-nan's teasing whenever she hit a sour note, which was often. The lack of quality of the music didn't help matters. Compared with the inspiring 'Horst Wessel Lied' and the anthemic 'Deutschland Über Alles', these songs were grating and shrill. Every so often the singers halted their musical butchery to drink, joke, and gossip. Like all hired men, they mocked their superiors – in this case Miss Dunbarton (you could tell when she spread her legs, opined the one called Skin crassly, because the furnace kicked on) and even President Eisenhower, whose fondness for Western magazines, remark-ed Brennan, revealed the poor white trash he truly remained inside – the same barefooted boy who had been born in Abilene and worked at a creamery, who in many ways had simply lucked into his current position of power.

The party broke up abruptly when a crackling of walkie-talkies informed Brennan that Dun-barton was on her way back through the security checkpoints. Within ninety seconds, everybody but Josette was gone, trucking loudly down the stairs. For the next few moments came quiet clunking sounds – probably the out-of-tune guitar being hidden away beneath the bed – and

74

then, after a very brief period of silence, the sound of the Philco being switched on.

Exhaling, Elisabeth closed her eyes.

Her mind was spinning. Tomorrow was Tuesday, her first day off. It promised to be busy.

FIVE

Yet for a long time, despite her exhaustion, she couldn't sleep.

The presence of enemy soldiers next door had stirred up old feelings. Of course the war was ancient history; and while she might take pleasure from avenging her *Fuehrer* against the cursed architect of D-Day, her motivations now were chiefly mercenary. Only rarely did an opportunity like this come along, offering sufficient recompense to set her up for the rest of her life, enabling an end to running from those who made a career of prosecuting Nazis.

Sleep, she thought, and punched fitfully at her pillow. Tomorrow she needed to be sharp. The past was the past. She must let it go.

Next door, the radio played softly. Farther down the hall someone talked quietly, and then laughed. But in her private quarters, Elisabeth was alone – no deprivations here in post-war America, where even the least of the hired help was given humble billets of her own. By contrast, her countrymen back in Germany were more desperate than ever, even hungrier and colder than they had been in the terrible years following Versailles.

The air in the tiny bedroom felt hot and dry. From somewhere deep in the bowels of the renovated barn, she could hear a furnace kicking and thumping. Windows were fogged with condensation. For a few moments she stared at a small plaque reading JESUS LOVES YOU mounted above the dresser. Then – the clock beside the plaque read 12:40 a.m. – she forced her eyes closed.

GETTYSBURG: NOVEMBER 15

Elisabeth rose early, ate a crust of toast with some butter, and struck off down the long driveway.

Passing near the towering grain silo, she slowed her pace. Up close, an observation she'd made from a distance was confirmed: no ladder ran up the silo's exterior. Hoops near the base were visibly less weathered than those near the top. A latched double-door in the dome was too far off the ground to be useful. At some point, she surmised, the tower had been shorter, and unloaded from the top by silage fork. It had since been built higher, and an air slide had been installed on the ground for easy mechanical unloading. But there would still be an interior ladder, a souvenir of the original form.

Emerging from the farm's main gate, she turned left, as if undertaking the four-mile journey into town on foot. After ten minutes, she reached a crossroads. Continuing straight would bring her into Gettysburg; a turn to the north would lead her around the perimeter of the Eisenhower property.

Tossing a glance over her shoulder, ensuring that the guard booth was out of sight, she took the turn. If caught, she would pretend simply to have lost her way – dizzy, simple girl that she was. Thus she managed to accomplish, by rough country road, almost an entire circuit of the Eisenhower farm. At the last moment, nearing the main gate again from the other side, she turned around and retraced her steps rather than be seen by the guard at the booth.

By the time she truly embarked on her four-mile hike to town, the sun was high in the sky and a few truant birds chorused merrily from the woods. Her flat heels thumped steadily against the uneven road, sometimes gritting on broken glass or discarded bottle caps or pieces of quartz. The day was one to encourage perambulation; she lifted her face to catch the fine morning sun. The forest around her reminded her of the glorious woods of home – although in comparison to the magnificent Black Forest, these trees were puny, and the colors washed-out. But, of course, she didn't think about home any more. *Never look back*, her father had once taught her – just about the only worthwhile lesson, when all was said and done, that she had ever taken from him.

The walk into town took almost seventy minutes, down a road arrow-straight except for a single hooking detour around a massive oak. During this time, only four vehicles passed. One was dusty, sideboards and windows caked with mud; she decided it probably belonged to a traveling salesman. The others held teenagers and tourists driving out to rubberneck at the Eisenhower farm, little realizing they had no chance of glimpsing the commander-in-chief.

Entering a residential neighborhood, she noticed a second-hand Oldsmobile parked on a front lawn, battered FOR SALE sign propped behind the windshield. Coming to a stop, she ruffled her brow. After a moment's deliberation, she moved up the front walk.

The young man who answered her knock would later tell investigators that he had initially been taken aback by this attractive young lady asking to purchase the Olds Rocket. The car was irrefutably a beast, appealing mostly to soldiers back from the war who had grown accustomed overseas to operating powerful military equipment. But as the young lady told her story, he began to understand the situation. She was buying the car at the instruction of her employer, a widowed German Jew named Josephine Booth who had fled the Nazis in the late 1930s, financed by the portable wealth of diamonds, and established herself in America. Having survived the Third Reich, Mrs Booth wanted an escape plan in place should history repeat itself. Seen through this lens, the young lady's interest in the second-hand Rocket – which with its 303-cubic-inch V8 engine and Hydra-Matic transmission certainly qualified as a fine escape vehicle – made perfect sense. And the diamonds she proposed to barter for the Olds were of the highest quality. When she agreed to leave one as a sample he might show a jeweler, his last doubts vanished. She suggested meeting again one week from that day, and if he found the diamonds acceptable, to go ahead then with the trade – conditions to which he readily consented.

Elisabeth proceeded toward the center of Gettysburg. The plaza in which she paused to orient herself – Lincoln Square, named after the author of the famous address given there ninety-some years earlier – divided the main street into two tributaries, York on the east and Chambersburg on the west. In the years since Lincoln's speech, the square had actually developed to become a circle surrounding a pavilion. Drugstores, movie theaters, bars, shops, and hotels crowded cheek-to-jowl around the perimeter. Occupying a position of honor in the center, beside an American flag and a large clock mounted on a wrought-iron post, stood an in-human-looking bronze statue of Honest Abe himself, with beard and stovepipe hat. Strange, thought Elisabeth, that they chose to honor this man who had done so much to spoil the purity of their bloodlines. Americans had everything backwards.

After identifying the bench in front of the Plaza Restaurant where she would meet her contact, she went shopping. To justify her day to anyone paying close enough attention, she bought a few personal items – a four-dollar skirt, an inexpensive box of chocolates, some toiletries and sundries, and a commemorative copy of Lincoln's speech. ('We cannot dedicate, we cannot consecrate, we cannot hallow this ground; the brave men, living and dead, who struggled here, have consecrated it, far above our poor power to add or detract.') Then she ventured farther afield, seeking pawn shops and five-and-dimes. From neighborhoods designed to appeal to tourists, she reached districts catering to students and factory workers; since the early nineteenth century, Gettysburg College and the Lutheran Seminary had operated in town, as had carriage manufacturers, shoemakers, and tanneries.

GOLD AND SILVER PAWN offered three used guitars for sale. For ten dollars and seventy-five cents, Elisabeth made a steel-string Gibson with a battered tweed carrying case her own. Inside a neighboring five-and-dime, she browsed shelves stocked with cosmetics, selecting items – make-up, false eyelashes, stockings, dark wig, spirit gum, rubbing alcohol, and a small jar of greasepaint – which she brought to the register. Ringing her up, the girl behind the counter whistled absently: 'How Much Is That Doggie In The Window?'

Precisely as the wrought-iron clock in the center of Lincoln Square ticked to twelve noon, Elisabeth settled down on the pre-arranged bench. She had waited no more than thirty seconds before a presence sat beside her. Although she didn't know her contact's name, she recognized him immediately based on the description – with his unusually tall frame, he was difficult to miss. After glancing at him briefly, she looked away, waiting to hear the identifying code phrase.

He looked over at her indifferently. 'Miss,' he said, 'can you recommend a place for lunch?'

'What are you in the mood for?'

'I'll defer to you.'

'I need a rifle,' she said, without glancing toward him again. 'Telescopic sight. Range at least three hundred yards. I won't be able to zero the scope, so it must shoot straight the first time.'

Very slightly, Richard Hart nodded.

'Now, the rub.' Speaking in a low voice, she explained exactly what she wanted – and then stood, leaving the guitar behind, and walked off without looking back.

In a small diner on a side street, she found a single-occupancy restroom with a door that locked. Inside, working carefully but quickly, she tested the disguise she had bought at the five-and-dime. Full at the sides and flat at the top, with the hairline far back, the wig lent a new width and roundness to her face. The effect was accentuated by subtle lines of spirit gum applied across the brow and around the mouth. Grease-paint circles beneath the eyes added another few years; smudges below the chin suggested jowls; false eyelashes and cheap stockings provided tackiness. When she had finished, the woman looking back from the mirror was familiar only in a strange, elusive way. Minutes before, an attractive blonde in her mid-twenties had entered the restroom. Now a brunette, puffy and middle-aged, turned her face this way and that, considering her reflection. The illusion might not pass close inspection, but once she was behind

81

the wheel of a moving car, it would suffice.

One hour later, having removed the disguise, she entered a car dealership across town: 'RENN/KIRBY, LICENSED SINCE 1933, GUARANTEES YOU WILL RIDE AWAY HAPPY!' Mr Kirby himself listened attentively as she gave her name – Jennie Tucker – and expressed her desire to buy an inexpensive motorbike for transport between Holland House, where, she explained, she was employed as a waitress, and Gettysburg College, where she was taking classes. As it happened, she was in luck; he just happened to have out back the perfect vehicle, which had belonged to his own daughter. And so Jennie Tucker rode away happy that very afternoon atop a used Huffy Whizzer Model 90, a motorized bicycle originally sold as a kit, for which she paid thirty dollars in cash. Feeling magnanimous, Kirby threw in a full tank of gas for the small engine mounted between seat and handlebars.

By half-past four, Elisabeth Grant had stowed her disguise and motorized bicycle in the woods to the east of the Eisenhower farm. She then commenced walking back around the perimeter to the west, so that upon arriving again at the gate, she seemed to be coming on foot from town.

Keeping vigil from his bedroom window, Francis Isherwood absently watched the girl walk up the long driveway.

Chaining his next cigarette from the butt of the last, he returned his attention to the porch on which Eisenhower stood painting. Moments later, a peremptory knock rattled the door in its frame. 'No smoking in the house,' called Miss Dunbarton.

Sighing, Isherwood pushed out of his chair. He opened the door to find the house matron standing in the hallway, glaring at him accusatorily. 'A special allowance has been made,' he lied. 'To facilitate effective surveillance.'

'Even if that were true, Mister Isherwood, it would not stand. My house, my rules. Take it outside.'

He gave her a crooked grin, which left her unmoved. She pointed stiffly down the hall. 'Outside.'

And so Isherwood took his cigarettes and his fedora and his cluttered thoughts out into the afternoon, where the breeze was cool and crisp. The fresh air turned out to be a blessing; he supposed he owed Dunbarton some thanks. Walking the firm ground, he wandered toward Farm One – Secret Service agents he passed along the way conscientiously reporting his every move via walkie-talkie – where he could keep monitoring Eisenhower.

Drawing near the screened-in porch, he changed his course a moment too late to avoid being seen. 'You there,' Eisenhower called. Standing behind his easel, the man again wore his red bathrobe, now with a military greatcoat draped over his shoulders.

Isherwood pointed at his own chest, raising his eyebrows: *Me?*

'Yes, you. Come here.'

So Isherwood moved closer to the sun porch, with the Chief's words beating through the back of his mind: *We're under specific orders from the doctors not to rile the President during his convalescence. He needs not only rest, but relaxation: everything sunshine and roses.*

'Afternoon, sir.' Suddenly, Isherwood was aware of two agents standing just around the corner of the house – Brennan and Skinnerton? – ready to intervene at the drop of a hat.

'Maybe from where you're standing, soldier. But from in here, it's a goddamned crap afternoon.'

Diplomatically, Isherwood said nothing.

'I'm a captive in my own goddamned home. And I don't take kindly to it. You want to give me one of those cigarettes?'

Isherwood hesitated. 'I thought you'd quit.'

'I did,' said Eisenhower archly. 'But good Christ, man, something's got to give.' With a dramatic sigh, he planted hands on hips and looked off to the west, where black birds wheeled restlessly. 'Do you know: the bloodiest battle in the bloodiest war in our nation's history was fought right over that ridge. Brother against brother, father against son. A travesty before the eyes of God, no doubt. But nevertheless, honorable deaths. Those men went out the way they'd lived, fighting for what they believed in. Better to die on your feet than live on your knees.'

Again, Isherwood held his tongue. When he looked around these gentle hills, he saw men being led like sheep to the slaughter; he saw pride and folly, vengeful ghosts, grieving widows, orphaned children. But Eisenhower evidently took a pleasant reminder of past glories, of flags being planted and medals pinned to chests. Somehow this man who had witnessed untold bloodshed on European beaches and fields still clung to his military values.

Or was the truth more complex? Of course Ike, the Supreme Allied Commander who had led America to victory during World War II, was and would always remain a soldier. And the President's fascination with Gettysburg's bloody history was infamous; he had eagerly talked the ear off many a captive audience while relating details of old melees. But the man's battle-ready image served a purpose, thought Isherwood: keeping the Soviets in line, allowing the President to engage in a game of nuclear brinksmanship which otherwise would have been impossible. As a lifelong poker player, Ike knew the importance of a good bluff. And some agents who had worked closely beside the man portrayed another Eisenhower, kept carefully out of the public eye, who had seen enough devastation in Europe and Japan to fully appreciate the value of peace. There was no denying that in his foreign policy he had certainly proven himself to be a great compromiser – and to his critics, a willing appeaser.

'Soon enough,' said Isherwood lamely, 'you'll be out and about.'

'Now you sound like the goddamned doctors.' But a flash of the famous grin crossed Eisenhower's face, just briefly. 'It's all bunk, son, if you ask me. A leader's got to lead by example. If that means putting himself at risk, so be it. Just think of Winfield Hancock. Stood and fought at Cemetery Hill, right over yonder, in the face of overwhelming odds, until Meade arrived to relieve him. Single-handedly held the high ground. His courage that day might well have won the battle, you know. And therefore, arguably, the entire war. In battle, high ground counts for everything.'

Isherwood nodded, thinking suddenly of Farm Two's grain silo, towering over the property like one of H.G. Wells' Martian Tripods. From such a perch, a shooter would have a clear line of sight of most of the farm, including the very sun porch on which Eisenhower now stood. A hunter could devise no better blind.

'Plenty of heroes made on this ground, son, and mark my words, they didn't get there by playing it safe. Why, Chamberlain's charge with the Twentieth Maine – that was as close to madness as a sane man can get. Yet there he went, giving the command: fix bayonets, he said, and put himself and his own brother right out front, too. Man realized that the left flank ended with him. Lose Little Round Top and they put the entire Union army at risk. Low on ammunition, high on casualties, with Rebs coming at him, wave after wave – but he rose to the challenge. Won himself a Medal of Honor, while he was at it. But do you want to know the truth? In tactical terms, it was a mistake. Man just didn't know any better. He was a professor of rhetoric, not a professional soldier. But sometimes that's what it takes to strike a vital blow – not knowing any better. And, what the hell, it worked.'

Isherwood nodded again.

'On the other hand.' Looking off over the terrain, reliving long-ago skirmishes, Eisenhower seemed momentarily content. 'Pride comes before a fall. And some good men made some goddamned prideful decisions during those four days, for which plenty of other good men paid the price. J.E.B. Stuart, for one, the glory hound: off joyriding instead of giving Lee crucial intelligence. A fine soldier, Stuart, but a goddamned grandstander. Liked to read about himself in the newspapers too much. And Pickett, the old dandy, making a charge that hadn't a chance in hell of success ... just over there on that ridge, son; we trained tanks for the Great War on that very same spot. Last in his class at West Point, George Pickett. Deathly afraid he'd miss his chance to fight here at Gettysburg.' A flinty chuckle. 'Man ought to be careful what he wishes for, am I right?'

'Yes, sir.'

'Of course, the charge wasn't really Pickett's idea. He was just following orders. But it wasn't Longstreet's mistake, either. Nope, that particular misadventure – twelve thousand men advanced, and fully half got cut down like wheat – that was Lee's fault. You'd be hard pressed to find a man of better character than Robert E. Lee, but the fact stands: that was his mistake, and his alone. Too much pride. Six thousand boys died in one hour. Cemetery Ridge earned its name that day, I wager.'

'Yes, sir.'

'Maybe there's a reason for me to be locked in this goddamned house, after all. A man's got to know his limitations.' He sighed, a visible puff on the cold air. 'But it chafes, son, I don't mind telling you. These pink walls drive a fellow out of his mind. Painted like a goddamned whore-house in here. And I haven't even had a real cup of coffee in two months. I went long enough without in England, drinking that ersatz crap, to last me the rest of my days.'

'I understand, sir. Spent some time overseas myself.'

'You served?'

'Yes, sir.'

'Good man.' Eisenhower peered at him afresh, and then shook his head. 'Men like you pulled the fat out of the fire. The old farts like me just sat back and took the credit.'

Again, Isherwood said nothing.

'And now here I am, adding insult to injury by making you listen to my bellyaching. Move along, soldier; you're dismissed. And thank you for not giving me that cigarette – that's a damned good call.'

Isherwood tipped his hat and dutifully moved on.

Once safely out of view of the porch, he lit another smoke. So that was Eisenhower, he thought. He felt gratified, and not just because the exchange would make a good story for Evy. It was one thing to defend Eisenhower the idea: the President who had guided America to victory abroad and a balanced budget at home, steering a steady course through D-Day, the death of

Stalin, the defeat of polio, and the end of the Korean conflict. But it was another thing altogether to defend Eisenhower the man.

THE CARROLL ARMS HOTEL, WASHINGTON DC

Joseph McCarthy's usual table inside the Grill Room was tucked into a back corner, where nobody could sneak up on him.

Although McCarthy's large head shook slightly with palsy, and his hand fluttered when he raised it in greeting, he was still powerfully built, evoking the boxer he once had been. Relatively young at forty-seven, he was also a sitting senator who radiated the authority of his position. Politically, he was dead in the water, yet his bearing didn't communicate that – and besides, thought Richard Nixon as he took a seat, politically, McCarthy had never been a realistic contender in the first place. This had not stopped him from becoming, at his peak, one of the three most powerful men in Washington, second only to J. Edgar Hoover and the President.

A house plant set too close to the chair brushed vexingly against Nixon's shoulder as he sank down; although the lighting was recessed, a bulb jutted from the ceiling at an uncomfortable angle, shining directly into his eyes. None of it was by chance. McCarthy liked every advantage, even among his so-called friends. Yet still he had his supporters – and despite the increasing political price paid for the association, the Vice President remained proud to count himself as one.

Keeping his composure in the face of these small insults, Nixon found and displayed a genial smile. Accepting a menu from a waiter, he consulted it briefly before passing it back with a small shake of his head. He had gained a few pounds since his Navy days, mostly in his cheeks, but tried hard to keep himself together. McCarthy, burdened by no such concerns, ordered another whiskey. Moments later the glass was added to the remnants of the meal spread across the table: two empty tumblers awaiting clearing, a plate still bloody from a vanished slab of steak, and residues of potatoes, onions, mushrooms, beans, slaw, and corn.

For a few minutes the men indulged in polite small talk, *de rigueur* in Washington. Although long-time cronies, they formed an undeniably odd couple, as if the star quarterback had taken up with the star hall monitor. McCarthy loved to drink, womanize, carouse, slap backs, and gamble, while Nixon drank even coffee with hesitancy, remained steadfastly faithful to his wife and her famous Republican cloth coat, and despite his best efforts couldn't summon much fondness for golf, let alone high-stakes card games. The balance of power between the two men was complex and always in flux. Just a year and a half before, Nixon had been the behind-the-scenes power broker pulling strings and promising McCarthy the White House. Then had come the spectacular flameout of Army/McCarthy – even as a youthful poker player, Fighting Joe had been infamously unable to resist bluffing on bad cards, and in front of a room filled with television cameras, he had finally overplayed his hand – and now McCarthy, made unelectable by his own impulsivity, was the one relegated to behind-the-scenes machinations. If either would one day take the public throne, it would be Nixon.

Their small talk encompassed Maryland's recent win over LSU, Washington socialite Alice Roosevelt Longworth's broken hip, and good-natured complaints about their wives. In September of 1953, to general bewilderment, McCarthy had married Jean Kerr, his mild-mannered aide. Had the marriage been a maneuver designed to distract from mounting rumors of homosexuality? A Hail Mary pass, to reverse the man's failing political fortunes? Or might it possibly have been the genuine article? Even Nixon, one of McCarthy's closest friends, didn't know for sure. In truth, he thought, there was probably no one simple answer. In Joe's world, facts and lies and wishful thinking all blurred hopelessly together.

With small talk out of the way, they began bellying up to the larger issues at hand. McCarthy complimented Nixon on his handling of the reins during the worst of Eisenhower's illness, when the President had been too indisposed to lead. The compliment, thought Nixon, worked on two levels. Superficially, the senator was congratulating him for proving his ability to govern competently at a difficult time. Subtly, McCarthy was applauding the surety with which Nixon had managed to hide his own ambition. Presiding over Cabinet meetings and tending the home fires, the Vice President had given the public impression of respectful stewardship, not of watchful readiness to pounce – an adroit maneuver, considering the reality.

'I'm just grateful,' replied Nixon disingenuously as dishes were cleared, 'that the worst seems past. I hear he's doing well, out on that farm of his. Pretty soon he'll be back to full strength.'

But he could not entirely keep the resentment from his voice; after all, he had not been invited to accompany Eisenhower during his convalescence. Instead, Chief of Staff Sherman Adams had been installed in the nearby town of Gettysburg. It was a slap in the face, another indication of the increasing disfavor with which Nixon was viewed by the administration.

After the waiter had gone, McCarthy looked around, making sure nobody was within hearing. The club catered to senators, congressmen, lobbyists, and various staffers who wanted to enjoy drinks, steaks, card games, and conversation away from prying eyes; tables were set at discreet distances from each other, and a background murmur drowned out individual voices. Nixon's Secret Service detail stood unobtrusively by the arched doorway, looking judiciously nowhere in particular.

Satisfied, McCarthy leaned across the table. 'Listen up, pal. Just between you and me: I hear things.'

Nixon squinted into the light, rustled against the plant, awaited elaboration.

'For starters: you're too close to a certain fire-breathing champion of liberty. Yours truly, pal. Here's the straight dope. Ike smiles to your face, tells you he's grooming you to take his place, and then cuts you out. He keeps you away from Gettysburg, makes plans to drop you from the ticket, and tries to pin every failure on your shoulders.'

'That's old news,' grumbled Nixon.

'Okay, so here's the headline. He's decided to run again – that's the scuttlebutt in the back rooms. Up until last week, he didn't know his plans for sure. Mamie wants him to give it up, you know. But all the waiting around, convalescing, drives him crazy. He claims he doesn't enjoy the office – too much politics, he says, too much glad-handing – but the fact is, he likes it better than the alternative. And here's the real kick in the nuts – you ready for this?' McCarthy leaned even closer, delivering a wilting blast of commingled whiskey and halitosis. 'He wants Anderson by his side: a *Democrat*. Can you get your head around that? He wants a Democrat, and he's going to ask you to *voluntarily step down*. Of course, that's career suicide for you. But he'll give you some patronizing bullshit about how it's for your own good, how you need administrative experience before your own run in '60, how he'll give you a good Cabinet position during his second administration – can you believe this crap? After you take care of things so swell while the old man rots in his sickbed, this is how he repays you?'

Coolly, Nixon leaned away. He did not want to respond to the bait, jumping like a dog at a bone for McCarthy's amusement. But the revelation had the ring of truth – Nixon had, in fact, suspected as much for a long time – and his fury, although masked, was beyond calculation.

Ike, the worthless traitor, the no-good rat – everything McCarthy had said was dead on the money. For as long as Eisenhower and Nixon had worked together, the elder man had accorded the younger no respect. Old enough to be Nixon's father, Ike refused to see his second-in-command as anything like an equal. He had called the Vice President 'immature', declaring him 'not presidential timber', worrying out loud about not having established 'a logical successor' – although none of it had been said, of course, to Nixon's face. Many considered Eisenhower the bravest of the brave, but Richard Nixon knew better. The President had a yellow streak a mile wide running down the center of his back.

But as the General had waffled endlessly before committing to his first run, who had been the one to cease splitting hairs, the one who dared tell him to shit or get off the pot? Only Nixon had done him that good service. And how had Eisenhower responded? With a furious dressing-down, the sting of which the younger man still felt to this day. Time and again the President had used his Vice President as a political tool: to mollify the right, bait the Reds, and handle the negative campaigning, while Ike cozied up with Democrats, city machines, labor unions, minorities, and egghead intellectuals. And then he dared describe Nixon as overly partisan, hanging his deputy out to dry in the press.

'He can't put enough distance between you and him,' McCarthy continued. 'What do you think that means, Dick? That he's getting ready to have you and the family over for dinner? Or does it mean—'

'Joe.' Nixon's tone stopped the man in his tracks. 'I get it.'

McCarthy paused. Seeing the cold light in Nixon's eyes, he smiled mordantly. 'Just trying to help out an old buddy,' he said. 'Consider it a friendly heads-up.'

'Sure.'

'That's not all.' Idly, McCarthy traced with one broad index finger a fleur-de-lis embossed on the tablecloth. 'There's another story being told, in these back rooms.'

'I'm all ears.'

'There are still some patriots in this country, you know. And they're not just going to sit back and let Ike get away with this.'

Nixon said nothing. The remaining members of the 'Loyal American Underground', as McCarthy called his personal web of seditionists, had lost their power when Joe had lost his, but there was no delicate way to put this.

'And there's Hoover,' added McCarthy. 'Don't forget Hoover. He's in your corner, Dick. He can make things happen – or he can get out of the way and *let* things happen.'

A sly pause. 'What things?' Nixon asked.

'Let's just say, you never know what's coming down the pike. Sometimes things have a way of working themselves out.'

Nixon shook his head. McCarthy's heart was in the right place – but he was a shadow of his former self, and good judgment had never been his strong suit. Nixon's slow tumble from grace within the Eisenhower administration had become all but irreversible. Only if the President suddenly died or became terminally incapacitated could the Vice President, inheriting the crown by default, become a serious contender for the upcoming nomination.

'My point is, things happen. Especially to old men with bad hearts.' A waiter passed by; McCarthy raised his finger from the tablecloth. 'Just keep it in mind – in case you were having trouble sleeping at night. Me, I sleep like a baby. *Garçon*: another aperitif, *s'il vous plaît*.'

PART TWO

Only Americans can hurt America.
                    Dwight D. Eisenhower

SIX

ROUTE 30: NOVEMBER 16

The reflection staring back from the rear-view mirror looked like hell: badly shaven, tie and hat askew, dark bags of fatigue brooding beneath weary green eyes. But the whites of those eyes were clear, and the breath, when Isherwood blew into a cupped hand, smelled of nothing except cigarettes and mouthwash.

He was ready for his close-up, he supposed – as ready as he'd ever be.

After tipping the service station attendant, he pulled back onto the road. One advantage to travelling at twilight was the scarcity of traffic; as soon he'd left Gettysburg, his Studebaker had become the only car in sight.

All through the day, sitting at his window and watching Eisenhower paint and write correspondence on the sun porch, Isherwood had resented the looming appointment with Max Whitman. How was he meant to do his job when hobbled by second-guessing and distrust? Besides, he had nothing to report – four days of asking questions around town and the farm had yielded precious little of value. But with the window down and a never-ending succession of cigarettes burning between his fingertips, he found himself glad to be away from the farm, out on the open road.

As he pressed east, undulating foothills evolved gradually into the steeper Alleghenies. In his rear-view, the lingering sunset lit the mountains gently from behind and beneath. The glow made him think of Evelyn – the way her hair hung in a loose spill, backlit by the goose-necked lamp, when she read at night in bed. He missed her fiercely. He wondered when – or if – he would get a chance to bestow the modest gift he'd bought at the chemist's. God knew he owed her more than a bottle of dime-store perfume. But it was a start. *Consider it*, he would tell her, *a down payment on bigger things.*

Flicking on the dashboard radio, turning up the volume to compete with the wind, he dialed past static, past a station playing standards, past static, past a rock and roll signal – WLS – coming all the way out of Chicago, past static. He found a weather report and headlines, both bracing: a cold front was coming in, and Big Four talks in Geneva had ended in failure. Snapping off the radio, he shook his head. A united Germany would encourage stability in the world. But reconsolidation seemed not to be in the cards. Sighing, he lit another cigarette from the butt of his last. He missed his wife; he missed his cats.

The Studebaker's headlamps carved a slice out of the accumulating mountain darkness. The engine labored as he climbed a particularly steep pass without slowing. As he crested the peak and started down, his stomach gave a vertiginous lift and corresponding drop.

Then sounded a very distant *crack*, flat and dry – if he hadn't been smoking with the window open, he wouldn't have heard it at all – and in the next heartbeat the Studebaker jolted painfully. The steering went slippery beneath his hands; the wheel spun wildly, and he lost control, careening hard to the left, plowing full-force into the guard rail.

Hart worked the bolt.

Then he paused. The Studebaker was riding full-speed along the rail, kicking up a ferocious shower of sparks. With any luck the barrier would let go and the vehicle would tumble into the valley, and gravity would finish Hart's work for him.

He returned eye to scope. His shot had been true; the car's left front tire was no more. The eerie shriek of shredding metal rang out across the valley. The blazing sparks and strange wail evoked a sudden memory: his father telling him a bedtime story, about the will-o'-the-wisp.

For a protracted moment the Studebaker trembled against the precipice, hood welded to railing. Then the remaining tires grabbed hold of the asphalt again, and with a pained wrench the car disengaged. For twenty yards the rear fishtailed in a clumsy burlesque. Slewing back into its original lane, then, the sedan drifted into a one-hundred-and-eighty degree pinwheeling skid. At last, facing ass-backwards, it ground painfully to a stop.

Hart clicked his tongue. Fate would require a gentle nudge, after all. But it should not be a problem. Any second now, Isherwood would step out to inspect the tire. Presenting himself in the full glare of headlights as he circled the hood, he would make an easy target.

Finger hovering against trigger, Hart held his breath.

For a long while, or so it seemed, Isherwood just sat, gripping the steering wheel, listening to the distant echo of shrieking tires and metal through the valley.

His mind had slowed to a deliberate crawl, as it had during times of action during the war. The air reeked of shredded rubber and spilled oil and fresh winter pines. He had lost his cigarette somewhere. He started to reach for another, and then slowly reconsidered – not with that oil-stink in the air.

A tire had blown out. He had gone into a skid, a bad one. But he had recovered, gentling the bullet nose back from the precipice. With the immediate danger now past, time should have returned to its normal, easy flow. Yet his perception kept scissoring each instant into microscopic units, as it had during combat. Because the danger *wasn't* past, his body was insisting to his brain. Appearances deceived.

The events leading up to the crash replayed methodically past his mind's eye. He had thought of giving Evy her perfume; he had switched on the radio. The weather was turning cold, and Big Four talks had failed. He had snapped off the radio, lighting another cigarette from the butt of the last. He missed his wife, missed his cats. He had gone up a steep hill and come down the other side, his stomach giving a commensurate lift and drop. Then had come a distant crack, and the tire had blown out. The crack had been flat and dry, he remembered, and if the window had not been open, he would not have heard it at all. And then he had come within a hair's breadth of going over into the edge, into the ravine.

Again he replayed the scenario. The flat, dry crack; the tire exploding. At last, sluggishly, the thought formed:

Someone had shot out his tire.

As the ticking of the engine slowed, his mind quickened. The shooter must be up on the wooded rise to the right of the road – which meant that with Isherwood now facing backwards, the man was behind him, over his left shoulder. And if Isherwood left the car without taking care, the sniper could ask for no better target.

He had only barely heard the rifle's report, and only by chance – any sane man would have kept his windows closed in this chill. And he had not seen the muzzle flash. So whoever had fired had taken care to find cover on the mountainside, to avoid discovery. The line of thought could be extended: whoever had done this had carefully chosen this stretch of deserted road, where Isherwood would hit the guard rail with such force that his death might look accidental.

And along *those* lines – here his eyes flicked to the side-view mirror, seeking a stirring in the night – the would-be assassin must have realized that there was no guarantee the car would go over the edge. So he would be prepared to help things along, if necessary, *mano-a-mano*.

Isherwood's hand moved at last: not for the cigarettes, but for his snub-nosed Colt Detective Special.

Drawing the gun from its holster, he held it in his lap. The enemy was out there in the night. But why wasn't the sniper shooting again, from his wooded rise, as Isherwood sat here behind the wheel, pondering?

Because the man didn't have a clear shot, of course ... and because he fully expected Isherwood, not realizing that he was dealing with anything except a blow-out, to exit the car and inspect the damage, presenting himself as an easy target in the headlights.

In battle, Eisenhower's voice said, *high ground counts for everything.*

After another moment, Isherwood reached for the latch, his hand remarkably steady.

Opening the driver's-side door, he slipped out of the car, staying low, avoiding the pooling headlights. He ran toward the treeline. No rifle fired. He slipped into dense woods, where the fragrances of pinesap and rosemary hung thick. He moved with surprising dexterity for a man so many years removed from active operations; not blundering, avoiding the worst of the crackling twigs and snapping branches. Some deep-seated instinct had come into play – the same instinct which had allowed him to sneak up behind the Nazi boy, on that long-ago night, with such cruel efficacy – placing his feet for him.

He climbed the hill in a straight line from the place where the car had stopped. He would find the high ground, like Chamberlain at Gettysburg, Philip II at Chaeronea, the Taborite at Hoøice. At worst, a stalemate would be attained. At best, he would find a chance to turn the tables on his unwitting enemy...

Up he went, beneath a moon one shade less than full.

Minutes kept passing, with no figure appearing in the headlights.

Hart took the scope from his eye at last. He wiped at his mouth with his handkerchief, hard enough to draw blood. Had the man left the car, under cover of darkness, and slipped away?

The more Hart considered, the more likely this seemed. So he should go down and find the man and finish it now, before another car happened by and complicated matters. Yes; that was what he should do.

Still he hesitated. Here on the rise with the high ground and the rifle, he retained every advantage. Walking downhill with the pistol, however, he opened himself to the possibility of a fire-fight. The will-o'-the-wisp, his father had said, tempted travelers from safe paths. The gypsy fortune-teller whispered ruefully in his ear: *You see here, how the ominous line crosses the life-line – a short life, this one; a pity.*

Another minute passed. Still the driver did not show himself. Shaking his head, Hart finally stood, slinging the M1903A4 Springfield rifle over his shoulder. Reluctantly, he unholstered his Browning 9mm. He checked the load, thirteen Parabellum rounds nestled inside a detachable box magazine. For a last moment, before striking off, he thought wistfully about his Buick, parked a half-mile distant. It was not too late to choose another place, another time.

But he had already failed the senator twice.

Setting his feet carefully, he started down the hill.

The forest around him rustled secretly. Branches shivered as animals fled his approach. Quiet gathered again in his wake. The night sky glistened in a thousand subtle overlays. Near the mountain tops, the stars faded to blue.

Before leaving the protective reef of forest and stepping onto the road, he took out the handkerchief and compulsively touched his mouth one last time. With renewed determination, then, he cleared all extraneous thoughts from his mind. At this moment there was only hunter and prey. If the man was still inside the car, Hart would get the drop on him. If not, the situation must be resolved now, before a passing vehicle interfered.

Raising the Browning straight-armed, he moved swiftly toward the Studebaker from behind, through the smells of spilled oil and scorched rubber.

The car was empty.

The door hung ajar; a small parcel sat on the passenger seat, still in its wrapping from the chemist's.

'Drop your weapon,' commanded a cold voice behind him.

Hart froze.

His testicles crawled up into his body; his belly

turned to lead. His own goddamned fault. He had followed the will-o'-the-wisp, tempted from his safe path like a fool. He had not heeded the fortune-teller's warning – and from somewhere far away, across the years, she cackled laughter.

Time slowed, turning thick and golden and sweet. He wondered if he could spin around quickly enough to snap off a shot before the man fired. One way to find out...

'Drop your weapon,' the voice ordered again.

The moment lingered, suspended. Something in the back of Hart's mind made an odd humming sound.

Then he spun: almost offhandedly, dropping to one knee, lifting the Browning. A thunderclap rent open the night. He reeled onto his back, the Browning spinning from his limp hand, into the road and then over the side, vanishing into the ravine. A tremendous pressure rose in his right shoulder. His numb hand was trying to fire a gun it no longer held, to empty thirteen Parabellum rounds in the direction of the silhouette he could now see standing not ten feet away: a dark shadow against darker trees, feet planted wide, fedora pushed back, pistol held unshaking in a two-handed grip.

Rolling, Hart reached to unloop the Springfield from over his shoulder. Isherwood fired again and a hot new pressure bloomed in Hart's arm. The rifle fumbled, dropped with a clatter.

When Hart reached stubbornly for the fallen rifle, a third shot rang out, kicking him meanly again in his poor right arm, the report echoing antically across the valley. Then he was tumbling backward, over the same guard rail against which the Studebaker had ridden. The metal was gouged and scratched and still warm. Yelping, he pitched down the steep drop. This wasn't right; it was Isherwood who was supposed to go over the edge, down this rocky slope, Isherwood in his Studebaker—

But it was Hart going down, flipping over now as gravity took more solid hold of him. His wounded arm bounced off a jagged rock, and he cried out sharply.

The world narrowed; time skipped, like a phonograph needle jumping a groove.

When awareness returned he was lying on his back, looking up at stars and an almost full moon. At first he didn't know where he was, although a sense of general urgency enveloped him. Trying to gain his feet, he found his head swimming. His right arm throbbed. One leg twisted beneath him at an unnatural angle. Falling onto his back again, he considered that angle with clinical distance. If that limb really belonged to him, then it was broken in at least one place. Thankfully, he felt no pain.

The world blackened again, like a sheet of paper catching fire from the edges inward. When he returned to himself, he had shifted position slightly on the cold ground. Now only half his field of vision was comprised of moon and stars. The other half was a dark, rocky mountainside, stretching up to a faraway guard rail. A silhouetted and fedora-topped figure leaned over the guard rail, small with distance, searching.

Hart almost giggled. He had tumbled down the

hill, suffering the fate he had meant for his target. The bright side: here at the bottom of the rocky slope, he was beyond Isherwood's reach. There was an undeniable dark humor to it all, a certain poetic justice.

Drifting for a time, he had difficulty separating fantasy from reality. A truck or similarly large vehicle stopped on the road overhead, brakes squealing; he heard tinny voices engaged in discussion. Or was that just a dream? The night sky wheeled dizzyingly, streaking the stars until they looked like shreds of tinsel hanging from a Christmas tree. He felt warm, then cold. A shooting star crossed his field of vision; and he took aim through his scope at a Nazi commander who wore glistening black boots and many decorations; and he took aim from a ridge above the George Washington Memorial Parkway at President Eisenhower, who cowered inside his bubble-topped Chrysler; and he foolishly followed the will-o'-the-wisp, the ghost-fire of legend, the pixie light, which beckoned lost souls; and the old fortune-teller bent close and declared, her voice like a seething nest of vipers, that he would have a short life, a pity.

Then he turned his head, slowly, and saw the sun starting to rise behind jagged mountains.

The light in the sky was unmistakably real. Cars passed on the road above, regularly if infrequently. Daybreak was near. The humming in his head was back, a nest of mad bees.

Isherwood was gone.

And Hart had survived the night.

He began the process of getting his functioning

leg beneath himself: painstakingly, using his one good arm as a lever. By the time he realized the task was impossible – if he wanted to move, he would need to crawl – the sun had risen higher in the sky, the low clouds beyond the mountains shading from pink to yellow.

And so he struck off in a clumsy slither, dragging his wounded leg behind himself, flopping his ruined arm uselessly, moving in the direction of the scenic overlook and his waiting Buick. He would survive this, he told himself. And next time, he would not underestimate his target. Next time, he would pay more heed to the warnings of the fortune-teller and the will-o'-the-wisp.

He slithered: scowling, cursing, weeping with the pain that now flooded his body, overwhelming, all-encompassing; and with every excruciating movement he cursed Jesus, Mary, Joseph, his own errors of judgment, and most of all Agent Francis Isherwood.

SEVEN

THE TREASURY BUILDING:
NOVEMBER 17
Behind his desk at 1500 Pennsylvania Avenue, Max Whitman stared philosophically into space, his broad mouth forming a thoughtful moue.

He pictured a beautiful young girl with hair the

color of autumn dusk, sitting just on the other side of the desk. *You're so handsome, Max. Letting you go was the worst mistake of my life. I'll never leave you again. I love you...*

The door to the reception area leaned open; and there stood Francis Isherwood, looking even less rested and more bedraggled than the last time Max Whitman had seen him. For an instant, the secretary couldn't keep the surprise off his face.

Then he recovered. 'Ish,' he said, managing strained bonhomie.

Stepping into the office, Isherwood let a long moment fall away. At last he said darkly: 'Need to see the Chief.'

'He's in a meeting. You, uh, should have called ahead.' Max glanced around furtively. Leaning across the desk, he dropped his voice. 'Where the hell were you last night? I was standing out in that damned pumpkin patch until the cock crowed.'

'Just let the Chief know I'm here.'

'He gave specific instructions not to be—'

'I'll wait.'

For the next quarter-hour, Isherwood shared the reception area with Max Whitman without once looking in his direction. At last a man wearing pinstripes emerged from the inner sanctum; Isherwood promptly stood. 'Better let me give him a holler,' Max started, but Isherwood had already breezed past him, moving into the office and closing the door resoundingly.

Max tried to distract himself by shuffling papers around the desk. If worse came to worst, he thought, it would be Isherwood's word against his. Unless, that was, they had evidence he didn't know about. Perhaps he had been photographed visiting the senator's mansion in Charlottesville, or talking with someone at the bar of the Mayflower Hotel. Perhaps he should just leave his desk, walk out of the building, and make a run for it. But those would be the actions of a guilty man. He would ruin any future he might still have in Treasury. And there was his wife to consider, his two precious daughters—

Sitting across the desk, the ghost of Betsy Martin wore her default expression, of concerned benevolence. But there was a distracted quality to it, Max noted, as always. Of course, that was how she had been in life too. Sitting alone with him in a parlor, she'd forever given the impression that half of her mind was elsewhere.

Still: that she would sit with him in a parlor at all had been a pleasant surprise. That had been the year of 'Brother, Can You Spare a Dime?' and 'In A Shanty in Old Shanty Town'. Unemployment had reached twenty-four percent, and the suicide rate had risen accordingly. The Depression had worked over the nation like a dog working a bone. Max's world, already painted in squalid shades of gray, had seemed darker every day ... and then there in the midst of the gloom had appeared this beautiful young girl wearing a fresh blue-and-white dress, with kohl pencil around her eyes and a sweet, disarming smile.

How had he ever found the gumption to walk

up to her, that day on the street, and strike up a conversation? The answer: he had been too young and stupid to know any better. And of course Emil Spooner had been by his side, egging him on.

'Go on,' Emil had urged. 'Look how she's standing. Look at those eyes. She's begging for it.'

'So *you* talk to her,' Max had answered.

Emil laughed at the absurdity. Short and scrawny, he had cultivated, that year, the affectations of a tough guy – the Emil who cared nothing for outward appearances was still decades away – wearing a straw hat far back on the crown of his head, as he had seen Pretty Boy Floyd do in photographs, and holding a Cherry Coke into which he had splashed some of his father's whiskey. Emil and Max had played hooky that day, pitching pennies and shoplifting from Woolworths. Now, in late afternoon, they had found Betsy standing on a street corner at the edge of Hooverville, near a hobo sleeping beneath a newspaper on a bench.

'She's out of my league,' Emil said. 'But I can tell she likes the strong, silent type. That's you, glamor boy.'

'What's she doing there?' asked Max, hazily, as if confused by his own question. 'What's she waiting for?'

'I'm telling you, buddy, she's waiting for *you*. She just don't know it yet.'

So Max forced his feet into motion, distracted, nearly getting run down by a streetcar after two steps. Licking his lips, he pressed forward, even as Emil laughed behind him. Approaching Betsy, he smoothed down his bushy cowlick.

As he drew near, she smiled. This confused him. Max Whitman was grindingly poor, even by Depression standards. Nobody would ever mistake him for smart, and his own mother didn't think he was especially handsome – yet, for some reason, Betsy was smiling.

'Hi,' he said.

'Hi.'

'I know you. You're Betsy.' He scratched his cowlick. 'I'm Max.'

She looked him up and down. 'I know *you*,' she said. 'You beat the hell out of Walter Addams, last year, in the school yard.'

Turning, Max gestured in explanation toward Emil Spooner, standing on the other side of the street. 'He called my friend an Abercrombie.'

'You sent Walt to the hospital, huh?' Her eyes gave a febrile glitter.

Max only shrugged.

'Want to buy me a Moxie?'

'Uh ... sure.'

She crooked out an arm. 'Lead the way, slugger.'

She had no brother or sister to look out for her. Her father worked late hours as a bookkeeper; her mother, occupied with mysterious errands from sunup to sundown, showed no interest in chaperoning. And for whatever reason, Betsy seemed only too happy to give Max a whirl.

They went to movies, sat in chairs of fumed oak in her father's parlor, and walked hand-in-hand around the block. At a local dance hall, they

114

swayed together across a packed floor to 'Mood Indigo', through smoky darkness and the fragrance of black market booze. She smiled up at him, all eyes and lips. 'I don't bite, slugger,' she said, and so he stole his first kiss.

And soon enough he stole more: in the back row at the movies, or in dark nickelodeons or public parks when nobody was looking, sneaking his hand up beneath her sweater or skirt until, cheeks flushed, she pulled away with contrived shock. Thus did the spring of '33 pass, with Max happily disbelieving his own good fortune, even as the rest of the nation writhed in agony and hunger pains.

One evening early in summer, she let it be known that she would take his ring. That night Max begged his mother to honor a promise she had made long before. Now that the moment had arrived, however, Mother proved reluctant to relinquish her engagement ring. At last she worked the stone grudgingly from one veined hand, passed it over along with an admonishment: *I hope you know what you're doing, with this girl*. The next afternoon Max slipped the ring onto Betsy's dainty finger. Together they admired the small European-cut diamond, the way it caught the light when she turned her hand.

Two weeks later, after a matinee of *The Invisible Man* starring Claude Rains, they stopped off at a soda fountain. Perched on a stool behind a marble counter, studying her own reflection in a large gilded mirror backing arching silver spouts, Betsy suddenly asked, 'Why are you friends with Emil, anyway?'

The question took him off-guard. 'Why?' he repeated dumbly.

'Yeah. Why? He's a wet sock.'

Max shrugged heavy shoulders. 'Long as I can remember, we've been friends.'

'But what do you *get* from it? You protect him from bullies and moolies. And what does he do for you?'

'You don't know Emil. One day, he'll do plenty for me. Hell, he already has.'

'Like what?'

'Like for starters: if not for him, I never would-'ve met you.'

That piqued her interest. She made a motion with her straw: *Go on.*

'He's the one told me to talk to you. See, Emil's got vision. He's got a lot of things – brains, and personality, and a good family name – but most important, he's got vision. He thinks big.'

'Huh,' she said.

'He's going places. And if I'm lucky, he might let me tag along. Best I can hope for without him, between you and me? An apple cart to push. That or the breadlines. But if we stay close – who knows?'

'Huh,' she repeated thoughtfully.

Looking back, he realized that with this conversation he had sealed his own fate. But with Betsy on his arm, his happiness had been so pure and simple that he had let down his guard, trusting her – and Emil – to behave honorably.

One Tuesday in early autumn, she had suggested a walk 'round the block. Max had gladly agreed. But soon enough, he knew that something was terribly wrong. For the whole first circuit she remained quiet, lost in thought. He talked loosely and foolishly to fill the silence, babbling on about *Grand Hotel* and a new college basketball rule that required the ball to be brought over the midcourt line in ten seconds. But eventually he ran out breath, and then she broke the news: she had decided to go steady with Emil, which meant she could no longer see Max.

He begged, threatened, and cajoled. Betsy only shook her head sadly. No matter what words he flung at her, she offered neither argument nor explanation. She just kept shaking her head, calmly, imperturbably. At the end of the walk, she returned his ring, affecting sorrow. But she seemed distracted, as always, with half her mind far away. At that instant, something curdled deep inside Max's stomach – the same thing which remained festering even today.

Later that night he found Emil sitting on a front stoop, nursing a Cherry Coke. At the sight of his friend coming down the block, Emil immediately read the situation correctly. Standing abruptly, spilling out drifts of sawdust which he used to prevent the jingling of coins in his pockets, he backed away, raising hands defensively. 'Max,' he said. 'Listen. She told me it was over with you...'

Max came to a stop at the foot of the stoop. 'It's not over.'

'She said she gave you back your ring.'

'She...' Max faltered, speechless.

'Buddy, listen. I never would have done it if I'd known you were still carrying a torch.'

'Well, now you know.'

'Yeah, but she's made her choice, hasn't she?'

Max waited for Emil to finish his explanation. It took him to a minute to understand that his friend *had* finished.

On the surface, the rift between them quickly healed. Emil swore up and down that he hadn't known Max and Betsy were still a couple, and within a few days, Max reluctantly gave them his blessing. Without Emil's support and contacts, after all, Max had no future worth mentioning. The friendship was one boat he could not afford to rock. And just three weeks later, Betsy met a guy from the Palisades and dumped Emil, and drifted out of both of their lives.

And as Emil's career took off, he indeed brought Max along for a merry ride. Becoming a prison warden, he made Max Whitman his second. Becoming Chief of the Secret Service, he made Max his personal secretary. For weeks, months, sometimes even years, Max would forget Betsy Martin completely. And yet still the vision of the beautiful young girl, with her blue-and-white dress and her auburn hair shimmering, would visit him at the most unexpected moments ... *I don't bite.*

Eventually had come 1953, and a stretch of dark days by which even the Depression seemed bright in comparison. His marriage had reached a nadir. The vision of Betsy had been with him constantly, and his resentment of Spooner had fermented into something pungent and intoxicating. More than once, after a long week of being bossed around by the Chief, he had shot off his mouth indiscreetly at the bar inside the Mayflower Hotel. With ears everywhere, it had been only a matter of time before certain organized people had heard of his complaints. Making contact, they had offered both a modest supplement to his government salary and a chance for long-awaited revenge against Emil Spooner.

Betsy was sitting across the desk again, smiling. *Don't worry about Frank Isherwood, slugger. He can't hurt you. Nobody can, as long as you've got me.*

The door leading out to the main atrium opened again.

Two Secret Service agents stepped into the reception area. Neither was on the Chief's docket for a morning appointment. 'Lou,' said Max with false cheer. 'Eddie. How's tricks?'

Lou Candless and Eddie Grieg just grunted, taking up position on either side of the door – preventing Max Whitman's escape.

'Here to see the Chief?' Max lifted his phone. 'He's in a meeting. But I'll see if he can make some room...'

When he rang Spooner's office, however, there was no reply. And in the next moment, two more agents had appeared inside the reception area.

'Fellows.' Max strove to keep his tone light. 'What's going on?'

No response. Then the door behind him opened, and the Chief stepped out of the inner sanctum. 'Max,' he said, 'go with these boys and answer a few questions, all right?'

Behind his desk again, the Chief let out a long, shaken breath. 'You're sure about this?'

Somberly, Isherwood nodded.

'But I've known him longer than I've known you.' The Chief gazed abstractedly up at the electric ormolu chandelier as he spoke. 'Longer than I've worked for the Service. I've known him my entire life.'

Lighting a cigarette, Isherwood withheld comment.

'Before we start on him,' Spooner went on tightly, 'you'd better be absolutely certain you-'ve got your ducks in a row. I mean one hundred per cent.'

'If someone else knew we were meeting, Chief, clue me in. Otherwise...'

'Maybe they had someone watching the farm. Maybe a signal was sent.'

'But without inside information, they wouldn't even have noticed me. And they sure wouldn't have known when and where I'd be on that highway.' Isherwood let a beat pass before stating baldly: 'Max sold us out.'

To Spooner, the office suddenly seemed too warm. He loosened his tie, unfastened his top button. 'We're talking about my oldest friend, Ish. And I still have to sleep nights.'

'And we both,' responded Isherwood evenly, 'have to protect the President. And if they managed to penetrate this office ... who knows where else they've infiltrated?'

The Chief shook his head. He clenched his fists, raised and then lowered them impotently.

'Good Christ,' he said. 'Good Christ. Who's supposed to run the fucking interrogation?'

'Candless and Grieg.' Isherwood watched a coil of smoke work its way across the desk. 'They're good men. And no matter how much you might want to play things close to the vest, we can't handle this alone – not any more. Way I see it, this attack by the highway tells us three things we didn't know yesterday. One, it's real. They're out there. Two, we're hitting a sore spot. We can't back off now. Three, Max knows something. We need to find out what.'

Spooner leaned back in his chair, closing his eyes.

'And this tall bastard by Route Thirty,' Isherwood went on, 'is another thread we can pull on. He left his rifle behind. Springfield M1903: standard issue during the Big One.'

Spooner's eyes opened. 'So he's a vet.'

'Ten to one.' Isherwood picked a flake of tobacco from his tongue. 'Man his height stands out. Give me some wheels to replace the bullet nose, and I'll hit some standard haunts – VAs, Rotary Clubs, VFA, American Legion. See if I can find someone who matches the description.'

Spooner pooched out his lips. He drummed fingertips against the desk blotter. 'And who guards Eisenhower while you're out playing gumshoe?'

'Start with Phil Zane. Kid's got grit. Lefty Marato, Leo Wayne ... all stand-up guys. They'll take a bullet without hesitating.'

'You'll vouch for them?'

'In a heartbeat.'

121

'I'd have vouched for Max, too. To hell and back, I'd have vouched for him.'

Isherwood said nothing.

Spooner rubbed at his brow for fully half a minute. His Adam's apple leapt. He took out a cigarette and spent another thirty seconds studying it. At last he returned from his higher plane of thought and started patting chest and thighs, seeking matches. Isherwood leaned forward, offering his Zippo.

'I don't care if you need to turn over every goddamned rock on the eastern seaboard.' The Chief exhaled a thrashing dragon of smoke. 'Find that cocksucker.'

Isherwood nodded.

CHARLOTTESVILLE

Beneath Richard Hart's cast, the broken leg throbbed and itched. Even worse was the wounded shoulder, which below the bandage burned and seethed. Worst of all, however, was the wound to the pride.

For a long moment, Bolin looked at him critically. 'Are you in pain?'

'I'll manage.'

'The doctor who worked on you...'

'A friend of the movement. Completely discreet.'

But Bolin hesitated – doubting Hart's judgment. And who could blame him? 'Well,' said the senator at last. *'Bois tortu fait feu droit.* Crooked logs make straight fires. Instead of being frustrated by a bad situation, the wise man finds a way to improve it.'

Hart nodded.

'The failed attack has doubtless made our friend Isherwood aware that he is a target. So there's no longer any need for his death to look circumstantial.' Insouciantly, Bolin inspected one manicured cuticle. 'You have no shortage of ... unsavory ... contacts, I take it, from your years on the street...?'

'I'll take care of him.'

'And the rifle in New York?'

'Not ready until Sunday.'

'That gives you time to finish what you've started.'

'Yes, sir.'

'Mister Hart: no more failures. Or I might begin to question my judgment of character.'

Hart squared his shoulders, setting his jaw. 'Yes, sir.'

Bolin watched him go, listened to the disjointed echo of the crutches – click-CLACK, click-CLACK, click-CLACK – bouncing back from the tall ceilings.

Outwardly, the senator remained calm. Beneath the surface, he felt considerably less at ease. Presently, he sighed, moving back into the study. Falling into the chair behind his desk, he doffed his spectacles and rubbed at the bridge of his nose.

Lighting a Viceroy, he found himself looking at a framed photograph on the desk. From the faded photo, his dear departed wife gazed back at him with pointed eyes. Her sepia gaze seemed to smolder with contempt. The daughter of one of the most powerful landowners south of the Mason-Dixon, she had never hesitated to voice her criticisms ... which may have been why Bolin so rarely mourned her passing.

But look what happens when I'm not around, those eyes seemed to say. *You've let this run away with you. And now it's all going to turn to ash in your hands.*

Coolly, he smoked. There had been missteps, he acknowledged tacitly; there had been missed opportunities. But Vera was mistaken. In the important ways, things remained under control.

You should have cut Hart loose long ago. Now he may have ruined everything.

But Vera was being uncharitable, as was her wont. The endgame was near. With the condition that Isherwood's death look accidental removed, it became a simple matter of attacking with over-whelming force. Hart could handle it. Then the only man in a position to interfere with the girl would be out of the way.

You try to put a good light on it, sniffed Vera. *But facts are facts. Your pansy failed again, and now Spooner's guesses have been confirmed. They'll realize that only one man could have betrayed Isherwood. Then they'll arrest and interrogate Max Whitman. And Whitman will turn on you, and you'll get just what you deserve for your incompetence.*

Again, she was mistaken. Whatever his ... complications ... Hart could finish Isherwood. And Emil Spooner had already proven himself hesitant, overcautious. After Isherwood's death, he would not move decisively in time to change

124

anything. In fact, the second brazen strike would send a clear message: nobody was beyond their reach.

Don't be a fool, said Vera. *Make provisions for the worst. Be prepared for any eventuality.*

Sharp-tongued she may have been ... but his wife had also been shrewd. It paid to prepare for worst-case scenarios.

Bolin grunted softly to himself.

Lifting the telephone, then, he made preparations: a car to the coast, steamship passage booked across the Atlantic, and a stateroom which would remain empty, creating confusion as to his true whereabouts – and another car to National Airport, where a twin-engine plane would spirit him to the Wulffs' allies in Argentina. He would remove himself from the equation until the deed was done, in case Max Whitman should crack. Only when it was finished would he return, to bask in his triumph. Any suspicion that fell his way then could be deflected by powerful allies newly ensconced in the White House. In the meantime, his staff would respond to inquiries with a simple statement concerning an unexpected personal issue.

After placing his calls, he moved to a Sergeant & Greenleaf safe hidden behind a landscape on the wall. From inside he withdrew two rolls of bills, which he pocketed, and various papers which could ruin the reputation his family had spent generations building. He carried the papers to the fireplace. Setting aside the brass screen, he reached for a platinum-encased poker and stirred the coals until the small, hot center was revealed.

Trading poker for bellows, he coaxed the small center into a lick of flame. He then selected slivers of kindling, dry and brittle, which he used to encourage the lick of flame into a lapping tongue. One by one he fed papers into the fire.

From the Rolodex on his desk he chose several cards, which he also brought to the fireplace. These were followed by documents removed from drawers, cabinets, and leaves of books. The pages burned quickly, sometimes lifting on a slight updraft before crumbling to ash. When all had crumbled, he replaced the brass screen.

He filled a snifter with brandy, lit another Viceroy, and summoned his butler. Young William arrived seconds later, with buttons on his red vest glimmering. His family had served Bolin's for generations, and Bolin trusted him implicitly to perform certain tasks.

William listened attentively to his instructions. Bowing from the waist, he departed to pack a suitcase as ordered.

Awaiting the arrival of his car, Bolin swished cognac around his mouth. His remote gaze returned to the photograph of his wife. Surely it was only his imagination, he thought, that she seemed now to smirk with satisfaction.

EIGHT

GETTYSBURG
Evening found Elisabeth and Josette together in Josette's room: Elisabeth sitting on the bed, paging through a recent copy of *Life* magazine and listening with half an ear to Fats Domino's 'Ain't That a Shame', while Josette preened in front of the mirror, inspecting from every angle the effect her new brassiere had on her figure. Outside frost-rimed windows, a cold wind rattled the panes in their frames.

As Elisabeth licked her finger to turn another page, Josette suddenly whirled from the mirror. 'I can't bear it any longer,' she said. 'I've got something to tell you.'

Nonplussed, Elisabeth looked up.

'Libby: I'm in love!'

Elisabeth forced a smile. 'Why, that's wonderful!'

'His name is James. Isn't that regal? People call him Jim – sometimes even Jimmy – but to me, he's always been James. And if we have a son and name it after him, I'll insist everyone use the proper form of the name: James, Junior.' Unself-conscious of her half-nudity, Josette sat down beside Elisabeth. 'I was trying not to say anything because I didn't want to sound foolish;

I know how it might sound. "Oh, there's scatter-brained Josie, in love again. Hasn't she already been engaged? Say it ain't so, Jo!" But this time is different, Libby. It's different because *he's* different. And now I realize for the first time what love really is.'

James, it transpired, was employed on the farm as a handyman. Quite possibly Elisabeth had even seen him – he lived on the first floor and worked mostly in the barns. Josette described an Adonis straight out of Greek mythology, broad of shoulder and chest, narrow of waist, strong of heart and mind. Not only was he good with his hands (here Josette manufactured a studied little blush), but he was ambitious; he had gone to college for half a year on the GI Bill before dropping out. At some point, he might even go back and finish his education. But responsibilities had intervened, in the form of his first wife, whom he had knocked up and then, conscientiously, married – until reality had intruded, and recognizing his own limitations, he had wisely filed for divorce. This development, as Josette presented it, was proof of his depth of character. Although they had known each other for ten months, their love had been consummated only the week before, most unexpectedly. She had been dispatched to deliver a dipperful of buttermilk to the aptly-named Maternity Barn—

Elisabeth refrained from commenting. The girl had taken a roll in the hay – quite literally, from the sound of it – with a self-admitted cad. If she had *truly* known how it sounded, she would not be congratulating herself.

'His kisses tasted like buttermilk. But then I found myself in a quandary, Libby; you can imagine. You don't want to make things too easy for a man, because nothing turns off an experienced fellow like a girl who goes all the way too fast.' Bending over, showing Elisabeth unsightly rolls of fat bunching up beneath the strap of her brassiere, she reached beneath the bed, pawing around – the guitar down there shifted in its case – and coming up with a bottle of schnapps. 'But you also don't want to play too hard to get and make him think you're not interested. So it was a matter of finding the right balance: encouraging him just enough, but not too much...'

Listening, Elisabeth maintained an attentive expression, even as it started to feel fixed and plastic. Let Josette make whatever mistakes in love she wanted; it was none of Elisabeth's concern. The important thing was that the girl keep trusting her. For the plan to work, everyone on the farm had to accept that they were friends.

The charade need continue for only a few more days. Then the gun would be delivered, the target eliminated, the mission complete.

The funny thing about kisses, Josette was saying, was that you never knew beforehand how they would be. The homeliest man on the planet might turn out to be the best kisser, or vice versa. Or you might hit the jackpot, as she had with James, and get the best of both worlds...

CHARLOTTESVILLE

Before climbing the stairs of the unassuming brick building – *BPOE* read a banner weakly illumined by a stuttering streetlamp – Francis Isherwood paused to check his reflection in a storefront.

The long day following a sleepless night showed in his face. Beneath the streetlamp's harsh light, every wrinkle and pouch was thrown into sharp relief. And he had thought he looked like hell before all this...

After a moment, he moved up the stairs. The block was crowded with similar unassuming brick facades, each flying an American flag and announcing its purview via marquee or neon sign: 'CAFÉ (Drink Coca-Cola In Bottles!)', 'ECONOMY CLEANERS (We Clean Rugs)', 'FURNITURE NEW AND USED', 'SEAFOOD RESTAURANT', 'MONITCELLO DRUGS', 'PIEDMONT REALTY'.

When he opened the door, the building breathed: shoe polish, disinfectant, Vitalis, coffee, body odor, tobacco. A swatch of nubby carpet covered only a thin wedge of the vestibule's wooden flooring. A circle of watery light ceded the corners to darkness. Slightly off to one side, a mop and bucket had been abandoned mid-washing.

An old man wearing an institutional janitor's uniform leaned against an arched doorway, facing away, listening to a speaker in the next room. Quietly, Isherwood joined him. From behind a squat lectern a man in his fifties, wearing a bespoke dark-blue suit, addressed a ragtag audience of about two dozen. Beneath faded lithographs of Washington and Lincoln, a folding bridge table supported paper cups, plates of muffins and cookies, and a percolating urn of coffee.

'There are still good fellows out on the front lines, of course.' The speaker chose one member of the audience after another with whom to make pointed, meaningful eye contact. 'Nationalists and patriots, fighting the good fight, beating back the tide. These are the men who battle every day to reverse the damage done by Ike's bipartisan appeasement, to correct the mistake of accepting compromise in Korea, to repudiate the sell-out at Yalta, to liberate the satellites in Eastern Europe, to purge the government of fellow travelers, to beat back the threat of *Brown V. Board of Education* before all our grandchildren become mud babies...'

The janitor snorted skeptically.

'But unfortunately,' the speaker continued, 'our President is not among these heroes. His form of Democracy, my friends, is nothing but Communism under another name. Expanding Social Security, resisting military interests, kowtowing to our enemies in Europe, standing aside as schools become integrated ... the man might most generously be considered a dupe. The truth is likely somewhat worse. He's as bad as Adlai Stevenson, with his holes in his shoes.'

The janitor used one arthritis-swollen finger to pick inside his ear, as if something there might be interfering with his hearing.

'The compromises of recent administrations have changed the course of the nation in ways for which our children and grandchildren will pay a price for generations to come. Who can

131

forget the spectacle of a Negro soprano per-
forming at Truman's inauguration? And as for
the so-called Republican, General Eisenhower;
well, it's no wonder that, up until the last second,
everyone thought he might run as a Democrat.
Take my word: scratch Ike and you'll find that
he's pink as a flamingo, just below the surface.
He's done everything in his power to expand
Frank D. Rosenfeld's Jew Deal. Now, I would
never make the mistake of denigrating Ike's
military record' – here the speaker paused
solemnly, placing hand over heart – 'but the fact
remains: the rising Soviet tide proves that
Eisenhower led us to victory in the wrong war,
fought against the wrong enemy at the wrong
time.'

The janitor muttered something derisive. But
many of the men in the room were listening intently, and Isherwood, watching them, felt a
twinge of profound disquiet.

'Integration, my friends, is an insidious movement fostered by the Reds, designed to sabotage
America from within. Greedy bankers and cor-
rupt politicians have sold the country out from
beneath the very veterans who risked everything
to defend it overseas. Jews grow ever richer,
while the rest of us can't put food on our tables.
And is it a coincidence that all Commies are
kikes, and all labor unions are in their pockets?'
He shook his head in disgust. 'And why is every
man in America pressed to stand either for
England or for Russia? Whatever happened to
Americans standing simply for *America*?'

An unruly murmur roiled the crowd. Isherwood blinked, lit a cigarette.

After finishing, the speaker circled the room, shaking hands. 'Hope I can count on your vote,' he said sincerely, and then to the next man: 'Hope can I count on your vote.' The assembly floated apart, reforming around the refreshments. Many displayed the appetite of men who had not recently eaten.

The janitor slipped back into the vestibule, where he picked up the mop and commenced slopping sudsy water across the wooden floor. Isherwood approached him, leaving his ID untouched. The man was pushing seventy, with a jaundiced complexion and angry set to his features. 'Evening,' Isherwood said easily.

The janitor showed yellowing teeth in a deeply lined face – an approximation of a smile – and kept mopping.

'I'm looking for someone, old-timer. Maybe you can help me out.'

A surly grunt.

'Tall fellow,' Isherwood said. 'Over six feet. Somewhere in his middle–late thirties. They say he can find his way around a Springfield rifle. He's been known to frequent VAs, Rotary Clubs, Elks and Kiwanis and such – anyplace he can get in out of the weather – although not for a few years now.'

The janitor stopped mopping. Unobtrusively, with his puffy fingers, he stuck a chaw of tobacco between cheek and gum. 'What do you want him for?'

'Well, sir, that's a long story.'

'Go on. Bore me.'

So Isherwood laid out the tale he'd told four other times, during the past fourteen hours, at waterfront bars and veterans' hospitals and Elks clubs and American Legion headquarters. His brother had served during the war – as had he himself – and had made a buddy overseas. Isherwood had never met this buddy, but he'd heard his brother talk about the man, and once he'd seen a photograph. Seemed the fellow had given his brother a gold money-clip when the latter had shipped back stateside, with a request to deliver said money-clip home to his family. But for some reason, Ish's brother had held onto the clip – and now that he had passed in a car accident, it didn't do to speculate too much about the reasons why, not speaking ill of the dead and all. Well, in searching through his brother's belongings, Isherwood had stumbled onto this gold clip. Remembering its history, he'd decided it was only right to do what his brother had never done and return the thing to its rightful owner. Hell, maybe it was his own strange way of grieving. But all he had to go on was a long-ago glimpse of a snapshot and a few old war stories. Nevertheless, he'd done his best, asking around VAs and clubhouses, hoping to get lucky. And he'd rung a lot of bells as he went, gathering more information on the man from people who remembered someone fitting the description. But nobody had been able to give him a name. And now the trail was growing cold, for during the past three years, nobody had seen this mystery man at all.

Pensively, the janitor leaned an elbow on his

broom. 'Sounds to me like you're talking about Dick Hart. Rifleman during the war. Tall drink o' water. Middle thirties, now.'

'Dick Hart,' repeated Isherwood carefully. 'Seen him lately?'

'No, sir, not for, oh, must be a few years now, just like you say. But once upon a time, he came through pretty often. Just as you describe – drifting around. Mebbe he found someplace to settle down and that's why we ain't seen him lately. I hope so. Nice fella.' The janitor unfolded a paper cup from a back pocket, hissed into it a stream of brown saliva. 'Not like some of these assholes,' he added, lowering his voice. 'They talk their poison right in front of me, the bastards, with no shame 't'all.'

'Takes all kinds,' Isherwood allowed.

'Hell. These America Firsters and Christian Fronters and KKKers – Coughlinites, all of them, just under a different name. Colonel McCormick would be proud, the old fuck.' He was gazing off now over the heads of the men, at the faded lithographs of Washington and Lincoln hanging near the lectern below red, white, and blue bunting. 'I fought myself – in the first war. And I seen some things in those trenches, boy howdy. But a man needs to let go of hate and move on.'

Isherwood nodded.

'But they're *proud* of their hate. That's the worst of it. Why, they turn what this country is all about right onto its head.' Another angry hiss of saliva into cup. 'When other nations fight, they fight for themselves – for their borders, for their men and women and children. And I don't begrudge them that right. But when Americans fight, we fight for all men. For everyone – for equality – for freedom.'

He stopped, gummily blinked. 'Why, I just made a goddamned speech, didn't I?'

'And a good one, sir.' Isherwood nodded toward the lectern. 'Damn sight better than that one.'

Embarrassed, the man looked away. 'Well, hell. If you find Dick, tell him Leo says hi. He might not remember me. But tell it anyways.'

As Isherwood left the clubhouse the old man was still leaning against his broom handle, looking distractedly up at the lithographs of Washington and Lincoln, and the red, white, and blue bunting above them.

GETTYSBURG

Bob Skinnerton manned the gate alone.

The private line running into the booth gave a piercing ring. Lifting the receiver he said, 'Skinnerton.'

'We're about to have some visitors.' Bill Brennan sounded annoyed. 'Agent Zane, replacing Isherwood, and two others. We're to make them feel welcome. That means they retain their sidearms.'

'But that's—'

'Direct order from the Chief,' said Brennan. 'Got it?'

Skinnerton sighed. 'Got it,' he said. But after hanging up, he groaned aloud.

Five minutes later, glowing headlights broke

136

the darkness. A full-throated engine gave a diminishing roar. Skinnerton reached for a foot switch, which triggered a high-intensity arc lamp, picking out the men inside the vehicle as it pulled to a stop.

The agent behind the wheel was young – mid-twenties – with sharp cheekbones, dark hair pomaded back straight from a high forehead, and a slight, short build. He handed over a leather shield. 'Agent Philip Zane.'

Skinnerton glanced at the ID, handed it back. As the agent started unlimbering his holster, Skinnerton shook his head. 'Chief called ahead. You've got a special dispensation.'

In the shotgun seat sprawled a desk jockey Skinnerton vaguely recognized, an older man wearing a charcoal suit. Handing forward his own shield, the man said: 'Agent Marato.'

In back was a third: burly, with a greasy fore-lock hanging over one eye. 'Agent Wayne,' he said, passing up his badge.

Skinnerton glanced at the IDs, handed them back, and opened the gate. Closing the barrier behind the Packard, he let out another long, slow breath. The barbarians, he thought, were taking over Rome.

Philip Zane set the holstered Colt onto the dresser.

He moved to the window and parted the muslin curtain, found a light glowing from the second story of the Eisenhower home. After watching for a moment, he dragged a chair over to the window. He would personally keep a vigil throughout the night. In the morning, a schedule would be arranged. He or one of his men would watch the President around the clock. While another rested, the third would keep watch exclusively on the towering grain silo, rising into the gloom farther out on Farm Two.

Three years spent behind a desk, thought Zane as he made himself comfortable, had left him tragically well-prepared for the job of sitting in a chair. But at least he was finally back in the field, and not just chasing funny money this time. And when he went home to Trudy and put his hand on her swollen belly, after this was all over, he would know that he had done something good out in the world at last, making a better place for little Michael or Mary, whichever it turned out to be.

He adjusted his short legs, smoothed down his pomaded coif. What would his bubbie say if she could see him now? Probably something like: *'Mit geduld boiert men durch afileh a kizelshtain.'* Translation from the Yiddish: *'With patience you can bore even through granite.'* Waiting behind his desk for the chance to prove himself, Zane had indeed shown the patience of the ancients. And not once had he complained. The first member of his family born in America, he had sworn to do whatever might be required to become worthy of this noble country, even if for an insufferably long while that had been nothing much at all.

But look at him now: working directly for the Chief on a secret mission, defending the President against a squad of assassins of which the regular Service patrols knew nothing. This was how he had always imagined life as an agent: danger, intrigue, critical assignments coming straight from the top. To a humble Jew born of Russian peasant stock, it was heady stuff indeed.

He studied the guard detail circling the farmhouse, the light burning in the window, the silo rearing up into the night. He could see why Isherwood, whose recommendation had gotten Zane out from behind the desk, had worried enough about that silo to make a point of mentioning it. Ish's instincts had always been good. During their brief stint working together, the man had already been on a downward spiral, nipping regularly from his flask and vocally resenting the bust back to counterfeit duty. But he had remained an effective agent, and his eyes had blazed with irrepressible dark humor. Zane had not been there to witness first-hand the day Ish, drunk on the job, had sealed his own fate by insulting the First Lady – mocking Bess Truman's aloofness, doing an impression of her awkward flat-footed stance, and mentioning her father's suicide, all while she stood just behind him – but the story had since entered into legend. Afterward, Ish had been placed on indefinite leave.

Zane covered a yawn. Even in the heart of the action, the job of a Secret Service agent was essentially voyeuristic: watch and wait, remaining awake and alert. But this was the price one paid for the honor of protecting America's chief executive. And he would not have traded it for the world.

As minutes crept past, he found his mind going to places he had previously deemed off-limits. If in fact a cabal *was* determined to remove Eisenhower, he wondered, what men might constitute its ranks? He could think of several – any one of whom, distressingly, wielded more than enough power to wipe young Philip Zane off the map like an inconvenient spill. Colonel Robert McCormick, the passionate and radically-isolationist publisher of the *Chicago Tribune*, came promptly to mind. Influential and ruthless, McCormick had resented FDR and his ilk (which Eisenhower, in refusing to dismantle the New Deal, had proven himself to be despite his Republican affiliation) for dragging the country into a world war he'd still considered unnecessary years after the fact. Although McCormick had died on the April Fools' Day just past, he'd left behind a legacy of slavering followers who remained willing and able to implement his ideals, and perhaps also his unfulfilled plans.

And that was only the start. Eisenhower had not become the leader of the free world without making some powerful enemies. There were bankers and business magnates like Kohlberg and Dwyer and Mordaci and the Wulff brothers, and Texas oilmen like Murchison and Cullen, and various and sundry munitions dealers and industrialists, all of whom saw little difference between the New Dealers and the Bolsheviks, and who could justify taking out the knives because America's nuclear monopoly had ended. And of course there were the politicians these men kept in their pockets: Jenner and Welker, who had lobbied hard to reverse Joe McCarthy's official censure, and Bridges and Dirksen and Mundt and Bolin and Potter, and key White House adviser C.D. Jackson, and publisher Mrs Garvin Tankersley...

Zane stretched until his back popped. He unfolded his legs, refolded them the other way, and sighed. Already he missed his wife. But, of course, this was the job he had signed up for. Exhaling again, clearing his mind, he focused on the lighted window across the farm.

Watch and wait.

NINE

THE TREASURY BUILDING:
NOVEMBER 18

Chief Emil Spooner woke, following a short catnap at his desk, with throat aching and eyes grainy; an overflowing ashtray just inches from his face made his stomach execute a sickly roll.

As he straightened, trying to collect himself, the telephone rang. Lighting another Winston mechanically, he reached for the receiver. His replacement secretary was young and inexperienced and, perhaps hoping to impress the boss with his resiliency, failed to modulate his chipper tone. 'Agent Isherwood to see you.'

Wincing, the Chief glanced at the clock on his

desk. The time was four minutes past six a.m.

Isherwood looked as wrung-out as Spooner felt, but a spark in his eye suggested progress. 'Found our man,' he confirmed, dropping a file onto the desk.

Before opening the folder, the Chief lit another cigarette, forgetting the one already burning in the ashtray. Turning back the cover, he found himself perusing a military personnel file. The subject, one Richard Thomas Hart, was pictured in a black-and-white photograph clipped to the first page. The Chief absorbed the image, trying to learn something from the face. The uniformed young man was photogenic, his face boyish and unlined. Frozen in time, his gaze was steady and phlegmatic.

Richard Hart had been born on September third, 1921, in Saint Clairsville, Ohio. Twenty years later, he had entered the United States Army at a recruiting station in the same small town. During the war he had served with distinction as a sergeant in Company B, Fifteenth Infantry Regiment, seeing action in Salerno and Lazio, and on the Anzio beachhead in Cisterna di Littoria. The Chief looked up. 'How'd you manage this?'

'I got a name from a janitor in Charlottesville. Then it was easy.'

'Huh,' said Spooner.

'Since the war he's apparently been drifting, mostly on the VA circuit. Worked an odd job here and there. But left precious little in the way of a paper trail. Never voted, or even registered, or owned any property. Never married, and hasn't paid taxes since 1945.'

Spooner flipped another page, to dental and fingerprint records. 'We'll Belinograph these to AFIS and ICPC. Put out an all-points with the photo and the name, see if he pops up anywhere.'

Isherwood leaned forward, claiming the Chief's forgotten cigarette. 'Anything from Max?'

'They've been putting questions to him all night. So far, he denies everything.' Lifting the phone again, Spooner hesitated. 'Ish: how long since you've gotten any shut-eye?'

Isherwood only shrugged.

'Going on forty-eight hours, I figure. Go home. Get some sleep. Meet me back here at oh-nine-hundred.'

Isherwood let a moment fall away. Then he leaned back, favoring Spooner with a weary gaze, and nodded.

ANACOSTIA
Each time the bell over the front door chimed, Richard Hart twisted around in the tattered lime-green booth.

The diner's clientele was working-class and varied, of Italian and Jewish and Irish descent. Time and again Hart turned back to his newspaper without recognizing the customer and resumed searching in vain for mention of a body recovered near Denver.

A peroxide blonde topped off his coffee without asking. He smiled up at her, sipped gratefully. The night had been long. His arm prickled; his leg ached. Scrabbling against the back of his mind was a thought he didn't want to face: perhaps the agent had forsaken a visit home, traveling instead straight back to Gettysburg. Behind the gates of the farm, Francis Isherwood would be all but unreachable...

The bell over the door chimed again.

Benny Lynch was dressed comfortably in gray slacks, white T-shirt, and scruffy green army jacket that had seen better days. He had snappish brown eyes and a narrow face that reminded Hart of a turtle. Five years ago, they had formed a brief partnership as pickpockets. Hart had been the less skilled member of the team, acting as steer and stall and duke man, while Lynch, quick and nimble, had handled the actual mechanics.

Lynch slid into the booth. Lighting a cigarillo with a cardboard match, he shrugged. 'Not sure.'

'What does that mean?'

'Man showed up. Right address. But wrong car.'

Frowning, Hart reached for his crutches. 'Hold the fort.'

Two minutes later he was out on the street, moving carefully on the icy sidewalk. En route to the Isherwood address he passed another man he'd recruited from the waterfront the previous day – a union buster named Morgenthau. Sitting inside a Hudson Commodore parked outside a Queen Anne-style rowhouse, the man held a military-grade AN/PRC-6 walkie-talkie loosely in his lap. Stationed around the block, five other men sat in similar circumstances, awaiting Hart's order. Where subtlety had failed, brute force would succeed.

Drawing near to Isherwood's home, Hart slowed. If the target saw him, the element of surprise would be lost. But beneath the low, even light of dawn, he perceived no sign of his prey. A petite young woman walked a dog; a courtly gentleman moved on and off the balcony of his rowhouse, dabbing at his nose with a tissue, bringing plants inside before the cold front arrived. Otherwise, the block slept.

Parked directly in front of Isherwood's porch was a spiffy late-model Mayfair. Across the street sat Hart's own Buick, in which Lynch had spent the night. Warily, Hart positioned himself behind a telephone pole near the Buick. A light burned inside Isherwood's rowhouse: a side window.

Hart watched. For a few minutes, the only movement he saw was that of sunlight gradually moving across porch, where ice shone. But at last a figure appeared behind the side window: Isherwood, opening cans on a counter as cats wound eagerly around him.

Hart scowled. While the hunter was bruised and broken, needing to hire out his dirty work, the quarry appeared to have come through the ordeal without so much as a scratch – and driving a smart new car to boot. The rowhouse looked cozy and warm. Inside would be a clicking radiator, a wallpaper pattern of spray roses, an upright piano in the parlor with sheet music open on its stand. Not just a house, thought Hart bitterly, but a home.

For another instant he watched, frowning. Then, using the crutch, he worked his way halfway back to the diner. He paused, took out his walkie-talkie, depressed the send button, and gave the order.

GAITHERSBURG, MARYLAND

For as long as the oblivion lasted, Max Whitman felt almost content: floating through a landscape of featureless white, revisiting his memories of Betsy Martin.

Every once in a while, however, a hole poked through the soft nimbus of insensibility. Then he became aware of less pleasant phenomena: a moist, moldy cellar, and blue-tinted cigarette smoke, and a burning lamp, and men beating him with brass knuckles and baseball bats, and clips attached to his nipples and testicles, sending jolts of agonizing electricity coursing through his body at regular intervals.

But after the shocks and the beatings came more comforting oblivion, which he wrapped around himself like a blanket. In this hazy netherworld, he was always a teenager and Betsy Martin was always on his arm, nibbling on his ear, whispering sweet nothings only he could hear. *I love you,* she said, and:

We'll always be together, and:

Who did you tell about your meetings with Agent Isherwood? and:

I don't bite, slugger, and she squeezed his biceps, which he flexed agreeably, grinning.

Then she whipped the back of his legs with piano wire and he cried out in agony; and the clips sent another thousand volts coursing through his body, making him jitter and jive; and

Betsy lit a new cigarette and talked in low voices with the men surrounding her, coming up with new strategies to get him to tell what he knew. Sometimes he surfaced enough to realize that she existed only in his mind. In reality she was married to a haberdasher in Connecticut, and he was in the cellar of a safe house somewhere outside Washington, being interrogated – often enough he had picked up the phone to send others to this same fate.

Who's in on it, Max? What are they planning? You may as well tell us; the game is up.

But those voices were shunted aside easily enough. Ironically, it was the very methods used by the interrogators which opened the escape hatch. After enough pain, Max was learning, the body threw a sort of interior circuit breaker, drawing numb senselessness close on every side. The worst these men could do was kill him – but they could never rob him of his memories. The blue-and-white plaid rayon dress, the kohl pencil, and hair like a fall of autumn dusk...

How did you communicate with them? How do they make contact? Why did you do it, Max?

Let them do their worst. Even if the inter-rogators threatened to put a bullet through the heads of his little girls, Max would not break. Because Emil Spooner would never allow that to happen.

The clips sent more voltage churning through his ruined body; and his bladder released, and he vomited convulsively, resoaking a chest already sodden with blood and sputum; and in his mind's eye, Betsy beckoned him closer, a knowing smile on her lovely face. *Ignore these goons, Max. They don't get it. But we don't need them. It's just you and me now.*

A blow rocked his head on his neck. He spat out a tooth. And despite everything, he grinned.

CIUDADELA, BUENOS AIRES

The Cessna 310 sailed from a turquoise sky onto a tiny runway at Aeropuerto Ciudadela.

Taxiing to a stop near a cluster of weather-worn Quonset huts, the plane discharged Senator John Bolin onto sun-kissed tarmac. Moments later a 1950 Chrysler Crown Imperial limousine rolled up. A back door opened, and Bolin climbed into air-conditioned shade. Two men sat across from him. One was about the senator's age: dark where Bolin was fair, smelling powerfully of Aqua Velva, wearing heavily-decorated military epaulets where Bolin wore his travel-rumpled white suit. The other was ten years younger, tall and fair and blond, wearing pale linen, dabbing regularly at his temple with a balled-up handkerchief.

'Senator,' said the darker man formally. 'It is my great honor to welcome you to Buenos Aires.'

The blond gave only a slight, cryptic smile, and again sopped perspiration from forehead with handkerchief.

They drove along poverty-stricken streets, past small mossy cottages. Heat shimmered in a faint milky cataract over low gray mountains. Looking through his window, Bolin impassively watched Argentina roll past: a pathetic garden, a rotting fence, an empty and filthy bird bath, children playing on an overgrown lawn. A set of wind chimes hanging from a peg gave a bitter-sweet jangle. Even through a miasma of cheap aftershave, the air inside the limousine smelled vibrantly of jacaranda and ficus.

At length they turned onto a road flanked by spider-like mangroves and humble bungalows, terminating in an abrupt dead end. Tucked into the farthest remove of the cul-de-sac waited a small house surrounded by leafy croton. The limo pulled into the driveway, and the passengers climbed slowly out.

The grand tour took all of three minutes. On a modest patio hidden from neighbors by a raw plank-board fence, then, Bolin sat with the men as a fat maid served a lunch of lobster *empanadas*, cinnamon *alfajores*, and *yerba maté*. Afterwards, they shared his Viceroys and listened to the sounds of the neighborhood: children yelling and crying, dogs barking, distant engines revving and falling. As they smoked, Bolin stole glances at the German. The handkerchief made endless ineffective movements to and from sweaty, sunken temples. The cheeks had the burst-vessel look of low-grade heatstroke. After ten years in Buenos Aires, the man looked no more accustomed to the climate than if he had arrived just yesterday. And he had relative youth on his side...

Bolin suppressed a sigh; a muscle leaped in his jaw. He removed his spectacles, polished them carefully against one sleeve, and replaced them. He had known, upon extending himself to get the

Wulff brothers' operative onto the farm, that he was opening himself to the possibility of exile. In taking the calculated risk, he had expected as a worst-case scenario luxurious German chalets high in the mountains. But this was dangerously near squalor.

Misreading Bolin's expression, the dark man gave a predatory smile. 'Never fear, *Señor*.' He lowered his voice to a melodramatic whisper. 'They say she never fails.'

Bolin looked at the man evenly. He considered suggesting that, considering the support his organization had given this man's cause – supplying funding, materiel, and planning for the *coup d'état* – he might have expected better lodgings. But surely the relics of the Third Reich, with their nearly-illimitable wealth, had received the best the Argentinians had to offer. And apparently, that wasn't much.

Bolin finished his Viceroy, dropped it to the patio beside a goggling plaster frog, and ground the butt beneath one heel. A plump buzzing fly landed on the back of his left hand. With an irritated flick, he dislodged it. After a few seconds he shook his head, compressed his lips, and reached wordlessly for another cigarette.

Only a few days, he told himself. Then his own *coup d'état* would be implemented; his allies would be installed in the White House, ready to pull strings on his behalf, and he could safely return home. Only a few days...

He could almost hear Vera laughing.

TEN

ANACOSTIA

Isherwood hung up the phone with more force than he'd intended.

For a moment he considered dialing again. Instead he turned, climbing the stairs, nearly tripping over a cat as he came off the top riser. A quick rest, shower, and change of clothes, and he would be on his way back to Treasury.

The thing to do, he told himself as he stripped off his jacket and unstrapped his holster, was make the most of the separation from Evy while it lasted. He was angry – that she wouldn't even answer his goddamned telephone calls, after all they'd been through, beggared the imagination – but she would come around in her own time, if she came around at all. Meanwhile, he could use the break to get some more sobriety under his belt. He could find a better bottle of perfume – Moonlight Mist, 'worth its weight in romance', might not do the trick – and he could give some serious thought to just how much more he had to offer. Once upon a time, they had talked seriously of starting a family. If he could bring up the subject again and convince her that he meant it, that might make all the difference...

Just as he was starting on his belt, the doorbell

rang. That would be Matilda Thorndike, from down the block, who had been caring for the cats. She must have seen the Mayfair parked outside and wondered if her services were still required.

He was already two steps down the stairs when he decided to turn back and fetch the Colt – a reasonable precaution, all things considered. Looping the holster over his head, he took a moment to swing it around so that the revolver lay in the small of his back – the better to spare young Matilda Thorndike any nightmares tonight – before thudding down the stairs again and answering the door.

Standing on his front stoop was a man decidedly not here to feed the cats. Thirtyish, about six feet tall, he had a boxer's broken nose and a sailor's tattoos encircling a thick forearm—

—and in his meaty right hand, aimed at Isherwood's heart, he held a small silver automatic.

Isherwood slammed the door; at the same moment, the automatic spoke harshly.

Fragments of wood peppered his chest and neck. Ignoring the flaring pain, he tried to work the bolt; but the sailor on the doorstep was smashing a piledriver foot into the door. In the same instant, glass shattered from farther back on the first floor, from the dining room, and Isherwood thought wildly: *Incoming!*

Moving on instinct, he found the gun in the small of his back, firing two shots through the flimsy buckling wood of the front door even as he became aware of a flickering shadow to his left, beyond the window of the living room. He threw himself down, thudding heavily onto the floor. One out front, he thought frantically, one out back (if not inside already), and one coming in from the west—

Glass shattered from the direction of the den.

The house had been surrounded.

Rocking up onto his knees, he saw from the corner of his eye the man who had broken the living room window, caught in the midst of climbing over the sill. Isherwood steadied his right hand with his left and fired, taking the intruder in the throat, spinning the man backward.

Gaining his feet again – his knees popped hollowly – he dashed forward, through the living room, toward the kitchen, with broken glass crackling underfoot. In a diamond-shaped mirror hanging above the bar he saw the front door burst open behind him. Turning without slowing, Isherwood snapped off a ragged shot, making the sailor withdraw.

A semi-automatic pistol was lying on the living-room floor, surrounded by broken glass. He scooped it up, barely slowing. The gun's previous owner sprawled half-in and half-out of the window, blood pulsing from his throat in a weakening freshet.

Isherwood's perception had again slowed to a combat-crawl, attaining the consistency of treacle. He felt a strange elation. Here, then, was his peculiar curse: under fire he was his best and worst self simultaneously. Heart pounding, mouth dry but electric, knees rubbery, eyes bulging from their sockets, he became the only

Francis Isherwood that didn't crave a goddamned drink.

Skidding into the kitchen, sending cats scattering in all directions, he seemed able to gather a
huge amount of information at once—

(two men were moving through the study; and
one more, he deduced from a groaning floor-
board, came through the dining room as well –
plus another came behind the one he had shot in
the living room, and the sailor at the door was
pressing forward again)

—and his body decided before his brain that
the bathroom was the place to be.

Thudding into the lavatory, he set the two guns
on the edge of the sink and then closed the door
behind himself, turning the lock, extremely
aware of the thinness of the plaster walls. But he
didn't plan on staying here long. He clawed the
cigarette lighter out of his shirt pocket. Clutching
the Zippo between clenched teeth, he popped the
top off the toilet tank and took out the bottle of
Jack Daniels he had stowed months before in
anticipation of a very different circumstance.
Setting down the bottle, he tore a jagged strip
from the bottom of his shirt.

Plugging the neck of the bottle with the strip of
cloth, he upended the whiskey briefly to soak the
material through. He spent a fraction of an
instant holstering the Colt and shoving the semi-
automatic – a Smith & Wesson Model 39 – into
his belt. Then he raised the bottle, corked by wet
cloth, in his right hand, and dropped the Zippo
from his clenched teeth into his waiting left
palm. He flicked the wheel; the flint sparked; he

touched flame to wet cloth; his foot rose and thudded against the bathroom door, rocking it open and popping off one hinge.

Before him in the kitchen stood three men: one facing the bathroom, two facing away.

As Isherwood threw the bottle, the man facing him fired. A powerful hand took hold of Isherwood's left side, somewhere between armpit and pelvis, and shoved backward and down. As he fell, he turned his head reflexively to avoid crowning himself against the sink, at the same time keeping a slice of kitchen in his field of vision – thus he saw the curtain of flame spring up, consuming all three men, two of whom fled screaming, living pyres, as the third, caught dead to rights, simply flagged and folded where he stood, instantly filling the air with the stench of charred flesh.

A blast of heat followed, intense enough that Isherwood had to roll over and protect his head with his left arm, which for some reason – ah, yes, because he'd been shot – didn't want to behave. Still, the arm proved capable of prioritizing, and managed to block at least the worst of the blast, although Isherwood sensed what felt like a very bad sunburn rising on his face and exposed forearm. Looking down, he saw without surprise that the arm was aflame.

Grimly, he found his knees again (*better to die on your feet than live on your knees*, Eisenhower advised) and jammed the burning arm into the water of the toilet, which gave a scabrous hiss. He felt awareness recede tentatively, a tide going out. Through sheer willpower, he pulled the tide back in.

With his right side propped against the wall, he pushed up to his feet. The fire was already flickering down as the alcohol evaporated. Only the body sprawled on the kitchen floor, with clothing just catching, burned with conviction. Gritting his teeth, Isherwood left the bathroom. He emptied the two shots remaining in the Colt into the man burning on the kitchen floor, then dropped the empty gun and drew the Smith & Wesson, cursorily checking its eight-round magazine.

From the direction of the study: scrabbling, crinkling glass. They were in retreat, he thought with a flash of disdain.

Instead of giving chase, he circled around the other way, to the study by way of the dining room. Before exposing himself in the doorway, he closed his eyes for a heartbeat and listened. Six men, as best he could figure, had entered his house. One lay dead on the floor behind him; one lay dead or dying propped in the living-room window frame. Two others were burning.

Raising the Smith & Wesson, he stepped through the doorway. He caught a man retreating, trying to climb back out through the dining-room window without resting weight against incinerated hands.

Near Route 30, Isherwood had shown mercy, aiming repeatedly for the gun arm – and let his assailant escape.

Now he took careful, deliberate aim at the spot where neck met back, and fired once.

The man folded bonelessly onto the parquet

oaken floor. Isherwood moved on toward the study. For the first time he became truly aware of the wound in his side – gaping and sucking, a red, wet mouth. The pain was jumbled in with a thousand other imperatives, and he found he could do a sort of magic trick, making the pain disappear, although he had his doubts about how long the trick would keep working.

Outside the study, he listened again. Snuffling, scrabbling. Gathering his courage, he stepped in, catching a glimpse of a dark figure slipping away through a shattered window. By the time he drew a bead, the figure was gone. *Run*, he thought acidly. *Run for your life.*

That left two.

Throwing the last vestiges of caution to the wind, he stalked back toward the foyer. Through the thin wall separating him from the staircase he heard a creaking step. He had lived in this house for twelve years. Countless nights he had scaled those same stairs while drunk, trying not to make a noise to rouse his wife. He immediately placed the creaking step as the fourth from the top.

Firing through the wall, he was rewarded by a thump of dead weight, followed by a series of shallow successive thumps as the body slid down from one riser to another.

Two huge strides brought him back to the foot of the staircase: a full turn 'round the house. A dead man sprawled upside-down on the stairs: the sailor.

He found the last one in the living room. Badly burned, the man was having trouble wrestling his dead accomplice out of the windowsill. As he

appeared unarmed, Isherwood considered appre-
hending him for questioning – but the tide was
retreating again; better to take no chances.

Coldly, he gunned the man down.

Then he had pushed too far, and his knees were
buckling beneath him. Landing on a floor
slippery with blood, he cursed loudly. 'Evelyn,'
he called. After drawing a breath, he tried again.
'Evy – help me.'

He wasn't sure if he had managed to say the
words, or only to think them. Then the tide
withdrew completely; darkness rushed in to fill
the cracks. In his last moment of awareness he
felt a cat's rough tongue against his cheek. He
remembered that Evelyn wasn't here to help
him. Then he was caught up in a violent black
undertow and drawn swiftly away.

GETTYSBURG

Miss Dunbarton stood in the kitchen doorway,
surveying her troops.

Maybe it was the sherry – but watching the
girls hustle about, preparing to serve lunch, she
felt a warm, almost maternal glow. After observ-
ing for a few moments, she stepped into the
room and clapped briskly. 'Attention,' she called. 'Attention, please.'

Activity clattered to a stop; half a dozen young
faces turned toward her.

'As we shall labor straight through Thanks-
giving,' pronounced Miss Dunbarton, 'and as we
shall then continue to work straight up 'til
Christmas, it has occurred to me that perhaps we
should pause to celebrate.' Eyes glimmering

puckishly, she looked from one girl to another. 'Therefore I am pleased to announce that tomorrow at six p.m. a holiday party for the staff will take place in the parlor. Curfew will be suspended; there will be drinking and music and dancing and, of course, plenty of food; perhaps we can even invite some special guests. The timing's a bit off, but better early than never.'

She beamed at her own small witticism. Her girls beamed in return, nudging each other with excited elbows. Josette and the new girl, Elisabeth, who had become fast friends, exchanged whispers. Miss Dunbarton considered admonishing them for impoliteness, but decided against it. At the moment she felt charitable even toward Josette, who listened to her radio every night in violation of the rules, and snuck men up to her room when Miss Dunbarton was off-premises, thinking nobody knew.

And what of the senator's housekeeper? Again, it might have been the sherry talking – Miss Dunbarton had put down more than her usual ration, between breakfast and lunch, in celebration of the season – but Elisabeth Grant had proven an agreeable surprise. She didn't flirt with the men, and except for her friendship with Josette she kept mostly to herself. She was pretty and charming and pleasant to have around. Any attitude she may have harbored had been kept out of view. She had done her work thoroughly and, as far as Miss Dunbarton knew, had broken no rules except for her late-night bull sessions with Josette. Overall the loss of Barbara Cameron, while inconvenient, seemed actually to

159

have been a boon for the farm.

Animated chatter spread between the young ladies; Miss Dunbarton officiously clapped again. 'Back to work!' she cried. A bit of the carrot, a bit of the stick; otherwise they would mistake her generosity for soft-heartedness. Give these girls an inch and they took a mile.

In mid-afternoon a ten-foot Douglas fir, freshly chopped from the backyard, was trundled into the parlor, dripping needles and instantly filling the herdsman's home with a sweet, citrusy smell.

Girls watched, wide-eyed and cooing, as men wrangled the tree into a five-legged stand and then drilled screws into the trunk, clamping it upright. The tree was the *coup de grace* to a parlor already decked that morning with tinsel, wreaths, garlands, mistletoe, and glittering ornaments. A Christmas scene had been impressively rendered in miniature on a tabletop, with a tiny compact mirror doubling for an ice-topped pond, and lace antimacassars giving the illusion of a snow-covered field.

Watching along with the rest, Elisabeth felt a flicker of scorn. Although some of her earliest childhood memories were of Advent calendars and sleigh bells, she had soon enough discovered the vibrant, primal pagan deities – Fricka and Brünnhilde, Wotan and Loge – and never looked back. Compared with nomadic wolf-warriors hunting in throes of bloodlust and ecstasy, with gold coins and haunches of meat and fleeing young women perfumed with sweat and terror, Christian symbolism seemed insultingly weak.

Here in America after the war, however, frivolity and indulgence were the rules, as per usual. And why not? They had all worked hard, Elisabeth included; their hands were callused with the evidence. And the unchallenging symbols of Christmas were comfortable and easily digested. A sorority had developed, binding them together – even Elisabeth felt a reluctant part of it – and so they deserved a night to celebrate. There would be men to kiss beneath the mistletoe, and whiskey by the barrel, and music for dancing, and no unwelcome reminders of the laws of nature, the redness of tooth and claw. In fact, someone had already switched on the turntable, and the room brimmed with Perry Como softly crooning 'There's No Place Like Home For the Holidays'.

As Elisabeth watched, Josette was boosted up, star in hand, by farmhands who couldn't resist the chance to sneak a glance under her skirt, winking and laughing. Then Miss Dunbarton entered the room, carrying herself with the extravagant precision of the tippler, and made a beeline for Elisabeth. 'Miss Grant,' she said. 'How are we, this fine day?'

'Very well, Miss Dunbarton. And yourself?'

'Very well, thank you.' The elder woman swayed slightly on her feet. 'Looking forward to tomorrow's party?'

'Yes, ma'am.'

'We'll need a hand serving and clearing. Everybody's pitching in. I'd like you and Josette during the first hour, please, from six until seven.'

'Of course, ma'am.'

For another moment Dunbarton glowed, oscillating, clearly full of Christmas spirits. 'Until later,' she said then, and weaved off toward Josette, who was being lowered to the floor, having finally pinned the star atop the tree. With Elisabeth looking on, they held a brief palaver. As Dunbarton headed for her next victim, Josette came toward Elisabeth, glowering.

'Some party,' said the younger girl beneath her breath. 'Sounds like we'll be working the whole time.'

Up close, Josette didn't look festive at all; she looked as if she'd been crying, with the skin beneath her eyes shiny and hard. 'Can we talk?' she added.

Dunbarton was distracted. The help was milling aimlessly, shirking chores in the general confusion. Nodding, Elisabeth followed Josette upstairs. No sooner had the door to the girl's bedroom closed behind them than she burst into tears.

Sobbing, she buried her face in Elisabeth's shoulder. 'James broke up with me this morning.'

Somewhat at a loss, Elisabeth patted the girl's broad back. 'Shh,' she said. 'It's all right.'

'No, it's n–n–not. He d–d–dumped me and I wasn't even – I wasn't even expect–pect–*pecting* it—'

'Take a deep breath,' said Elisabeth. 'Settle down.'

Instead of a deep breath, Josette took her bottle

of schnapps from beneath the bed. 'Ah, *fuck*,' she said eloquently, wiping at her eyes. She widened them and tilted her head back, trying to spare her mascara. 'What is about me, Libby? What makes people walk all over me? It's like I'm wearing a sign around my neck: *kick me*.'

Elisabeth said nothing.

'It's always been that way,' Josette plowed on, 'for as long as I can remember. There's always been a James. There'll always *be* a James.' She uncapped the bottle and guzzled vindictively. 'Luke, my fiancé, said he loved me. Until he got what he wanted, of course. You know what *that* is. And then he dumped me. And he laughed while he did it. That's what happened this morning, Libby; James snuck in to see me, and we got a little drunk, and then we made love, right here, right on my bed; we made love, and then as soon as it was done...' The tears rose again, choking her. 'As *s–s–soon as it was d–d–done—*'

'Oh, honey, don't.'

'—he s–s–said – he s–s–s–said—'

'He's not worth it.' Elisabeth hugged the girl. 'Shh.'

Moments passed. The sound of Josette's crying blended with the plangent hum of wind through the house's eaves – lower-pitched than usual, more spectrally alive – and the voices and music from downstairs. At length, Josette gave a final-sounding snuffle. She relaxed her clinch with Elisabeth, but did not let go completely. Drawing back a few inches, she left her hands on shoulder and waist.

'I ask for it,' said Josette in a dull monotone.

'It's my own damn fault. I ask for it, and I always have.'

'It's not your fault, honey.'

'Don't lie to spare my feelings. I may be a lot of things, but I'm not stupid. I ask to be taken advantage of, and then I ask to be dumped.' A tendril of snot hung quivering from one nostril. 'And it's always been the way. If there's a louse within a thousand miles, I'll find him. And I'll fall in love with him. And then I'll cry like a fool when he dumps me. Oh, I thought I was doing it right this time, Libby. I waited to go to bed with him until he said he loved me. Now I realize: it was all just an act. It was all one-sided, the whole time. But I bought the whole story. Hook, line, and sinker. Like the fool that I am.'

Elisabeth shook her head. 'It's in the past,' she said firmly. 'Never look back, Josie.'

Josette's eyes shone. Despite her best efforts, her mascara had run in two black smears down her round cheeks. 'Oh, Libby,' she said, with a sad little laugh. 'I'm such a mess.'

'You're going to be okay.' Elisabeth embraced the girl again, harder, and smiled. 'I promise.'

ELEVEN

Never look back.

Doubtless good advice – but with her eyes closed and the scent of crisp resin lingering in her nostrils, the advice became indistinguishable from the recollection of receiving the advice.

She could see her father now, standing before the Christmas tree in their isolated cabin by the lake, trying to find the perfect bough off which to hang a glittering ornament. Elisabeth had been but five or six, overflowing with enthusiasm to help. Running toward the tree, she had slipped on a shred of tinsel, crashing hard against the plank-board floor. A moment later she had been up again, laughing. Then her mother had grabbed her from behind, twisting her arm up sharply, revealing blood trickling down her wrist where a splinter had broken the skin. *Look at that, Elsa. Look what you've done to yourself. You must be careful. You are delicate!* Concern had underlain the words, but they had come across as angry, and Elisabeth had burst into tears.

Five minutes later, rubbing his daughter's wrist as she sat on his knee, Father had leaned in close and whispered beneath his breath. *Don't be upset, Liebchen. Your mother means well. You are all she has; you are her entire world. But I know that you are not so delicate as you might seem. When you get hurt – by the floor, by Mother's tone, by anything – you must just shake it off. Never look back.*

She had taken the words to heart. Later, alone in her room, she had turned them over, treasuring them – as she had treasured the tree they had trimmed, and her small Advent calendar with its chocolates and little toys and songs written on scraps of paper. She had not yet learned that these were the old ways, the crutches of the weak, and that she must leave them behind.

Before sending her to school each morning, her mother bundled her in layer upon layer of clothing, as if protecting a piece of fine china against breakage. As a result Elisabeth walked stiffly, lurching awkwardly through the school yard. Her fellow students teased endlessly, calling her Dresden, and Chinadoll, and Frankenstein's Bride. The worst offender was a chubby brute named Inge, mannish even before puberty, a full head taller than her classmates, stocky around the shoulders and neck. Elisabeth tried to ignore the taunts, focusing on her lessons. She was a good student. After passing the Abitur, the graduation test, with flying colors, she would attend the University of Munich, where she would study biology. Then at last she would rise above her tormentors, proving her superiority.

But a change had been washing over the Fatherland – a great, irresistible tide. The first manifestations had been subtle. More coal became available; Elisabeth could no longer see her breath as she sat behind her desk in school.

She encountered more horses and dogs, during her daily walks to and from the lakeside, as animals were less often butchered for meat. One day during her seventh year, a portrait of Adolf Hitler appeared in her classroom, and soon after, a Nazi flag. Many adults seemed uncomfortable with these developments, which to Elisabeth made no sense. They had complained bitterly about the deprivations following the War – but now that someone had arrived to show them the way out, they resisted. Her father compared Hitler to the Pied Piper of Hamelin, who with his flute led children to their doom. Her favorite teacher refused to start his class by *heiling* Hitler, insisting instead on the old greeting of: 'Good morning, children.' Her mother cautioned against joining the *Hitlerjugend*, claiming that the family could not afford the monthly dues of ten pfennig, and that the mandatory meetings would interfere with chores and church.

But those who resisted were fighting a losing battle. By the time she'd turned eight, Elisabeth could see that clearly. One Sunday, a contingent of *Hitlerjugend* brazenly disrupted church services by standing in the graveyard outside the basilica and playing trumpets. Later that month, a squad of Hitler Youth – one hundred boys wearing full regalia – appeared at the door of her science class to insist that the teacher begin the day with the proper greeting. She saw the fear in Herr Hofmann's eyes. And from then on, days began by *heiling* Hitler, after all.

Yet still Elisabeth tried to follow her parents' directives. Mother had drilled into her head that she was weak, fragile, and dependent, and so going against their wishes had seemed inconceivable. All through her ninth year, as the tide roiling the Fatherland had spilled over borders into Czechoslovakia and Poland, she strove to be faithful and obedient, and kept to herself. But then had come a fateful week that changed everything: starting with a confrontation with Inge in the school yard, and ending, at Elisabeth's first youth rally, with the revelatory Karl Schnibbe, the boy who had shown her the way to a better life, a better self.

Inge, like many schoolchildren, had been emboldened by the change in the wind. Never before had the youth felt so free to flaunt the orders of the elders. And so the mannish girl dared bring her abuse to the next level, lying in wait after class and then ambushing the strange, stalking figure of Elisabeth. As girls gathered around, chanting encouragement, Inge tackled the smaller child as she tried to walk home, bringing her down onto hard cobblestones.

Elisabeth would never forget the feeling of Inge's rock-solid body plowing into her: like running into a brick wall. Then she was down on cold cobbles, disoriented. Unyielding ground scraped at her back and Inge's heavy fists pounded into her face, and she felt pain, distress, fear, and, worst of all, hot shame at her own weakness.

When the beating was finished, the girls withdrew, laughing and pointing, and Elisabeth stumbled home in tears. There her mother received her not with sympathy, but with anger. Elisabeth, insisted Mother, should have known better than to wrestle with girls like Inge. She should have kept her distance, protecting herself. She was fragile, and Mother could not always be there to hold her hand.

With disgrace boiling inside her, Elisabeth was sent to bed without supper. Waking in the middle of the night, she found her pillow soaked with blood from a shattered eardrum. But she did not report the blood to Mother, who would simply have reprimanded her all over again. Instead she turned her pillow to the cool, dry side and then lay awake: seething, plotting revenge.

Two days later, against her parents' express orders, she attended her first *Hitlerjugend* rally.

The young man leading the event was nothing less than mesmerizing. Sixteen or seventeen, he possessed a beautiful face, with ice-blue eyes and cheekbones like razors, and an astounding physique, sculpted from endless military drills and athletic tournaments, and displayed to fine advantage by his fitted brown uniform. Intellectually, he was no less impressive, putting the most important tenets of Nazism into terms she could easily understand. Campfires and parades and storytelling and uniforms and flags and badges, he explained, his baritone ringing powerfully out across a crowd of hundreds without artificial amplification, were only the beginning. The Hitler Youth stood for much more. Only the most select German children could become members of the *Jungvolk*, and only after procuring an *Ahnenpass*, a stamped and sealed official document proving their racial heritage. Then, after taking the oath of the Blood Banner, the cream of German youth would succeed where the elder generation had failed. They would cast aside the ancient poxes vexing the Fatherland and run out any cowards who adhered to the old order. To these privileged members of the *Herrenrasse*, the master race, belonged the future.

After the oration was done, she screwed up her courage and approached him, planning only to ask for information about the next meeting of the *Jungmädel*, the Young Maidens. But turning his dark eyes onto her pale face, Karl Schnibbe saw something – even beneath the bruises and the layers upon layers of clothing and the strange Frankenstein gait, he saw something. Later, she would wonder what exactly he had recognized in her. It had been something that at the time she had not even recognized in herself. Perhaps in her flecked turquoise eyes he had seen a smoldering ember of hatred. Or perhaps he had sensed a beauty, in her high pallid cheekbones, and a potential in her untapped body. Whatever the case, he acted on his instincts immediately, with all the grace and ease one would expect of a natural leader. He took her hand and kissed it. Two hours later, he led her into a musty stable halfway between the rally and her home, where, surrounded by chaff and stamping horses, he made her into a woman. She had been two days from her tenth birthday.

Of course, she had not appreciated the subtleties of the experience; she had been altogether too young. But she had felt the pressure of his hard body against hers, and the intensity of his gaze locking onto her face, and the sudden sharp pain and attendant promise of a whole new world unfolding. In his view she was not a porcelain doll who stalked clumsily from place to place, a young girl inviting abuse and cowering from harm. She was a strong and beautiful and proud German woman. When abuse was to be dealt, it would come from the *Herrenrasse* toward the *untermenschen*, and not the other way around. Some basic equation about life had changed; something always unbalanced had come at last into symmetry.

Upon Elisabeth's arrival home, Mother chastised her for staying out too long. They argued, and then Elisabeth – with years of frustration and anger suddenly spilling out, and strengthened by her new-found inner symmetry – spat in Mother's face. There followed a shocked, disbelieving moment of stop-time. Then Mother ordered her daughter out into the cold. No such disrespectful offspring of hers would sleep under this roof. Father objected, but Elisabeth paid no attention. Instead she went to Karl, who gladly took her in.

Lying now in the second-story room of the herdsman's home, listening to Josette's radio and the distant rattle of radiators, Elisabeth felt all over again the thrills of discovery which had followed in rapid succession. During the ensuing weeks she had become a sophisticated adult, a National Socialist, and a fully-realized proud member of the master race, all at once.

Night after night, she had received private lessons from Karl, not only on the mechanics of love – although there had been plenty of that – or on the philosophy of National Socialism and the need to move beyond weakness and passivity – although there had been plenty of that too – but on her own potential. He helped her recognize that she was not weak, but strong. At first, having absorbed her mother's lessons all too well, she protested. Telling Karl about Inge, she gave voice to fears that fighting back might result in an even worse beating, and irrevocable damage. But Karl laughed. He had a beautiful laugh, ringing and confident and rich. *Liebchen*, he said – having appropriated her father's term of endearment as effortlessly as he'd appropriated everything else – *I promise you: stand up to the bully, and everything will be all right. For too long we have let ourselves be pushed around – by the architects of Versailles, by the scheming Jews, by the frightened elders. Now it is* our *time. Weakness and pity and fear are for children, not for us.*

And he had been right; he had been right about everything. She discovered this on a pleasant autumn afternoon in 1940 when she turned the tables on Inge, waiting in ambush for the bigger girl at the end of the school day. Elisabeth used a horseshoe to crown the cow, knocking her down and then smashing her face to bloody pulp without bruising so much as a knuckle. Inge had never again caused a whit of trouble. Moreover, she had refused to identify her assailant to the *Schuldirektor*, and so Elisabeth had tasted for the first time the power which came with instilling fear.

By then she had become, under Karl's guidance, a different Elisabeth: confident and graceful and lovely, with an easy smile on the surface but a hard core underneath. After two months in the Young Maidens, where she studied femininity, dancing, hygiene, and charm, Karl announced that, with her special talents, she was destined for more. He extended her training through fox hunting and into rifle sniping, hand-to-hand combat, and rudimentary trade-craft. Then he graduated her, declaring that the student had surpassed the teacher, and gave her over to the *Sicherheitsdienst*, the intelligence division of the SS, to complete her education under the guidance of the legendary Herr Hagen himself. Beneath Hagen she learned the finer points of espionage: languages, accents, codes, lip-reading, lock-picking, surveillance, and more.

And then she went off to war, albeit in a special capacity, along with the rest of the patriots in Germany: missing the caresses of Karl and Hagen, but eager to make the sacrifice for a future without compromise. Installed in Great Britain, sending back regular reports with her suitcase wireless, she threw herself into her work. For her parents, she spared nary a second thought. Her father had taught her but one valuable lesson, after all, in all the time she had known him, and she had taken it to heart.

She would have liked for her memories of Karl Schnibbe to end there. But a tragic postscript had come four years later – and that, too, swam back into her mind now, in the luxurious comfort of post-war America. It had been in Berlin, during the final days of the conflict. The promise of

National Socialism had gone appallingly unfulfilled; a dark destiny had closed in, along with the advancing Red Army, to claim all those who had given themselves to the cause.

Risking everything to return to Germany from England, Elisabeth had discovered upon arriving that there was nothing worth returning to. Berlin was all ruins and dust, burning automobiles and dazed refugees, trophy hunters darting between patches of shadow, and rotting corpses littering the streets – human, horse, and dog. The once-glorious Unter den Linden had been reduced to mounds of concrete and shattered glass. Bodies hung motionless from lamp-posts – deserters from the eastern front, made into an example by roving Werewolf bands or their own SS troops. Yellowish, chemical-smelling smoke lurked in dense clouds. Elisabeth moved warily through the streets, seeking a prearranged rendezvous with a group of elite operatives who would find sanctuary in Argentina. And there amidst the dregs of National Socialism – between a group of well-dressed women standing amongst suitcases arguing over a car, and a squad of adolescent boys, recruited by Hitler in desperation, goose-stepping through the devastation – she stumbled onto a familiar face.

Karl Schnibbe was a pathetic shadow of his former self. Face streaked with blood, uniform torn down the entire length of his torso, he recognized her and flung himself forward with unbecoming desperation. *Elisabeth*, he pleaded, grasping her shoulders. *They are almost upon us. You have a way out? Take me with you, please;*

take me with you, bring me along—

A single gunshot to the temple sent him sprawling away. She felt not the slightest flicker of remorse. This was not the real Karl, after all, but a hollow shell of a once-great man. The real Karl would have wanted her to end it this way. He would have thanked her for her mercy.

A burst of static from next door, like a punctuation mark; then Josette's radio switched off. Even the radiators fell silent. Night settled, heavy and empty.

Decisively, Elisabeth shut off her mind as well. Despite one's best efforts, the past was bound to come creeping back up from time to time. But those memories belonged to a different life, a different world. Then she had been Elisabeth Hübener, of Wittlich – and for a time in England, Elizabeth Morgan of Shropshire. Now she was Elisabeth Grant, of Maryland. And she had enough concerns to fill her plate without reminiscences. She must claim her weapon; she must finish her job; she must secure her future.

But the sharp scent of fir lingered in her nostrils, and the memories tried to poke up again. Coldly, she pressed them away. After a few minutes, she drifted away from the overheated little room and into a pleasant dream. High in the silo, she took aim; and, on the sun porch below, Dwight Eisenhower fell to his knees, a bullet through his brain, a fine pink mist fogging the air behind his head. *Never look back.*

TWELVE

WALTER REED ARMY MEDICAL CENTER,
WASHINGTON DC: NOVEMBER 19
Spooner produced a folded newspaper from a
hip pocket. 'Second column, halfway down.'

The paper was yesterday's *Denver Post*. Halfway down the second column, Isherwood found
an article headlined *'POLICE ID VICTIM IN
BODY PARTS CASE'*.

NOVEMBER 18, 1955 – BY STAFF
REPORTER
JEROME WINSTON

Police have identified the man whose head,
body, and hands have been found in various
locations across the Denver area over the
past two weeks.

Authorities have named Arthur Glashow,
24, employed as an underchef in the kitchen
of the Cherry Hills Country Club, in Cherry
Hills Village, Denver. On Tuesday night a
detective said that there have been no arrests
and there are no 'persons of interest' in the
case.

Detectives were seen at Glashow's second-
floor apartment at Villa Park for several
hours on Tuesday afternoon, and witnesses

reported them taking items from the home, where Glashow lived with his wife, Deborah Glashow, 22. Denver County coroner's officials declined to provide additional details because police have placed a security hold on the case, which prohibits them from releasing information.

It was not clear whether the man was first identified through a tip. Coroner's officials said on Monday that they were unable to obtain fingerprints, but a knowledgeable source reports that a distinctive birthmark was recognized.

The bizarre case began unfolding just over two weeks ago, when a man walking near South Platte River on 4 November discovered a disembodied human hand...

Isherwood twice reread the critical line – *under-chef in the kitchen of the Cherry Hills Country Club* – and then tossed the paper aside. Putting his legs over the side of the bed, he turned to the dresser where the nurse had put his civvies.

'Whoa,' said the Chief. 'Slow down.' He indicated Isherwood's pepper-shot neck and chest, blistered skin and gauze wrapping, and blood-spotted bandages.

'I'm fine.' Lips skinning back from teeth, Isherwood slipped a leg into his slacks. 'Had a whole night to rest. Bullet passed through, they doped me up with painkillers ... and you need me out there.'

'If you think you're up to it, Ish, nothing would please me more. But it's not quite that simple.

There's the little matter of the DA. Five men died inside your house yesterday.' Spooner shrugged, taking out his cigarettes. 'I think we can finesse some breathing room – self-defense, after all, and Arnie's a reasonable man. But he'll want a deposition, at least.'

'And then everything becomes a matter of public record. You ready for that?'

'Of course not. But I can only stonewall him so long, and it's easier to claim you're indisposed when you're in the hospital. Still...' Spooner exhaled a rafter of smoke toward the ceiling. 'I'll swing something. Meanwhile, there's more. Last night the cops – same fellows who responded to the report of gunshots from your neighbors – picked up a local tough, down by the waterfront. Hands cut all to hell on broken glass. After a little encouragement, he 'fessed up. He was part of the team that hit your place. And he gave a description of the man who hired him: very tall, mid-thirties, dark hair. Beat up, using crutches, as if he'd recently taken a bad spill. Ring any bells?'

Trying to work his other leg into the pants, Isherwood paused. 'Richard Hart.'

'Bastard's gunning for you, all right. But now we've got every cop in the forty-eight states looking for *him*. They've got a name, photograph, fingerprints. And a vehicle – sighted outside your place in Anacostia. Parked there all night, but gone as soon as the fireworks started.'

With a grimace, Isherwood finished climbing into his pants.

'Long as we've got the boys in blue working

178

on our behalf,' Spooner went on, 'I'm doubling down. If these guys cover their tracks by cutting up corpses, it makes them slippery – but it also qualifies as a *modus operandi*. We can use that against them. Any other body parts float, we'll hear about it.'

'What about Max?'

'Keeping mum. But I'm heading over there myself from here, see if I can knock some sense into him. If you're really good to go, Ish, I could use you back at Treasury, covering for me.' He tapped ash into a drinking glass on the night-stand. 'Say, where's your better half? Thought I'd see her here.'

A pause, filled with beeping monitors and the faint sound of a woman crying from down the hall.

'She's in Florida,' said Ish at last. 'Since September.'

'Well, hell.' Spooner cleared his throat. 'I'm damned sorry to hear that.'

'Life goes on.'

'Sure.' Spooner seemed on the verge of adding something else, and then smoked again instead.

Another moment passed. The crying down the hall faded away to snuffles. Isherwood reached for his shirt.

GETTYSBURG

Staring into the mirror, Josette hollowed her cheeks, turned her face right and then left to inspect her chignon, and smiled brightly at her own reflection. 'How do I look?'

'Perfect.'

'But I must look *pluperfect*. I must make James realize beyond a doubt that he's made the biggest mistake of his life.'

'One look at you, and he'll be desperate to win you back.'

In fact, Josette had indeed made a commendable recovery from the previous day's waterworks. Wearing a black crêpe de chine which flattered some curves and concealed others, with make-up too heavy only in the aquamarine mascara edging her lashes, she presented an attractive figure. Only the fixedly forced smile detracted from her allure.

Josette turned left, then right, then left again. 'I look fat,' she decided.

Sitting on the bed, Elisabeth fidgeted with a fold of her pale gown – borrowed from Josette, it hung off her slender frame like a mainsail. 'You look beautiful.'

'What if he's mean to me? I won't be able to take it. I won't survive. Oh, but what if he ignores me completely? That would be even worse.' With one pinky she removed a fleck of lipstick from a corner of her mouth. 'You're so lucky, Elisabeth. You're beautiful and calm and elegant. Everybody admires you, you know. All the men want you. And all the girls want to *be* you.'

Elisabeth said nothing.

Josette turned from the mirror. 'Just please don't desert me tonight,' she said. 'Whatever happens, stick by my side. Hold my hand. All right? I'll owe you, Libby. Anything you want, I'll owe you.'

GAITHERSBURG

The Chief gazed blankly out a tinted window.

The black Cadillac Fleetwood passed a red-bricked firehouse, the imperial dome of City Hall, and the now-empty county fairgrounds, barren and lonely beneath a cold wind. Achieving the residential west side, the car slowed, cruising through an upscale neighborhood of cropped lawns and stately towering oaks. When they passed a deserted baseball field, Spooner's mind made a sudden cross-connection: Max Whitman as a lumbering youth, drawing back a broom handle during a game of stickball. Max had not been the fastest among them, nor the most coordinated. But he had definitely been the strongest, and when he did manage to connect with a pitch, people ducked and windows got broken. By contrast, Emil Spooner had been quick but delicate, some might have said puny.

The Cadillac turned into the driveway of an ordinary two-story brick colonial with a gated picket fence. Leaving the car, Spooner moved slowly up a flagstone walk. The parlor was sparsely furnished, lacking a woman's touch. A low-ceilinged hallway led past a wall of generic framed family photos. Beyond a scrupulously sanitized kitchen stood a padlocked cellar door. As Spooner watched, Lou Candless keyed the padlock open.

During one game of stickball, a tall kid named Freddy Carlson had accused Spooner of cheating. Sharp-featured, crafty, with small, hot eyes and an angry red birthmark covering his right cheek, Carlson had advanced quickly, tearing the broom handle from Spooner's surprised hand. But then Max Whitman had come trotting over from the manhole cover which doubled for third base, seizing the broom and breaking it neatly in two over Carlson's head. The kid had gone running home with tears streaming down across his birthmark. And the funny thing about it, Spooner thought now, was that he *had* been cheating that day. He had taken advantage of the lack of chalk to claim that the pitch had gone outside the strike zone, when in fact it had been dead on target.

Lou Candless stepped aside, gesturing the Chief forward and down.

Through the cellar darkness drifted odors of blood and sweat and smoke and urine and ordure and ancient, exotic-smelling mosses. A single bright lamp faced away from the cement stairs, picking out chains and clamps and baseball bats and coils of wire hanging from the wall. On a metal tray table rested scalpels and syringes and ampoules. In one corner hulked beneath a tarp an ominous shape, barely larger than a shoebox.

Coming off the bottom step, Spooner ducked a thick cobweb. He caught Eddie Grieg's eye, and nodded.

Grieg climbed the stairs, leaving Spooner alone with the man in the chair.

Hands fastened behind back, ankles bound, Max Whitman seemed to remain unaware of the Chief's presence for two full minutes. At last he raised his head sluggishly, his broad cheeks distended with bruises, face swollen almost beyond recognition. Beneath a mask of blood, his blue eyes glinted.

He met Spooner's gaze and gave a hideous, gallows humor smile, lacking two front teeth.

The Chief took a step closer. 'Max,' he said.

Whitman just kept grinning: a flower missing two petals.

Spooner regarded the man from a new angle, lifting his chin, trying to see something he had never before seen. Then he realized this might be perceived – rightfully – as looking down his nose. He made his head drop, tucking chin into chest.

Whitman laughed hoarsely. He choked on blood, and the laugh gurgled away. Shadows formed peaks and valleys on his swollen face.

'Max,' said Spooner again. He grappled for the right words. But that was like grappling after something falling into a deep well – hopeless – and all he could manage was, 'Why?'

Whitman turned his head, spat red onto the bare cinder-block floor. 'It's not ... me.'

'It had to be you.'

'No.' The macabre grin widened. 'It's ... *you*.'

Spooner frowned. He checked his rising temper. 'I don't understand,' he said plaintively. 'I gave you everything. I trusted you.'

Another hoarse laugh.

'Help me understand, Max. What are you talking about?'

Whitman sneered. *'Her.'*

'Who?'

'You don't even ... know. That's worst ... of all.'

'What are you talking about? Help me—'

183

'Help you ... *understand*.'

'Yes.'

'Rot in hell.'

Silence.

'It's not just us,' said Spooner at length. 'This isn't just about us.'

No reply.

'It's about our sworn duty.' Spooner paused. 'It's about our families. Do you want your family to pay the price for your mistakes, Max?'

'Take your ... empty threats,' said Whitman. 'And take your...' A spasm of coughing, followed by another messy expectoration of blood. 'Self-righteousness,' he managed. 'And take ... your goddamned ignorance ... and your sworn ... *duty* ... and shove them right up ... your bony ... back-stabbing ... ass.'

For another long minute, Emil Spooner faced his aide without speaking.

Then he turned, and climbed the stairs again.

Emerging into the sunlit kitchen, he found Candless and Grieg.

'The gloves come off,' he said hollowly.

CENTREVILLE, VIRGINIA

Richard Hart ran his eyes restlessly over a latticework of cracks in the motor court's ceiling.

He saw himself walking by a riverside, with his father and older sister. Daddy was whistling a spry tune: 'If You Knew Suzy'. Then his sister whistled a few bars. And then, naturally, young Richard tried to take a turn. But when he pursed his lips, no sound came out except a thin, reedy whisper. His sister laughed cruelly. *You know*

184

what they say about a boy who can't whistle, Daddy! And Father glanced over, wearing an expression Hart would never forget: sorrowful and abstract and far-seeing, as if he was looking not at his son but through him, at something distant, hazy, and very sad...

Receiving in Charlottesville the news of Hart's failure by Route 30, the senator's face had looked just exactly the same.

A car pulled out of the Esso station next door. Headlights splashed away; the motor court's ceiling darkened. *Fade to black.*

Then another car pulled up to the pumps, and the ceiling was illuminated again. Cracks shifted; the curtain lifted.

He was a few years older than he had been by the river, paying two bits admission at the fairground. A calliope played, steam hooting. Grease and sugar and oil and roasted corn wafted on the air, and sawdust and manure and frying peppers and onions. The roller coaster and carousel creaked dangerously. Hollow pops sounded from the shooting gallery. Barkers cried hoarse pitches. Geeks, bingo, strongmen, bearded ladies, mirror mazes ... and the gypsy fortuneteller, her breath sweetly rancid. Fingers leathery as she traced his palm. Eyes crusted with opaque cataracts. She leaned in close. *A short life, this one; a pity.*

The car next door pulled away. *Fade to black.*

He flipped over, groaning. The thin motor court mattress played hell with his already broken body. But Myron would not be ready with the rifle, in New York, until morning. The only option besides the motor court was returning to the senator's mansion, facing the man with news of his latest failure – and seeing again that disappointed expression. And that was really no option at all.

Headlights splashed, and the cracks rearranged.

The scene now was the lodge in Charlottesville: the first day he had encountered Senator Bolin, the day which had given meaning to the rest of his life. *BPOE* read the banner, *Benevolent and Protective Order of the Elks*. Hart had gone inside, that afternoon, seeking only shelter from the cold. But among a hodgepodge of local businessmen and laborers and drifters he had found the senator, tall and noble and patrician, spotless white suit flowing like liquid, striking a dramatic pose behind the lectern. John Bolin belonged to a dynasty of Virginia gentry which stretched back to the Mayflower – his ancestors had defended their plantation, tooth and nail and flintlock and musket, against Indians and Redcoats – and his stance communicated this noble lineage.

Positioning himself in one dark corner, Hart listened. The senator spoke passionately about the dangers of integration, the feebleness of current foreign policy, the need to retake America for Americans. Then he mingled with the crowd, smiling grimly, shaking hands. His grip was just as Hart expected, strong and firm and uncompromising. His spectacled gaze was clear, charged with a peculiar paradoxical energy, both cold and hot. Hart volunteered on the spot to join the senator's cause in whatever capacity might be available. Bolin looked back at him evenly, somewhat skeptically, and asked if he had been a veteran...

Hart's breath came out with a shudder. He flipped over again. Reaching for the low night-table, he lit a cigarette. Stabbing it out angrily, he lay back again and stared at the cracks. Must sleep, he thought. Must rest. Must stay sharp ... Matter of life and death.

But superstitions flickered behind a thin scrim in the back of his mind – fortune-tellers and will-o'-the-wisps and bad providence – and he heard his sister's cackle: *You know what they say about a boy who can't whistle, Daddy!*

Headlights flooded the ceiling; the cracks shifted again. A narrow back alley, an intimate lounge, and a shadowy figure – Hart himself – stepping through the door.

The bar's patrons – all white, male, well-dressed, and studiously respectable-looking – engaged in muted conversation, which died away upon Hart's entrance. Many wore green carnations in their lapels. Others wore red neckties or pinky rings. The bartender's hair was cut like Caesar's, lying in a straight line across his forehead. As the man mixed Hart's drink, he used an unfrosted glass – a signal inside the subculture indicating that the recipient was to be considered suspicious until further notice.

Opening a tab, Hart nursed the Martini, keeping head down and shoulders rounded. Slowly, banter around him recommenced, cautiously at first, and then with increasing freedom. By the time he finished his first drink, a man at his elbow had engaged him in conversation on the subject of the Brooklyn Dodgers, who after what seemed like eons of 'waiting 'til next year' had finally had their year. By the time he finished his second, the man was inviting him to a private house-party just around the corner – catnip to a vice cop; either the man had thrown caution to the wind, or was giving Hart enough rope with which to hang himself. Regretfully, Hart declined. He was just here, he said, to lay the dust. As a traveling salesman, he'd spent a long day on the road, and a bustling party sounded like a bit much. His next drink came in a chilled glass, sending a clear signal to the bar's other patrons: all clear.

He saw himself picking up his drink and ambling over to Arthur Glashow, who looked something like the actor Howard Keel, and wore a bracelet representing the Greek letter lambda. Hart indicated Glashow's Martini and raised his own. 'Great minds,' he said. 'Dirty? They're best when dirty.'

'I've never had one dirty,' Glashow answered.

'Well, your time has come. My treat.'

Shadows flickered; then Hart saw himself sitting beside Glashow at the bar, checking his watch. 'Got to get back to my hotel before the witching hour,' he said, 'or I'll turn into a pumpkin. It's just down the street...'

Arthur Glashow checked his own watch. 'Gee, it's about my time, too.'

They settled the bill and left the lounge together, stepping out into a balmy Indian summer night. After casting a cautious glance over his shoulder, Hart reached for the man. Of course, Hart was no queer. He did what he did in that alley only for the cause. Earlier in life, he had done it when necessary only for a roof above his head on a rainy night. And back in the hotel, he continued doing it only for the sake of the camera hidden behind the one-way mirror...

You know what they say about a boy who can't whistle, Daddy!

And two weeks later, when he put a single bullet into Glashow's hairline just below the right ear, dismembered the corpse, and scattered it between three bodies of water, he did it only for the senator. By then he had grown somewhat fond of Glashow, who had faithfully followed instructions, and had deserved better than a shot in the back of the head. But the senator came first. The senator always came first.

Through slatted blinds, headlights continued to shift, advancing and receding. Again, the cracks in the ceiling dissolved, swirling to form a new picture ... but this time, Hart's attention remained on the window, behind which lights moved. An instinct was clamoring, from the deep place where superstitions take root. Nothing seemed to have changed...

... but something was wrong.

He levered himself off the mattress in darkness, following an intuition which hardened in the space of a heartbeat to a certainty.

They're here.

He got a crutch beneath himself, crossed the room, and pulled down one slat of the blinds.

189

There – by the hedges on the far side of the parking lot, beside his Buick, beneath a few plump flakes of falling snow: a police cruiser.

And inside the lighted motor court office: a blue-suited officer, talking with the desk clerk.

As Hart watched, the clerk pointed toward his room.

THIRTEEN

GETTYSBURG

Most of the revelers seemed to have gotten a head start on the celebrating; well-oiled voices and laughter drowned out the music from the phonograph.

Weaving back and forth through the throng, hauling armfuls of lambswool and Harris Tweed, Elisabeth saw much giggling, flirting, and slapping of rumps. Scotch flowed freely, along with wine and beer and Martinis and highballs. From the kitchen doorway Miss Dunbarton watched over the proceedings ceremoniously, skirt ballooning out above an absurd crinoline.

Just before seven, someone switched on a floodlight mounted outside the north-facing window, catching the year's first snowfall in an unexpected frieze. The partygoers paused, overcome with the timing. For a few seconds Bing Crosby's was the only voice in the parlor, singing, appropriately enough, 'White Christmas'.

Then girls shrieked, men laughed, and a cheer was raised, along with countless glasses.

When their shift ended, Josette led Elisabeth by one elbow to the powder room.

As she touched up her make-up, the younger girl babbled on nervously about the men at the party – Bill Brennan was looking particularly handsome tonight – and the fact that James had not yet made his arrival. Probably, he was waiting, she said, to make a dramatic entrance. Everything was a calculation with him. That was the problem with attractive men; they thought of nobody except themselves. Next time she fell in love, she would find someone intelligent but ordinary – why not? What did she care for looks, really? At one point in her life, sure, but you only had to burn yourself so many times before you learned not to reach for a hot stove. What she needed was a good *average* man, a Jim Anderson type, a hard worker and steady provider, not some kind of film star gigolo. And speaking of hard work, had Elisabeth noticed what a lousy job Jane Carlson had done cleaning the parlor that afternoon? A good half-inch of dust remained everywhere. The Hummel figurines looked as if they stood in a snowdrift. Jane was a nice enough girl, but you could only cut corners for so long before it came back to haunt you ... but here she went, blabbing again: her very worst trait.

Adding a final unnecessary flourish of mascara, Josette batted her eyelashes in the mirror.

'Now,' she said bravely, 'let's join the party.'

Together they left the powder room. The bash was on an upward swing, with groups of girls waiting to be approached for a dance, and groups of farmhands and agents drinking, trying to gain courage to approach them. In the center of the parlor, an area near the Christmas tree served as a dance floor for those bold or drunk enough to make use of it.

Smiling with determination, Josette headed straight for the bar, where she downed one scotch in a gulp and then took another to mingle. Elisabeth stuck close, holding an Old-Fashioned she didn't plan on touching. As long as she stayed near Josette, she could avoid falling into any conversations of her own. Getting through the evening with the least possible interaction was her goal. As soon as escape seemed feasible, she would claim a headache and slip off to bed.

They floated through the crowd, picking up threads of conversation. 'You'd think some of the glamor of having him around might rub off,' one girl told another, 'but you'd be wrong; the old battleaxe makes sure of that.' Two farm-hands engaged in a lively, not to say contentious, debate, with one giving credit for the Bums' recent victory to Johnny Podres for pitching his game seven shutout, and another loudly yielding that honor to left-fielder Sandy Amoros, for running down Yogi Berra's long fly ball and thus enabling Pee Wee Reese to catch Gil McDougald at first. A clutch of Secret Service agents, look-ing ill-at-ease in checkered sports coats, watched the snowfall through a window. 'Question is,' said one sagely, 'will it stick? If it warms up just five degrees, you won't find anything on the ground by tomorrow afternoon.'

Josette sidled up behind Bill Brennan, who was examining Jane Carlson's stocking. 'Well, you just can't see the seam at all,' he asked, 'can you? Here, lift that ankle up a little bit higher and let me take a closer look...'

Becoming aware of a presence behind him, he turned. 'Why, if it isn't Sister Rosetta Tharpe. My, but you clean up nice.'

Josette giggled. 'You ain't so bad yourself, Bill.'

He slung an arm over her shoulder. 'How's tricks, dollface?'

'Now that my shift's over,' she said, 'just fine. Bill, I want you to meet my friend Elisabeth. Libby, Bill Brennan.'

Brennan drank in Elisabeth appreciatively. 'Hubba, hubba. Are your legs tired, honey?'

She blinked. 'Sorry?'

'Because they will be. You're going to be running through my dreams tonight.'

Josette rolled her eyes. 'Bill's a charmer – in his own mind.'

'I have my days,' he admitted.

As Josette chatted with the man about *Howdy Doody* and Buffalo Bob, Elisabeth felt a knot of tension loosen in her gut. If this buffoon was their head of security, she thought, she had given them altogether too much credit.

THE TREASURY BUILDING
Dry-swallowing a pill, Isherwood spent a

193

pensive moment examining the vial in his hand.

The doctors had prescribed codeine – so why couldn't he take a drink instead? As soon as the idea occurred, it began to seem terribly reasonable. He'd already proved he could function without booze. The whiskey would be purely medicinal. One good slug would clear his head; he pictured clouds parting, clean sunlight shining through. Even the accouterments of the act – the burst of cork leaving bottle, the woody smoky flavor hitting his nose before his tongue – would do him a world of good.

Something inside him gave an ugly clench. *It is the greatest art of the devil*, Baudelaire had said, *to convince us that he does not exist.*

Slipping the vial back into his pocket, he looked up and saw that from behind the desk the Chief was watching him intently. When the phone rang, Spooner reached for it without taking his gaze from Isherwood's face.

'When?' asked the Chief. 'And,' he prodded. 'And.' He took out his pack of Winstons, shot one onto the floor, crooked the phone between chin and shoulder to retrieve it. 'How many? ... Right. You know where to find me.'

He hung up, tightly smiled. 'Hart,' he said, and crossed his fingers.

GETTYSBURG

Philip Zane listened to a series of clicks as the operator patched through the call, a weird underwater peeping, and then the ringing of a faraway telephone. Three rings, four – a woman answered sleepily. 'Hello?'

194

'Person-to-person from Mister Zane,' interrupted the operator, 'for Missus Zane.'

A microscopic pause. 'This is she.'

'Your party, sir,' said the operator, and rang off.

'Honey,' said Zane eagerly.

As his wife catalogued her latest complaints – aching back, bloating and blotching, torrential sweating, inadequate bladder – he made sympathetic noises, keeping one eye on the Eisenhower house through the window of the Secret Service office. Upon finishing, she segued without missing a beat into a touchy subject: 'I had lunch with my father yesterday. He says Melvin's on his way back to California come the new year; his mother's ailing.'

Zane felt his stomach bottom out, as it did every time this subject came up. 'I'm sorry to hear that,' he said carefully.

'About his mother, or about the spot opening up?'

Both. 'What do you think? The mother.'

'I think you meant both.'

No fooling Trudy, of course. But it didn't take Einstein to figure out that Zane, having achieved the pinnacle of the American Dream, would not eagerly abandon the position to work as a manager in his father-in-law's hardware store.

'We talked about this,' Trudy was saying.

'We did,' he conceded.

'You said you'd think about it.'

That was before he had gotten out from behind the desk. 'I'm thinking.'

'Honey, we can't bring a baby into this world without a father. At least in the store nobody's

195

asking you to step in front of a—'

'*Zeeskyte,* I've got to run. Sorry. Love you.'

He hustled back toward Farm Two beneath the light snowfall, dodging baleful looks sent his way by the skeleton crew on duty watching the President – anyone who could slip away to join the party had done so.

Entering the herdsman's home through the kitchen door, he avoided the thick of the festivities – men and women swaying in clinches as Nat King Cole murmured 'A Blossom Fell' – and reached the staircase. Settling back down in his chair by the bedroom window, he risked lighting a cigarette: against the rules, but the house matron would have her hands full downstairs.

He should have known that Trudy would press the issue. But he had hoped for a few more pleasant moments of conversation before they got there.

His wife had grown up in Westchester, he reminded himself, playing tennis and croquet, attending cotillions and mixers, serving Martinis to her father each night when he came home from work. Her parents had no memories of the old country, no pogroms, rapes, or murders in their past, no recollections of hiding in cellars to express political or religious opinions. America would never mean to Trudy – or to their unborn child – what it meant to Philip Zane. And that was good, of course. He would not take away her sense of security for anything. Still, he sometimes wished that she understood more what America, and so this job, meant to *him*.

He sighed. The sound of tipsy merrymaking

drifted up from downstairs. Companionship, a drink, a festive atmosphere to balance out the solitude ... the party was what had made him sneak away to call Trudy in the first place. But, of course, this was the job for which he'd signed up. This was the job he wouldn't trade for the world.

Angling his chair slightly in the direction of Farm One, he cracked open the window, exhaled smoke into a cold swirl of snow flurries, and settled in. *Watch and wait.*

CENTREVILLE

Hurrying away from the motor court, leaning against the one crutch he'd had time to grab – the only thing, except for coat and wallet, he'd saved from the room – Richard Hart felt a sweet, sugary fear coursing through his body, a fear glutinous in its purity.

Neon signs lining the highway tinted the falling snow aquamarine, coral pink, emerald, and tangerine. Despite the proximity of a major thoroughfare, the night possessed the preter-natural stillness of the moment before an auto-mobile accident. Reaching the edge of the road, Hart paused to look back behind himself. Two more patrol cars had pulled into the parking lot. Beneath fat, tumbling flakes of snow, four offi-cers were massing outside the room he had just clumsily vacated via the bathroom window. Two others approached the parked Buick, guns drawn. The desk clerk stood outside the motor court's office, beetling his brow and wringing his hands.

A car came whizzing down the highway. Licking bloody lips, Hart propped himself against the single crutch and stuck out a thumb.

The car whickered past.

He set the crutch and moved off, humping down the road's gravel shoulder. His pulse beat in the hollow of his throat. Cold wind sliced surgically through his coat, clothes, and skin. Despite the chill, clammy sweat-spiders crawled over his chest and back. The crutch slipped against ice, and he nearly fell. Cursing, he regained his balance. His broken leg beneath the cast sent a pulse of distress. A sense of unreality descended. These were the ingredients, he thought, of a particularly lurid nightmare.

A distant thud as the cops put shoulders against door in the motor court behind him.

Another pair of headlights was coming down the highway. He turned again, stuck out his thumb. *Please, God—*

Spraying up a curtain of cold slush, the car – a peach-over-white Nash Metropolitan – pulled over onto the gravel shoulder.

GETTYSBURG

'Don't look now; it's him.'

Elisabeth looked. A new group of men had appeared, wearing blue jeans and chambray work shirts. 'Which one?'

'The tall one. Is he coming over here?'

He was – a curly-haired, cherubic man of about thirty, sporting a handlebar mustache in an effort to make himself look older. 'Brace yourself,' Elisabeth warned.

Josette forced an enthusiastic grin onto her face. 'Probably, it's for the best,' she said merrily. 'Because when I get on my way, I wouldn't want to be held back by – why, speak of the devil! James, please meet my friend Elisabeth; Libby, James.'

'Libby.' He took her hand and gave it a lingering kiss, making Josette squirm. 'My, my. Libby.'

One of his friends pressed rudely through the crowd. 'Jimmy, whatcha drinking?'

'What *aren't* I drinking?' James laughed roughly. 'The price is right, ain't it? I'll take one of everything.'

As the friend shouldered off toward the bar, another farmhand promptly materialized to take his place. 'Like rats on a hunk a cheese, over there. Nothing like free booze to bring out the best in people, huh?' His eyes were glued to Elisabeth's décolletage. 'Say, honey, you ready for a dance?'

'Sorry. I got a bum ankle.'

James threw an elbow into the man's ribs. 'Sal, I told you. You gotta work up to it. A little class works wonders.'

'I just asked for a dance.'

'Yeah, but look at what you're dealing with here. This here's the epitome of feminine pulchritude.'

Elisabeth turned, seeking escape, but found herself hemmed in on every side.

Soon the friend returned from the bar, bearing drinks and a joke he'd heard in line: where was Solomon's temple? On the side of his head.

Josette managed a fake, tinkling little laugh. The best Elisabeth could summon was a dimple. The crowd pressed close around them, warm and smothering. On her right, a frizzy-haired scullery maid named Caroline Dreyfus fell into heated discussion with Sal about the merits of venison. (Too tough, she declared, and Sal informed her that she'd never had it cooked correctly.) On her left, Josette tried to involve James in a conversation about scotch and soda versus gin and tonic.

But he ignored her, staring hungrily at Elisabeth. 'I could use a smoke,' he said, as if they were the only two in the room. 'Let's sneak outside.'

He turned, heading for the side door, assuming she would follow. Falling into step behind him, Josette shot Elisabeth a beseeching look. Elisabeth said into her friend's ear, 'I've got a headache. Think I'm just going to...'

'Oh God, don't you dare! Don't you *dare* leave me alone with him!'

'Josie—'

'I mean it,' Josette hissed, and grabbed Elisabeth's hand.

Seeing their trajectory, others fell into their wake. Now the dance floor was packed; couples held each other close, the music had gotten louder, and a first Christmas ornament had been broken. Dunbarton, who should have served as the voice of reason, was nowhere to be seen. Glancing at a Waterbury clock on the mantle as they passed, Elisabeth was surprised to find it not yet eight p.m.

In the yard outside, a motley group of six –

Josette and Elisabeth and Caroline Dreyfus, and James and two other farmhands whose names Elisabeth hadn't caught – moved toward the nearby oak. None had stopped for overcoats, and except for Elisabeth all shivered in the snow, for the most part grinning good-naturedly as cigarettes were handed around and then chivalrously lighted. James finished his drink, produced a flask, and swigged. He passed the flask to Josette, who although holding a scotch in her other hand drank and then passed it to Elisabeth, who had lost her Old-Fashioned somewhere. She pretended to drink and then passed the flask to the man standing beside her, a gangly fellow of about forty, drowning in a tweed jacket at least two sizes too large.

Noticing Elisabeth's bare arms, the gangly man said, 'Cold?' He put an arm around her shoulders, squeezing her close.

'Hey Earl,' said Josette scornfully, 'give her your coat, why don't you, if you want to be a gentleman?'

'Better yet,' said James, 'let's go into the barn. It's warm, and we can smoke without worrying about Dunbarton.'

Elisabeth shook her head – but Josette was looking directly at her, significantly.

The group moved off beneath languid snowflakes, across frozen ruts of earth.

THE TREASURY BUILDING
Isherwood could hear the voice on the other end of the connection: pinched, adenoidal, strained.

Spooner covered his eyes with one hand.

'Sergeant,' he said carefully, 'I don't see how that's possible.'

An insectile reply.

'Well,' said Spooner, 'fucking *find* him,' and he slammed a fist onto the desk with enough force to make the picture of Joe DiMaggio behind it go crooked.

ROUTE 650: NORTH OF CENTREVILLE

'Hope you got the license plate,' said the man behind the wheel, glancing over at Hart in the passenger seat.

Hart laughed. 'Boy,' he said. 'You don't want to get me started. You wouldn't believe the weekend I've had.'

The man driving the Nash Metropolitan was in his late sixties, heavily sideburned, with white tufts of hair sprouting from prominent ears. 'Do tell,' he said. 'I could use a good laugh.'

An infinitesimal pause. 'Well,' said Hart then. 'I'm heading up north to see my sister, coming up Route Fifteen, and this Mack truck jack-knifes in front of me – yesterday morning, this is. So by yesterday afternoon, I'm in the hospital, my car's on the way to the junkheap, and I've got forty bucks in my wallet. Worse, I got this bang on the head. Confuses me. The doctors do a quick patch-up and tell me the worst is past. But I'm looking at a bill that means taking out a second mortgage, so I decide to get on my way, ride my thumb up north.' He laughed again, s h a k i n g his head ruefully. 'May not have been the best decision,' he admitted, 'what with the crutch and the weather. But I'm not thinking too straight. Yesterday morning, my biggest problem was what to eat for breakfast. And now...' He trailed off.

'Where's your sister at?'

'Boston.'

'I can get you as far as Union Station, how's that sound?'

'Sounds good. I appreciate the lift.'

He glanced in the side-view mirror as he spoke. No sign of sirens yet – but they would find the ruffled bed, still warm. But the snowfall was too new to hold tracks; they would not know which way he had gone. If he could reach the train station, he could give them the slip.

They passed shadowed factories and body shops and grimy little stores selling propane and auto parts, made almost pretty by a thin blanket of white. 'Relax,' said the driver suddenly.

Hart looked over. The man was smiling at him. 'Life's too short, son. Count your blessings. You're out of the weather, you still got your health for the most part – could've been a sight worse, that's for damned sure – and pretty soon you'll sit down at your sister's table and she'll fill you up with good hot food. Man's got to look on the bright side.'

Hart smiled back.

'Me, I learned that the hard way. Lost both my parents to the Spanish flu. One day they're healthy as horses; next they're telling me they don't feel right. Well, I was busy, the way people get in their mid-life. I didn't have time to worry about some sniffles, a runny nose. So I told my mother to put some extra blankets on the bed and I'd check back again in a few days. But by the time I checked back, they were both gone ... What I'm trying to tell you is, stop and smell the roses. It all seems so goddamned important now, whatever it is. But don't let it get away with you. Just like the song says: it's later than you think.'

Hart nodded. *A short life, this one; a pity.*

Minutes later, beneath a snowfall already slackening, they passed over the city limits of Washington, DC.

FOURTEEN

GETTYSBURG

The Maternity Barn was the largest and, excepting the tool shed, nearest of the outbuildings to the herdsman's home.

Empty at the moment of livestock, the barn's interior was nevertheless heated, divided into pens – two large and many small – with the floor covered by loose straw and, in some places, soft animal bedding. In the center stood an office with closed doors and windows, surrounded on three sides by stacked bales of hay. The air smelled robustly of chaff, dust, and fragrant manure.

Stepping through the doors, the group of six seemed by some secret signal to have paired off:

James and Elisabeth in the lead, Caroline Dreyfus and the tall gangly man called Earl behind
them, and Josette, with the third man, bringing
up the rear.

'My queen,' said James cornily, and removed a
bale of hay from the stacks, which he offered
Elisabeth as a chair. Once she was seated, he
heaved off a few more bales. As they all sat, the
flask made another circuit; a bottle of rum had
appeared from somewhere to join it. Elisabeth
felt as if she occupied the small, sober center of
an increasingly rowdy hurricane.

'Wish I had my guitar,' said Josette thickly.
She looked flushed, and her chignon was coming
loose.

Disregarding her, James faced Elisabeth
squarely. 'So, *bella*,' he said. 'How is it I never
met you before?'

'She's new,' Josette said. 'She replaced Babs.'

Leaning forward, he brazenly put a hand on
Elisabeth's knee. 'We'll have to make up for lost
time,' he said, and squeezed.

Elisabeth smiled emptily. She covered James'
hand with her own, left it there for a moment,
and then gently slipped both hands off her knee.

Caroline and Earl had fallen into a discussion
about Daphne du Maurier, whom both had read
and liked. The third man was trying to rope
Josette into conversation about the lack of food
at the party. 'I don't need filet mignon or snails,
you know. But a chicken sandwich might have
hit the spot...'

But Josette paid him as little attention as she
was receiving from James. Her eyes, wet and

wounded, bored into Elisabeth. The farmhand tried a new approach. 'Say, Josie, you ever look at the newspaper? 'Cause I was just reading about this case outside Cleveland. Real interesting thing. This guy named Sam Sheppard, this surgeon, they think he may have killed his pregnant wife. You read about that?'

'You got classical bone structure,' James was telling Elisabeth. 'You look like an old painting. Anybody ever tell you that?'

She dipped her head modestly.

'You're not too good at getting compliments, are you?' Surreptitiously, he placed his hand back on her knee. 'You oughtta work on that, baby, if you don't mind my saying.'

'Another thing I read in the newspaper,' the third man told the back of Josette's head, 'about this other doctor, Salk. He came up with this thing to stop polio, you hear about that? But they done a mass, whaddya call it, incalculation of schoolchildren. And I'm thinking, what if this causes an outbreak? Because I'm not sure if you know, but these incalculations, is what they call them, actually these are a sample of the disease.'

Josette turned to face him at last. 'Sample of the disease?' she said muzzily.

'It's a true fact, Josie. It's a little piece of polio, which they inject right into these kids' arms...'

With Josette momentarily distracted, James pressed his attack, sidling closer to Elisabeth on his bale, chafing her knee. 'You like music, honey? Me, I love Benny Goodman. Next time he swings through Philly I'm gonna go check it out. If you want to come with, I'll try to score an extra ticket.'

'Oh, that's sweet,' said Elisabeth.

'Yeah, but whaddya say?'

'Thing is, I've got a fellow back in Virginia.'

'Virginia? Might as well be Mars.'

Maintaining her empty smile, Elisabeth again dislodged his hand. She dragged her bale a foot away from him, closer to Josette, and then glanced at her friend, hoping the gesture had not gone unappreciated. But the younger girl still looked wounded.

Now Caroline and Earl talked earnestly about the difficulty college women had in finding a husband, while the other man spoke again to the back of Josette's head, complaining about the back-breaking labor they had done that afternoon, filling the corn crib. Voices grew ever more strident, and a fug of cigarette smoke hung heavy in the air. James scooted his bale closer to Elisabeth again. 'Come on,' he implored. 'Don't play hard to get.'

Abruptly, Elisabeth stood. 'I'm going back to the party,' she announced. 'Josie, come with me.'

Josette hesitated. After a moment Elisabeth turned, heading out into the night alone; in a flash, Josette was by her side.

During their minutes inside the barn, the snowfall had stopped. A diffuse glow lit the cloudy sky. Elisabeth started back toward the herdsman's home, but Josette brought her up short with a hand on one arm. 'Let's go for a walk, huh? I need to clear my head.'

Elisabeth bit back an argument. They wandered aimlessly away from both barn and house, in

207

the general direction of the bullpen and corn crib. For several long moments, they strolled through the cold without speaking. Josette hummed a few tuneless bars of 'Darling, *Je Vous Aime Beaucoup*'. She took out a cigarette, dropped it, bent to retrieve it, and stuck it between her lips upside-down. 'Libby,' she said sulkily, 'you and James never ... you know. Did you?'

'Oh, for God's sake. He was flirting with *me*, Josie. Not the other way around.'

'Sure. And who could blame him? You're gorgeous.'

Elisabeth reached out, turning the cigarette around before Josette could light the filter. A moment passed, during which their crunching footsteps were the only sound. A match flared, illuminating Josette's heavy mascara and slightly drooping eyes. Then Josette said: 'You're a good friend, Libby.'

Elisabeth scanned for sarcasm, found none. Josette took her hand, and they kept walking. Each time the wind shifted they could hear music and rowdy laughter, chopped by the breeze. By now there would have been some pairing-off, thought Elisabeth, some hanky-panky between the girls from the herdsman's home and the healthy red-blooded American Secret Service boys. She wondered if she might take a chance, sneak onto Farm One, and finish her work this very night. With luck and courage, she might be gone before sunrise.

Tempting – but foolish. In just three more days, she could do it right.

As if reading her mind, Josette asked, 'How

208

much longer you planning on staying here?'

'Hm? I'm not really sure. I just started ... A while, I guess.'

'Well, I won't be here much longer. I've got to get out.' Josette stifled a small, ladylike belch. 'And I'm going to. Real soon now. I'm going to Tinseltown, like Babs.'

'Gee. Some day soon, Josie, I'll see your name in lights.'

'Yeah,' said Josette avidly. 'Right opposite Clark Gable's. Right up there on a marquee.' She stumbled, quickly righted herself without losing her grip on Elisabeth's hand. 'Although sometimes I wonder: how many girls go to Hollywood and end up on the streets? Prettier girls than me, too.'

'Oh, but you're beautiful, Josie.'

'That's sweet of you to say. But I know it's not true. *You're* beautiful. That's why James is all over you. Me, I'm just fat. Oink. But,' she rushed on before Elisabeth could protest, 'I'm also talented. I've got star quality. That's what my mother always said; that's why she named me after a film star. But then, mothers always think that about their daughters, don't they? Anyways: I should probably start my career on the stage, I'm thinking, before I go into the movies. The theater rewards talent. The movies chew it up and spit it out. And I've got more talent than looks.'

Elisabeth said nothing.

'So I'm thinking maybe New York, or Chicago, or London. You know: the theater cities. To get my foot in the door.'

'It sounds exciting.'

'Or Paris.' Josette reached beneath her crêpe de chine and hoisted up a falling bra strap. 'I've always dreamed about Paris. Have you ever dreamed about Paris, Libby?'

A flash of a memory: one dark night in a Saint-Michel graveyard, while working her way from Great Britain back to Berlin. She had snuck up behind a resistance leader, silently drawing a knife while the man was distracted by a map... 'Paris,' Elisabeth echoed faintly.

'What girl hasn't? Well, then, why don't you come with me? Oh, it'll be so much fun! We'll have the time of our lives. What an adventure! I'm born for it – my mother knew it, I think, when she chose my name – and you've got a certain sophistication, don't you? A kind of European flair. You'll fit right in. We'll get a little garret together in, what do they call it, the fifth *arrondissement*? Do I have that right? The left bank? The artsy place. The Latin quarter. Oh, and we'll have affairs – beautiful affairs with beautiful Frenchmen. *Très sophistiqué.* We'll smoke Gauloise and walk through the rain and go to art galleries and such. And you can help me pick out outfits for my auditions, and I'll help you get your modeling career off the ground. Oh, we'll just have a ball. An absolute blast. And I'll get some valuable experience in the theater so that when I *am* acting opposite Clark Gable, I'll be ready.'

They walked, holding hands.

'We'll get up early,' Josette continued after a moment, 'and drink our morning coffee in a little café. And we'll watch the sun rise behind the Eiffel Tower. I picture fog. Do they have fog in Paris, or is that only London?'

Elisabeth couldn't help but smile; she wiped it off her face before her friend could notice. 'I think they've got fog everywhere.'

'I picture fog and beautiful men and pretty dresses and lots of cigarettes and coffee and wine and dancing. And music and salons and artists and those little hats, what are they called, berets. And no more Miss Dunbarton! No more sweeping and mopping! Can you picture it, Libby?'

'You know,' said Elisabeth, with the smile flickering back, 'actually, Josie, I think I can.'

THE TREASURY BUILDING

Spooner was trying to coordinate, using only local police, a contingent to interview every guest at the motor court, another to set up strategic roadblocks, another to check bus and train stations, another to cover Washington National and Friendship International airports, and another to trace the Buick found in the motel's parking lot.

'Then call in some favors, man, for the love of God.' The Chief shook his head. 'Don't you know who I am? Listen: if I wanted to use G-Men, I'd use G-Men. I want to use *you*, and I don't want to have to get the President out of bed to make you hop to. That's right, I said the President. Well, Sergeant, which fucking President do you *think* I mean?'

His frustration was contagious. Isherwood paced the office, snapping his Zippo open and shut, *snik snik, snik snik*, and working his way through an endless chain of cigarettes. Passing by the window, he paused to absorb the view – not the postcard-ready scene visible from the reception area, but a sandstone pavilion, small parking lot, and stretch of 15th Street NW.

On a chilly Saturday night, vehicular and pedestrian traffic moved in cycles: slackening, so that for a moment everything was still beneath the diminishing snowfall, and then picking up again as the next swell of diners or drinkers or late workers spilled out onto streets and side-walks. Richard Hart, thought Isherwood, was somewhere out there at this very moment. Perhaps in one of these very passing cars...

The cigarette between his fingers had burned half to ash. The Chief was still shaking his head. 'No, I can't tell you that. But I *can* tell you what to do next. Now listen close – got a pen? I want any reports of stolen vehicles, stolen food or clothing, unexplained assaults ... a matter of national security, pal, and that's all you need to know ... are you writing this down? ... stow-aways, hitch-hikers, dead bodies...'

UNION STATION, WASHINGTON DC
The Metropolitan pulled over. 'Here you go,' said the driver.

'Much obliged, sir.'

'Pleasure's mine, young man. Good luck to you. And remember what I said: stop and smell the roses.'

They shook hands. Hart climbed out, cumber-somely, and watched the car go. Then he turned his attention to the train station's six-hundred-foot façade and triumphal arch, with three American flags riding high on burnished poles, and a steady stream of visitors moving in and out despite the hour.

Inside, the horde was even thicker. Speckled among civilian garb he saw official uniforms: police, seamen, railroad conductors, an occasional Marine wearing dress blue. Beneath a high vaulted ceiling, a schedule informed him that the next train to New York would not depart until 10:15 p.m. After a few seconds of consideration, he turned toward the rectangular bar set dead center in the bustling Main Concourse. Fugitives ran, he thought; fugitives hid in corners, shadows, cars, houses, apartments. Fugitives did not remain in broad, well-lit spaces crowded with authorities. But sometimes the best way to hide was in plain sight.

On his way through the main hall he passed a drunk, sprawled across cold marble and talking to himself. 'Mother,' the derelict muttered. 'Mr and Mrs America, you say, and all the ships at sea. But Mother: Mr and Mrs America live right next door.' He chortled. 'Five-star generals and admirals right next door, Mother, living with the Cheesecake Girl and Ginger Rogers, if you'd just open your eyes and *see...*' The man's hat lay ignored on the floor. Hart snagged it with his crutch, lifted it in one smooth motion, barely slowing.

At the bar, laying the crutch out of the way against the floor, he pulled the brim of the hat low over his eyes. Ordering a Martini, he focused exclusively on his drink. Hide in plain sight, he thought again. Audacity worked wonders. Once he had heard a story about an old-time magician who would 'levitate' a young lady in front of a large crowd. With her body floating in the air, the conjuror would declare that no mirrors or wires were assisting the trick. Then he would call a child from the assembly, lifting the youngster up directly beside the floating lady so the kid could vouch that indeed there were no wires or mirrors. Up close, the child would see thin cords, imperceptible from a small distance, supporting the illusionist's assistant. But at that moment the magician would growl directly into the child's ear: *Breathe a word of this, you little shit, and I'll track you down and teach you how to keep your motherfucking mouth shut!* At which point the child's mouth would fall open; and the magician would beam to the audience, which would take the child's expression of astonishment as proof of magic, and well-deserved applause and cheers would sweep the arena.

The bar began to fill up. Hart studied the crust of olive brine on the rim of his glass, avoiding being drawn into conversation. Police drifted through the shifting crowd. But with the crutch on the floor, the coat draped over his shoulders and cast, and the hat pulled low over his face, Hart did not merit a second glance. He was starting to feel confident. He had no cigarettes, no vehicle, and no weapons; but he also had nothing to weigh him down. He had used an alias in the motor court's registry, and he'd left behind nothing to indicate his origin or destination. Years of drifting had left him light as a feather, thin as smoke.

He waited until his train was within minutes of departure. Then he retrieved the crutch, slipped it beneath one arm, rearranged the coat to conceal it, and moved as smoothly as possible toward the platform. Two Martinis poured with a heavy hand had given him poise. At 10:12, he stepped directly past another uniformed officer and onto the train.

The car was unexpectedly crowded. But the throngs worked to his advantage; he melted in, vanishing. On his right, a young man with bulging eyes read a newspaper. On his left, a severely-drawn young woman gave her full attention to an Agatha Christie mystery. Hart stared at the seat back before him, rocking gently back and forth with the motion of the creaky old car as they pulled out of the station, heading north.

Several times during the first forty-five minutes, newspaper vendors passed through the car, dressed like mourners as they hawked the *Washington Post*. Then the vendors stopped coming; the young man on Hart's right dozed, and the young woman on his left, finishing her book, promptly started reading again from page one.

He closed his eyes. Now was his chance to catch some rest. But he couldn't sleep, and soon enough he opened his eyes again, looking through bleary windows at the passing night.

THE STORK CLUB, NEW YORK CITY

The usual angst the Vice President would have

felt upon entering the Cub Room – a shrine to the decidedly un-Nixon-like virtues of drink, night-life, gossip, glamor, and celebrity – was com-pounded by the uncertain nature of the business that had brought him here.

His misgivings were hardly relieved when he caught sight of the FBI Director's table. Associ-ate Director and close pal (nudge-wink) Clyde Tolson favored Nixon with a jealous eye as the Vice President approached. Two stolid middle-aged women looked at him as if he were some-thing good to eat. Taking a seat, Nixon recog-nized one as Ethel Merman, the First Lady of musical theater and a frequent guest at the Eisen-hower White House. His discomfiture increased a notch. A close friend of Hoover's, the diva suffered from a legendary penchant for loose talk. At least Winchell, the slime-mongering kike, was missing in action tonight, thank God.

Smiling warmly, Nixon tried to set aside his concerns. He engaged in the *de rigueur* few minutes of courteous small talk, starting with an explanation for his presence – he had been just down the block at a fund-raising dinner and had heard that Hoover was holding court in the Cub Room – and moving on to brief chit-chat about the pleasures of the theater. Did Miss Merman realize that Nixon had met his darling wife on-stage? It was true. Seeking to drum up business as a young attorney just starting out in Whittier, he had joined the local theater group, where he had found himself cast in the mystery *The Dark Tower* opposite a pretty new teacher named Pat Ryan. Tall, slim, and graceful, Pat had caught his eye immediately...

The crowd moved around them in a smooth, unobtrusive flow, guided by the sure hand of Sherman Billingsley, the club's founder, owner, and premier *bon vivant*. Passing by the table, Billingsley tossed a chummy nod to Merman, for many years his mistress and still a favorite companion. On the other side of a glass partition, the orchestra started in on a mambo; on the small dance floor, people gamely began to cha-cha-cha. Cigarettes girls and white-suited waiters circulated fluidly, smiling and serving with glints in their eye.

At length Nixon managed to communicate with a lift of his brow that a private moment of Hoover's time would be appreciated. The songstress took the hint, suddenly recalling business in the main dining room. Picking up a mink stole, she seized her friend by the elbow. Tolson departed more reluctantly, only after an expressive nod from Hoover, and only after pausing to snag a shrimp from a cocktail at his place.

America's Top Cop then regarded Nixon with such a flat and unapologetic stare that the Vice President fidgeted in his seat.

'John,' started Nixon. 'There's a matter I want to discuss. But it's ... delicate.'

Hoover's gaze was hardly sympathetic. Considering their history together, this was unsurprising. Although Nixon had been careful to speak only admiringly of the Director in public, they had not always been allies behind the scenes. The defining moment of their relationship had come seven years before, after the discovery of top-secret government documents inside a hollowed-out pumpkin in a Westminster field. Whittaker Chambers, the ex-communist who had led investigators to the pumpkin, had identified a former State Department official named Alger Hiss as their source. In the feeding frenzy which followed, Nixon and Hoover had jockeyed ruthlessly for the honor of crucifying Hiss. Only when Truman's Justice Department had tried to quash the case had Nixon and Hoover grudgingly joined forces, resulting in two convictions of perjury against a man who had been one of FDR's closest confidantes. To this day, each resented having shared his prize with the other.

'Few days ago,' Nixon went on after a brief pause, 'I had lunch with Joe. And he was talking about Clay and Hoffman and those fellows. And he says, you know, that they'll drop me like a hot potato, if only they can find a reason.'

Hoover's dark eyes betrayed nothing. Again, Nixon was unsurprised. Secrets were what got J. Edgar Hoover out of bed each morning, what he thought about as he drifted off to sleep each night. They were his *raison d'être*, and he bartered them carefully, lovingly, and always to his own advantage.

'But Clay and Hoffman,' Nixon continued, 'aren't my concern. In fact, it's the flip side that's got me worried – the patriots, Joe calls them. The men, and I quote, who "won't let Ike get away with this".'

Hoover's bulldog face revealed nothing.

'So.' Nixon shot his cuff, fiddled with the link.

If Hoover was going to make him come right out with it, they would never get anywhere. That the Club was wired – by Hoover, by Winchell, by Billingsley – was an open secret. Sensible men took care what they said within these bugged walls. He decided to try another approach. 'I'm here because you know what goes on, John, better than anybody. A man can't take a number off a restroom stall without you hearing about it. And so I'm wondering if you've, er ... heard anything. Which you, uh, might care to share.'

The heavy brows rose slightly. 'Such as?'

'Well, that's the question, isn't it? Look: what Ike's trying to do to me isn't right, not by a long shot. But if certain men were to – let's say – take action on my behalf – well, that might not be right either. If you follow. Depending, of course, on the nature of the action...'

'You're talking circles here, Dick.'

'Joe implied some things.' Nixon shrugged. 'I'm not sure I liked the sound of them.'

'You're not sure,' Hoover repeated – slowly, almost mockingly – 'you liked the sound of them.'

'That's why I'm here. Sometimes it's hard to know what's real and what's just a man's imagination. But if there's...'

The look on Hoover's face – ironic, half-amused – made him trail off.

Don't forget Hoover, McCarthy had said. *He's in your corner, Dick. He can make things happen – or he can get out of the way and* let *things happen.*

Nixon blinked. He had been driven here tonight by pangs of conscience. If Fighting Joe McCarthy had gone off the rails, if some desperate eleventh-hour plot had been hatched against the President in smoke-filled rooms, then the Director of the FBI should know. For Eisenhower, despite his myriad flaws, was a decent man. He deserved more than a stab in the back from his own trusted generals.

But Hoover, Nixon saw suddenly, *did* know.

Hoover watched understanding dawn; one corner of his solid mouth ticked up with a glimmer of humor. He produced a cigarette lighter embossed with the Stork Club logo – bird wearing top hat, carrying cane – and lit a Chesterfield.

'Dick,' he said around the filter, 'it's a tough business we're in. And between you and me: I'm goddamned sick of watching everything we've worked for get handed away to subversives. I've given up too damned much for this country. Now, you're a stand-up fellow, Dick. I think we could do a lot worse, as a nation, than you.'

Nixon opened his mouth, closed it again with a snap.

'Stand-up fellow,' Hoover said again. Leaning across the table, he thumped Nixon's shoulder fraternally. 'And a bright one, too. Bright enough to realize that sometimes all you've got to do is keep your mouth shut and let the cards fall where they may. We've had our differences. But we'll work things out in the end, when it counts.'

Nixon nodded dumbly. He smiled: first to cover his confusion, and then to cover feeling small. Despite his esteemed title, it seemed that he remained in many ways as unsophisticated as a naif. Although he had shown a willingness to bend ethically when necessary, rising to national prominence along similar lines as Joe McCarthy – baiting Reds, encouraging innuendo and guilt by association – apparently, he was but a schoolboy who had stumbled into a pick-up game with the big kids.

He stood, still smiling, and firmly shook Hoover's hand – a professional handshake, two solid pumps – and then turned away, weaving through the crowd, tossing a rakish, joking salute to Billingsley on his way out.

GETTYSBURG

The more Elisabeth willed herself to sleep, the more awake she felt.

She forced her eyes to remain closed. JESUS LOVES YOU, read the wall plaque; yes, yes, she knew that; she didn't need to be reminded. What she did need was rest. The next few days would tell the tale.

Yet she couldn't sleep; although the last noises from the party were finally falling quiet, her mind kept humming along.

She must have faith – not in Christ, the false prophet, but in the destiny that was her birthright as a pure-blood Aryan. Mastery over subhumans was her inheritance and her due. And so she must believe: she would find success.

To us, the privileged members of the master race, Karl had said, *belongs the future.*

He had not been talking about an ordinary life, with a cross-breed as a best friend. He had been talking about luxury beyond imagining: Mitropa railroad cars and pure-blood lovers, diamonds and precious gems by the heap, mountain chalets and opulent ballrooms. These were her legacy. To settle for less – for coffee and fog and Frenchmen – would be cheating herself.

With the sound of the party quiet at last, the night seemed eerily empty. Something was missing ... Josette's radio, of course. Drunk, the girl had fallen asleep without even tuning in her favorite rock and roll station for a nightcap.

Elisabeth did her best to shake her doubts away. Everything she had done, and still would do, would prove worthwhile. All the choices she had made would be vindicated. She deserved more than an ordinary life. She deserved only the best.

Yet still she lay awake, struggling in vain to rest as the sun rose outside her window on the morning of Sunday, November twentieth, staining the eastern sky the color of blood.

PART THREE

In the councils of government, we must guard against the acquisition of unwarranted influence, whether sought or unsought, by the military-industrial complex.

Dwight D. Eisenhower

FIFTEEN

The sight of Betsy's pale lovely neck, as she lifted her hair so that Max Whitman could work the clasp of the necklace, made him ache in a place deeper than his bones.

After she let auburn hair fall back to her shoulders, she turned and smiled. 'Do you like it?'

In answer, Max took her in his arms. As they kissed, he felt her mouth curve into a smile. He returned the smile, happy and content in a simple, amazed way. He thanked God for his blessings. Life was, after all, so very fragile.

Recently, he'd had a dream – a terrible dream. In the dream, Betsy wasn't truly his at all. She was only a hallucination, brought on by three straight days of degradation and deprivation. And his boss and best friend Emil Spooner had betrayed him, in this dream, and Betsy herself had turned out to be a no-good whore, falling into bed with whatever boy could offer her the fanciest night out on the town ... and eventually marrying a haberdasher from Connecticut, of all things. *A haberdasher from Connecticut.* You couldn't get more ordinary, more compromising, if you tried.

And Max himself had children, in this dream:

two beautiful daughters, the most precious little angels a man could ever wish for. A smile from one of the girls could turn a bad day neatly on its head. And the funny thing was, he felt even luckier to have these girls, in the dream, than he felt in reality to have Betsy – and that, it went without saying, was very lucky indeed.

But in this dream, he had done a very stupid thing. He had given in to his baser instincts – jealousy, desire, ambition – and fallen in with some very bad people. And the hell of it was, his beautiful little girls would be the ones to pay the price. Because the last chance to make things right had passed. Now he was caught. If he confessed, he'd fry. If he didn't confess, they'd beat him to death right here in this moldy cellar. And either way, his little angels would be left without a father.

A tear tracked down his cheek, carving a channel from smears of blood.

For a moment, his vision cleared. With his one remaining eye he saw Lou Candless and Eddie Grieg sitting on chairs in front of him, harshly backlit. Lou and Eddie were looking at him pityingly. They knew his daughters; once upon a time they had all been friends, equals. They had played ball together, shot the shit by the water cooler, picnicked with their families. But time was like a river and it rushed on, and sometimes the river took unexpected turns, and then you ended up here, in a dingy little cellar with instruments of interrogation – chains, clamps, baseball bats – hanging from the wall, with your former friends impelled by duty and honor and justice to

226

beat the living crap out of you until you choked to death on your own blood and bile.

Lou and Eddie exchanged a glance. 'Coming around,' said Lou softly.

Eddie held a cup of water to Max's parched lips. 'Have a drink, Max.'

Max drank. The water was cold and painful and drove a spike into his brain. He coughed, withdrew, vomited.

'Help us stop this.' The pleading note in Eddie Grieg's voice sounded genuine. 'Please, Max. Tell us what we need to know.'

If Max could have chuckled, he would have. It was far too late to stop. He had long since made his choices.

Behind Eddie and Lou sat Betsy Martin, nodding. *That's absolutely right, Max. That's my big, strong fella. Don't let these pricks push you around. That's what I love most about you – your strength.*

'Please,' begged Eddie again.

It's almost over now, said Betsy. *Forget your daughters. Forget your wife. Let this end, and you'll be free. We'll start over. We'll start a family of our own. It's okay, slugger; I don't bite.*

Ah, but it was sad. Because he did love his little girls, so very much.

Eddie sighed. Finding Lou's eye again, he nodded. Lou stood, blocking out the harsh light. Something in his right hand slithered and jangled.

Max retreated back into fantasy. He and Betsy were going out to dinner, and she was wearing the necklace he had given her. The restaurant was a modest little place with wine bottle candlesticks, with great pools of multicolored wax spreading over the tables. And cockroaches and spiders and maggots climbed over the wax, and when the waiter brought their plates, the meal itself was a dead rat, splayed on its back, pinned open like a student's dissection project.

Betsy took a forkful of entrails and angled it toward his mouth. *Eat up, Max. This is what you've bought, after all. For the wages of sin are death, but the gift of God is eternal life. Let go, Max, and come along with me. And we'll be together like this. Forever.*

He shook his head. It was all a mistake. He didn't want this; this was not his fate. He would surface again. And he would tell them everything. It was not too late.

But the candlelight was fading, the darkness closing in. *Too late*, he thought distantly. *Too late, too late, too late...*

And Betsy, forcing the viscera and offal into his mouth, was smiling.

Eddie Grieg raised a hand, preventing the next blow before Lou threw it.

Stepping forward, he laid two fingers against Max's thick neck. As he searched for a pulse, something crawled in the pit of his gut. He focused back on the task at hand. With the same two fingers, he lifted Max's chin. The bleared remaining eye was still half-open, but the light inside was dead.

'He's gone,' Eddie said.

228

THE TREASURY BUILDING

Entering the office one hour later, Lou Candless deposited a thin dossier on the desk without ceremony. 'Final report on Max.'

Before picking up the Manila folder, the Chief cultivated a layer of intellectual distance, impenetrable as enamel. He met Isherwood's gaze squarely. Then he looked down and opened the file. The document covered half of one single-spaced page and reported nothing of value. Max had carried his secrets to the grave. Was it wrong that Spooner found that respectable? One thing about Max Whitman: even as a boy on the playground, he had never let anybody push him around.

Covering a cough, Spooner ground out his cigarette and set the report aside. This had not been the way things were supposed to go. He heard, faint with distance and years, a remote echo of an ancient stickball game: *whisk-crack.*

Lou Candless stood quietly before the desk, seemingly distracted by the picture of Joe Di-Maggio hanging crooked behind the Chief. 'You're relieved,' said Spooner shortly. 'Eddie, too. Get some rest.'

When the agent had gone, Spooner spent a few moments looking over the report again. The questions put to Max had been scrupulously recorded, as had the methods of encouragement implemented. Left to the imagination was the toll they had taken on that massive body, and of course the motivations behind the betrayal in the first place...

Her, Max had sneered.

Who?
You don't even know. That's worst of all.

He lit another Winston, immediately felt nauseated, sent out smoke on a dry, rattling cough. The phone gave another buzz. He grabbed the receiver. 'Spooner.'

As he listened, his secretary came in, carrying two steaming cups. Isherwood sat blowing ripples across the surface of his coffee, watching from the couch as the Chief grunted monosyllabic sounds of encouragement. After emptying the ashtray, the secretary left. Seconds later, the Chief hung up. Tenting one hand over his eyes, he sighed.

'Maryland PD,' he said at length. 'Found a man who picked up Hart, last night, outside the motor court. Get this: he's an administrative assistant in their third precinct. Saw the APB this morning and said, "I brought that man to Union Station."'

A moment passed.

'Ticket vendors,' Isherwood said then. 'Conductors. Newsboys. Anyone who was on-board any train leaving Union Station last night...'

Spooner nodded, looking into his coffee desultorily. From a lower drawer he removed a freshly starched collar, used silver studs to pin it to his shirt. Then he reached again for the phone.

NEW YORK CITY
At the sound of the bell, Myron Kemper bolted upright.

Operating on instinct, he pulled a gun – his favorite pistol, a modified double-action Colt

230

Python with a six-inch barrel – from beneath his pillow. Once the Python was trained on the door, he reached with his free hand for the glasses beside the bed. Balanced on the bridge of his nose, the thick spectacles brought the world into focus. He saw that the six locks running up the inside of the door-frame remained intact.

The bell sounded again; he leapt out of bed. A calendar tacked to the wall announced the day as Sunday, the twentieth of November. He had a meeting scheduled this morning, clearly marked – yet he had overslept. Disruptions of schedule made Myron Kemper nervous. As he processed the situation, an asthmatic wheeze rose from within his shallow chest.

Four strides brought him across a cramped apartment whose every level surface was covered with drills or barrel vises or borescopes or roll pins or torque drivers or carbon dies or gun components. Through the spyhole, he saw the face of the man who was ringing his doorbell. Warped by the curvature of the lens, foreshortened by the man's extreme height, the features formed a funhouse travesty – small slanted eyes, impossibly straight nose, and bizarrely huge chin – but Myron nonetheless recognized the visitor as one of the few men he trusted in this world.

He stuffed the Python into the back of his pajama bottoms; the elastic retained just enough tension to hold the two-pound weight. With practiced movements he opened the six locks, one after another. 'Richard,' he said. 'Sorry. I over-slept...'

Absorbing his friend fully, he trailed off. Only

231

a few days had passed since their last meeting, but Richard Hart presented a very different figure: leaning his entire weight against a crutch, right leg encased in a thick plaster cast, skin peeled from cheeks and temples, one eye blackened. Beneath a hat brim pulled low, the determined crimp of Hart's expression spoke of intense pain.

A tight steel cage closed inside Myron's sternum. He was not good at handling unexpected developments. He was much better with the cold, logical processes that came with designing and modifying firearms, which was why he had gone into this line of work in the first place.

Richard Hart managed a smile. 'It's not as bad as it looks,' he said, and then after a moment: 'May I come in?'

With a jerky nod Myron stepped aside, closing and relocking the door behind his guest, forgetting in his shock to feel self-conscious at his own striped pajamas. From long habit they endeavored their customary greeting, rolling back shirtsleeves (Hart, on his crutch, clumsily) to reveal matching tattoos. The unit insignia of the Fifteenth Infantry Regiment depicted a gold Chinese dragon and red acorns, rendered against a blue and white coat of arms. They pressed their forearms together briefly but significantly, a sacred rite.

'Sit down,' said Myron breathlessly. 'Let me get you a chair.'

'No, Myron, I'm in a hurry. Have you finished?'

Despite his surprise at Hart's appearance,

Myron found it within himself to be insulted. 'I said I would, didn't I?'

As he went to fetch his work from a back room, Myron turned over in his mind the irrational alarm he felt at seeing Hart in this condition. Of course the man was one of his few friends, so it was somewhat natural to react with emotion ... but this went deeper. They had been the only two in their company to emerge entirely physically unscathed from the war. On some unrecognized level, Myron had perhaps come to believe that they were specially blessed. But if Richard Hart could be injured by the world, so, too, could Myron Kemper.

Returning to the front room carrying the case, he was taken aback all over again. Propped by a workbench, Hart was absent-mindedly examining one of Myron's pet projects – a customized German Luger loaded, in an outré touch, with gold-plated bullets. Bludgeoned and battered, Richard Hart seemed a mockery of the respectable man he had recently become. After the war, like many others, he had fallen on hard times. But lately he had found an upscale crowd and made a new man of himself: always neatly groomed, well-dressed, reminiscent of one of the wealthy businessmen Myron saw through his window come cocktail hour. Sometimes Myron would watch those businessmen, strolling down the sidewalks with a secretary on each arm, through the cross hairs of a high-powered scope. Absorbing every detail of their placid, self-satisfied faces, he would relish a feeling of secret power. They had everything Myron lacked –

pretty girls on their arms, wedding bands indicating wives at home, and no doubt nice suburban houses somewhere out on the Main Line, complete with kids and dogs – but Myron had something even better. He had their oblivious faces trapped in his cross hairs. All he need do was squeeze the trigger...

Richard Hart had offered a connection to a world from which Myron felt acutely excluded. But now Hart looked as maltreated as Myron himself felt. The disappointment was unexpectedly profound.

Forcing his mind forward, Myron laid the tweed case across a workbench and hit the catches. Business came first. 'A nice job,' he said with a touch of smugness, 'if I do say so myself.'

Setting down the Luger beside another of Myron's pet projects – a scalloped twelve-inch blade – Hart focused on the case. Inside, the Gibson nestled against fraying red velvet, to all appearances an ordinary guitar, with a slightly-nicked pick guard indicating gentle use.

'Looks good – yes?' Myron removed the instrument from the case, carefully fingered an open E chord, and strummed once. 'And sounds good. Yes?'

There was no denying, as the chord reverberated and lingered, that it sounded good – in fact, to Myron's satisfaction, the guitar sounded even better than when he had received it. In the course of doing his work he had corrected a warping of the neck and replaced a bent truss rod, discovering in the process a lost calling as a luthier.

'We can't break it open – this is for a single use only – so you'll need to take my word for it,' Myron continued, 'but the rifle exceeds your specifications. I found more than enough space inside the neck for a twenty-four inch barrel. Therefore I would feel perfectly comfortable firing this weapon from up to four hundred and fifty yards, using the ammunition you'll find inside the headstock – eight .30-06 cartridges – assuming my target was medium-sized big game.' He let the euphemism hang in the air for a moment, competing with the last reverberations of the chord, before moving on. 'The barrel and the truss rod are one and the same, so once the rifle is assembled, the guitar won't play. But I assume you won't be using it to serenade anybody.'

Hart nodded briefly.

'Here,' said Myron, tapping the saddle bridge at the base of the guitar's body, 'is your scope. Just pop it out and turn it around. The assembly mechanism is self-evident. Zeroing the sights won't be possible, you said, and the user thus has concerns about accuracy. So just to be on the safe side, I've grooved the barrel a few extra times: eight in total. This weapon therefore possesses the spin stabilization of an Olympic-level instrument. As no conditions were made concerning weight, I've used a bull barrel; thus we avoid extra flex and vibration, further increasing our accuracy.'

Hart made a noise of acknowledgement.

'All in all,' concluded Myron a bit prissily, 'this was hardly a challenge. The only difficulty came in the haste with which I was required to work.'

Hart said nothing. Having expected more praise for a job clearly well done, Myron sniffed. Returning the guitar to its case, he closed the catches. 'Okay?'

'Excellent. As always.' Rearranging his crutch, Hart produced a buff envelope from an inside pocket, which he silently passed over. Myron opened the envelope and riffled through bills with fingertips. Forty, sixty, eighty...

'Is this a joke? We agreed on a fee of one—'

Looking up, he blinked. His eyes had been averted for only a moment – but Richard Hart held the Luger, aimed at Myron's chest.

Myron started to laugh. But the sound caught in his narrow chest. Instead, he raised his eyebrows questioningly.

'Turn around,' said Hart coldly.

'Richard – what is this?'

'Turn around.'

Slowly, Myron turned. He heard the clumping of the crutch; then the modified Python was plucked from the back of his waistband. The safety came off with a small but audible click.

'Wait,' he just had time to say, before a cold barrel pressed against his temple.

'Who knows about this rifle?' asked a steady voice in his ear.

Myron's tongue flicked out, frog-like. 'Nobody,' he answered, 'of course. If this is a joke, Richard, it's in very poor taste.'

'A manufacturer, supplier, warehouse...?'

'You know I keep all my equipment on-site.'

'Do you keep records?'

'What *is* this?' asked Myron in disbelief, twisting around.

The Python's barrel rapped against his temple, convincing him to cease the movement. Why, thought Myron, Richard Hart was betraying him; it was happening right now. The one man he'd fully trusted...

Suddenly, he felt like crying. Hart was the same as all the others. How could he have been such a fool?

The moment extended interminably. Was his so-called friend going to shoot him, or simply steal his work? As Myron wondered, he felt warmth rising in his ribcage – but the warmth seemed the least of his problems, unrelated to the gun as it was, so he shuffled it mentally aside.

If Hart planned on shooting, he would have pulled the trigger by now. So this was a common robbery. That made the humiliation all the more bitter. But not pulling the trigger, thought Myron, had been a fatal mistake. For once Richard Hart completed his theft, he would leave the apartment, descend the switchback staircase, and step out onto the sidewalk. And then Myron would have every chance to frame his friend's face in the cross hairs of a sniper's rifle. And if the street was empty enough – and on a Sunday morning, it just might be – he would do it. He would pull the trigger. He would blow Richard Hart's brains all over the sidewalk. In fact, he was *glad* this had happened. Too many times had he targeted a gray-flannelled businessman outside his window, only to ultimately put up the gun unfired. Now he would find the chance to actually consummate the act, to experience the thrill of that ultimate secret power—

The balmy torpor spread through his right flank. In his last moment, Myron glanced down and was shocked to see his pajamas soaked through with coppery blood.

Then he slumped, folding onto the floor.

After wiping the scalloped blade clean on bloody pajamas, Richard Hart returned knife to workbench with one hand. Looking at the body, he repressed a shudder of self-loathing. Myron, like Arthur Glashow, had deserved better. But the senator's protocol for covering of tracks had been crystal clear – and the senator came first. The senator always came first...

A pack of cigarettes rested on a nearby table. Helping himself, Hart looked thoughtfully around the cluttered workshop/apartment. The place overflowed with vises and benches and tools. If you needed to dismember a body, he thought darkly, you couldn't choose a better place.

SIXTEEN

GETTYSBURG

The parlor glowed softly from gentle sunshine, still-lighted table lamps, and the flickering electric baubles of the Christmas tree; on the turntable, a needle danced across the run-out groove in an endless scratching loop.

Miss Dunbarton spent a long moment standing at the base of the staircase, absorbing the scene incredulously. At last her paralysis broke, and she moved gingerly forward. At the sound of her footsteps a couple leapt up from behind the couch, smoothing down rumpled clothes. The maid muttered an apology and ran upstairs. The Secret Service agent looked stricken, hung his head, and made for the side door.

Before she could find the heart to press on, Dunbarton bolstered herself with the hair of the dog. Then she set her jaw and pressed into the worst of the devastation, pausing to lift the needle from the turntable as she passed. Shards of broken ornaments and drinking glasses crackled underfoot. The smell of smoke was everywhere; her prohibition had been not only disobeyed but outright flouted. Give these girls an inch, and they took a mile. But the fault was partly her own. She had miscalculated her own consumption and retired earlier than intended – and now she was paying the price.

The Waterbury clock was still intact on the mantle, thank goodness. She kept surveying. Upstairs she found one of the new agents, Philip Zane, seated by his window behind a door hanging ajar. They exchanged brief good mornings before the house matron moved quickly and a bit shamefacedly down the hall.

All of her girls looked green around the gills; one refused to be roused except to tell Dunbarton to stop her goddamned knocking. That girl would not keep her job for long, of course. But considering the current mess, firing was not a luxury that could be indulged. Assembling her charges in the hallway – even the slugabed came sullenly to join the line – Miss Dunbarton conveyed her immense displeasure with a toxic glare. Then she urged the girls to visit the kitchen, enjoy a quick breakfast of black coffee, and get about cleaning the mess they'd made, applying themselves first to wherever they had conducted their most sordid transgressions.

As the girls filed past, heads hung low, she noted one who seemed more alert than the rest: Elisabeth Grant, the new girl. Although Elisabeth's eyes were rimmed red with fatigue, she did not seem hung over; her chin was held up, with pride. Briefly, their eyes met, and in the girl's clear gaze Dunbarton sensed reproach for her fellows. The house matron gave a small, admiring shake of the head. A few more like that, she thought, and the farm would run in a manner befitting the President they all served.

THE TREASURY BUILDING

When the phone rang, Isherwood struggled into a sitting position.

He watched from the couch as Spooner lifted the receiver. The Chief looked even more cadaverous than usual: thinning gray hair disheveled, prominent skull clearly defined beneath. The fresh new collar had already been marred by a dusting of dandruff. In the center of the high forehead, an impression from the desk blotter suggested a flesh-colored watermark. Hanging up after half a minute, Spooner moved a thumb slowly, morosely, across his lips.

'Something?' asked Isherwood.

'Less than nothing. Every conductor and ticket vendor must be blind.' Spooner gave a sad, gravelly laugh.

The phone rang again. Resignedly, Spooner reached for it. Despite a tickle in his throat, Isherwood lit a cigarette. He had not been aware of falling asleep, but now he felt slightly refreshed. He tapped ash into a half-empty coffee cup on the floor by his feet.

Spooner seemed encouraged by whatever he was hearing. He sat straighter, nodding; his sallow cheeks filled with color. 'You're sure?' he asked, and picked up a pen. 'Spell your last name for me.' He listened again. 'Would you swear to that in a court of law?'

After extracting a promise of silence, he hung up and addressed Isherwood in a murmur despite the fact that, with the office door closed, nobody could hear them. 'State trooper from Charlottesville – saw the APB for Hart and recognized the face. Last year, he says, at a fund-raiser for the Patrolmen's Benevolent Association, Richard Hart was accompanying Senator John Bolin.'

Isherwood was suddenly wide awake. 'John Bolin,' he repeated.

'Part of the Bridges and Dirksen and Mundt crowd. McCarthyites.' Spooner smiled sternly. 'The Wizard of Ooze and his tin men.'

For half a minute, both were silent, absorbing the implications.

'So what now?' asked Isherwood. 'Waltz into the Senate chamber with a warrant for Bolin's arrest?'

'On hearsay from a state trooper? Fat chance.'

'Let Eisenhower in on it, then. President trumps senator.'

'Last resort. Remember: doctor's orders.'

Isherwood jetted smoke from each nostril. 'We're looking for a thread to pull on. Here it is, with a bow tied around it. You want we should just sit on our hands?'

'We need Hart.' Spooner kicked back in his chair, rubbed a palm blearily over his face. 'He's the smoking gun – literally. Once he fingers Bolin, we've got cause. Then we lean on the good senator and roll up the whole mess.'

Again, the men looked at each other in silence. Wind moved outside the window with a numinous sigh. A girl in an office down the hall laughed loudly, stridently.

'We've got feelers out,' said Spooner eventually. 'High and low. I say we sit at the center of our web and wait for another strand to quiver.

It's our best move.'

'Get some eyes on Bolin, at least.'

'Negative. We can't risk putting him on guard. We wait.'

Isherwood bit his tongue. Too many years spent behind a desk had ruined Spooner's nerve; but argument would be wasted breath.

The girl down the hall laughed again, raucously. Isherwood wished he knew what was so goddamned funny.

GETTYSBURG

As afternoon turned toward evening, Elisabeth and Josette stood shoulder-to-shoulder, cleaning dining-room windows.

'You know,' said Josette suddenly, 'I was pretty zozzled last night.'

'Boy, me too.'

'But I meant what I said. We should really do it. Go to Paris together.'

Elisabeth spritzed, wiped.

'Libby? Why so quiet?'

'Just thinking.'

'About what?'

Elisabeth shrugged. 'Sometimes,' she said slowly, 'it's easier to plan something than to actually follow through. That's all.'

'Sure. But we'll have each other to lean on. That'll make all the difference. It won't be easy – but that's what will make it exciting.'

Rags squealed against glass.

'You're my best friend, Libby. There's nobody I'd rather go with.'

'That's so sweet.' An awkward silence; Elisabeth was forced to add, 'You're my best friend, too.'

'Then let's do it. Let's go, right away.'

Elisabeth laughed. 'Now?'

'Tuesday's your day off, right? You can talk to the travel agent, find out some prices.'

Elisabeth moved on to the next window. 'Maybe we should think about it some more.'

'But that's what I've been doing for years: thinking. Thinking about Hollywood, or London, or Chicago – just thinking, thinking, thinking. Before I know it, I'll think myself right into being an old maid. The chance will have passed me by. I've done enough thinking.'

'You're crazy, Josie. Anybody ever tell you that?'

Josette tapped her head, smiled craftily. 'Crazy like a fox,' she said. 'Promise you'll ask?'

Elisabeth stifled a sigh and nodded.

NEW YORK CITY

A young couple braved the chilly wind to enjoy a romantic stroll along the Hudson River.

When the young man suddenly stopped, took both of the girl's hands in his own, and awkwardly leaned in for a kiss, she closed her eyes, as she had been taught was proper. As the moments passed, however, she began to feel increasingly self-conscious – who knew what friends or family might be walking the river? The docks were populated not only with longshoremen and sailors, but with ordinary people who were enjoying the view and the fresh evening air and the lights on the water. And all it took to ruin a girl's reputation was a single scurrilous rumor. In spite of herself, then, she opened her eyes, even as the kiss continued, to run her gaze restively over the gray-brown water of the Hudson, lit from both shores, slopping against pilings ten feet below.

Suddenly, she gagged, tearing away and noisily vomiting.

The young man blushed, mortified; although he didn't know what he had done wrong, his girlfriend's reaction was clear. And so it came as almost a relief, moments later, when he turned and saw the human hand, messily severed from an absent body, bloodless and fish-belly white, tangled in a fishing net amongst the pilings.

THE SULGRAVE CLUB, WASHINGTON DC

As the moon rose on the evening of November 20th, Richard Nixon and a handful of reporters listened, inside a private club of yellow Roman brick and cream terracotta, as Senator Joseph McCarthy promised a blazing comeback – and not a moment too soon, the senator assured his audience, for he knew from confidential sources of a plot communist forces had been waging inside the highest echelons of the American government.

But the attention of the spectators wandered, Nixon noticed; they had heard this script too many times before. More than one toyed distractedly with a dessert fork or leaned over to whisper disrespectfully in a neighbor's ear. The Vice President also noted that McCarthy was spilling his drink as he wove his tall tales, and that, alarmingly, a trickle of slobber rode un-noticed from one corner of his broad mouth. The powerhouse Fighting Joe who had infamously slapped columnist Drew Pearson inside this same swank club five years before was no more. And unless the man changed his habits dramati-cally, Nixon could not help thinking, Joe Mc-Carthy might not be long for this world.

Behind the tinted windows of a Lincoln Continental traveling down K Street one hour later, the Vice President stared out at the baubles of the capital at night, muscles in his jaw bunch-ing fitfully. When different loyalties pulled a man in opposite directions, it was damned diffi-cult to know how to react. He had come so very far in this game. And yet he still had so very much to learn.

But however the cards fell, Dick Nixon would land on his feet. The country to which he had promised himself demanded no less. In his own estimation he was one of the few men – perhaps the *only* man – able to keep his moral center under such perfidious conditions. Born into a house his father had built with his own two hands, a Quaker house in which drinking and dancing and swearing had been strictly forbid-den, Nixon had been infused with a sense of right and wrong strong enough to survive the warping required to be effective in Washington. The trick, he realized more every day, was to bend in the proper places. One embraced smaller evils for the greater good. And so to win his first seat in Congress he had smeared his rival Jerry Voorhis by waging a vicious whispering campaign, implying Voorhis's endorsement by communists. Stumping against Helen Gahagan Douglas in 1950, he had sunk even lower, distributing a pink flyer that simultaneously attacked her voting record and – by dint of its color – her gender. Caught maintaining a privately subscribed expense account of questionable integrity, he had taken to television airwaves, conducting a tasteless public financial striptease, opportunistically using his children and cocker spaniel puppy to sway public opinion back in his favor. Such ethical compromises were necessary, he had learned, in order to reach a height from which a man might do real good. *Uneasy lies the head which wears the crown.*

Political allies were not friends. And loyalties were not black and white. He had made promises to McCarthy and to Eisenhower, to Pat and Tricia and Julie, to himself – and most of all to America – that could not all be honored. One had to pick and choose.

The trick was in making the right choice.

SEVENTEEN

GETTYSBURG: NOVEMBER 21

At a few minutes before noon on Monday, the more conscientious of Gettysburg's teenagers sat in class on Old Harrisburg Road, listening for the bell that would signal lunch.

Joe 'Buddy' Buchanan sat in a drugstore on the outskirts of town, nibbling on a hangnail and pressing the soda jerk to add more syrup to his Coke. When his usual charming smile failed to accomplish this goal, Buddy tried a glare, and that did the trick; the pimply jerk's head must have filled with images of switchblades and brass knuckles, for he reluctantly gave an extra few pumps. 'Hope you like it sweet,' he mumbled as he passed over the soda.

Buddy Buchanan tossed him a pally, but not unthreatening, wink. 'You know it, nosebleed.'

He took his time with the Coke, enjoying the jerk's squirming beneath his gaze. Wandering out to his hopped-up Bel Air a few minutes later, long legs switching beneath pegged jeans, he lit a cigarette and wondered how best to spend the long day stretching out before him. That night he had a race with a screamer over from Abbottstown, so he didn't want to get too blotto; but that meant a whole dull afternoon to be killed without the benefit of booze. He supposed he could hit the matinee at the Odeon, but he had already seen the James Dean flick playing there nine times. That left the railroad tracks, where he could peg empty cans at rats, always good for an hour or two's diversion; or maybe Carl's, where he could flirt with a roller-skated carhop wearing a too-short skirt. Either way, he was bound to run into some friends who would keep him occupied until it came time to head over to Table Rock for the race. It was a plan.

Lost in thought, he didn't notice the stranger's approach until the man addressed him. The stranger was a certified square, wearing a soiled gray suit, which after laundering would not have seemed out of place on Buddy's father. He was also a gimp, hunching his considerable frame low over a crutch. Drawing close to Buddy's car, looking around shiftily from beneath the brim of his hat, he said: 'Hey, kid. Want to make a few bucks?'

Buddy blinked. He nearly answered, *What are you, queer?* But crutch or no, this guy looked as if he might mean business. Sometimes you found men like this, who had seen too much in a war, who would now kill you as soon as look at you. And was that the bulge of a gun, beneath the man's lapel, or just a pack of smokes?

'You deaf?' asked the man. Rejiggering his crutch to allow more freedom of movement, he removed a pack of cigarettes from a pocket nowhere near the bulge.

'Naw,' said Buddy, pushing off the fender and making himself stand tall. Despite the effort he still found himself looking up; the stranger, even hunched over the crutch, towered above him. 'I ain't deaf.'

'So I'll ask it again. You want to make a few bucks?'

'Depends.' Buddy tried to inject a suggestion of threat into his voice. With each passing second, however, he was feeling less intimidating than intimidated. 'What do I gotta do?'

When the square reached into another pocket, Buddy nearly flinched. But all the man withdrew was a crisp new portrait of Ulysses S. Grant. Handing it over, he explained his needs with a few simple words. Once it was done, Buddy would be rewarded with a hundred bucks on top of the fifty. Needless to say, the arrangement would remain just between them.

Buddy grinned. A buck-fifty from nowhere; he could hardly believe his luck. 'Daddy-O,' he said, 'you got yourself a deal.' *Even if you're crazy as a bedbug*, he thought, but diplomatically did not add.

NEW YORK CITY
Leading Isherwood to the edge of the dock, the cop named Barlow sent his cigarette pinwheeling into the water.

'Something like this,' Barlow said, 'barely raises an eyebrow 'round here any more. We get chunks of people washing up every week or so. Makes you wonder what the world is coming to.' He lit another cigarette. He was a beefy man, slightly cross-eyed, with a shaving cut on a grizzled throat. 'But the Captain says we got a standing order from DC to report any floaters, so here we are. Must be important, to send a Fed in person ... and take up a dredge crew's valuable time.'

Isherwood let the implied complaint pass without acknowledgement. As they came to a stop, he wrinkled his nose. The rotting fish-stink dislodged by overturning the river's bottom was staggering – or was that just the usual stench of the Hudson? By contrast, the Potomac seemed downright unspoiled.

'Hand's down at the medical examiner's,' remarked Barlow casually. 'But without fingertips, we got nothing. Pretty standard syndicate technique, y'know. They cut off the head and hands, take the fingertips somewhere else – probably to a pit with some lye – and bash in the face so you can't get an ID or a good dental. Makes us run around in circles. Guess they like to watch us chase our own tails. But when you big Federal boys say jump, we jump. Although I tell you, pal, if we find anything to match the hand, I'll be a monkey's uncle. Sixteen years on this force and not one—'

A sharp whistle from the river interrupted him. He scowled across the brackish water as a winch raised a prehensile claw. Moments later, the catch broke the surface: a deflated Goodyear tire.

Barlow turned back to Isherwood. 'Not one time,' he finished, 'have we come up with two parts that match.'

Again, Isherwood said nothing.

'Hell, don't think I'm complaining. I get paid the same either way. So gimme a hint, pal.

What's the big deal about some poor sap's hand?'

Another whistle cut off the reply: the snagboat bringing up another trophy.

This time the recovered object was not easily identifiable. Isherwood watched as it was examined, loaded into a low boat, and rowed back to the dock. Only after the find, wrapped in algae, was lugged up onto the planks could Isherwood identify it as part of a human body – a skinny torso with arms and legs, lacking head and hands. His abdominal muscles gave a queasy grind.

'Well, I'll be dipped in shit and rolled in breadcrumbs,' said Barlow conversationally. 'Willya look at that.'

Isherwood took a knee beside the corpse. Peeling back strips of algae, he found himself regarding a faded tattoo on one hairless, undernourished forearm: a gold Chinese dragon and red acorns, rendered against a blue-and-white coat of arms.

BOCA RATON, FLORIDA

Picking listlessly at her Blue Plate Special, Evelyn Isherwood tuned out her sister's prattle.

All through dinner, as Helen talked about Italian mule sandals and poodle cuts, Evy had gone back and forth in her mind over well-trod ground. *In sickness and in health*; *for richer and for poorer.* But, of course, there came a time when a girl would be absolved of such promises, she thought. After too many nights spent lying awake, waiting to hear the key in the lock; after too many promises given, too many second chances squandered.

Nonetheless, a packed bag waited in the bedroom closet back at her sister's house. At any moment, Evy might decide to hop on a Greyhound. She would do it without providing warning to her sister or to Ish, or even to herself. She would appear in the doorway of the house in Anacostia, taking everybody by surprise, and say, *One more chance, Ish. Just like you wanted.*

Closing her eyes for a moment – the better to tune out her sister – she pictured Ish as he'd looked on the day they had met. Handsome, assured, cigarette burning casually between fingertips, hat cocked far back on his head, he had made a dashing figure. She had been a girl of just twenty-two, standing at the crosswalk of a busy DC street, trying to coax her Scottish terrier into motion. But the terrier had other ideas, planting her paws stubbornly. Evy tugged, urged, excoriated, exhaled with frustration. Then Ish appeared beside them, wearing a minimal smile. 'Got to use a strong hand,' he advised.

Evy ignored him. Her days were spent working in her father's stationery store, her nights cooking and cleaning at home; nothing in her life had prepared her to receive hard-hearted advice from a strange man on a public street. She continued trying, ineffectually, to coax the dog into crossing the street.

'She's got all day,' remarked Isherwood. 'Do you?'

At that, Evy turned on him. 'What do you want me to do, drag her?'

'Or pick her up.' Isherwood smiled again. 'And then join me for tea. How about it?'

For better and for worse. To have and to hold...

Still: there had to be a limit. There had to be a time when a girl gave up and moved on.

Back and forth over familiar ground she went; and her sister, careless and blithe, talked now about Marilyn Monroe and Joe DiMaggio, and how anyone with two eyes in their head could have seen it coming.

THE TREASURY BUILDING

Beneath the light of the chandelier, the Chief opened another military personnel file, his mouth forming a judicious crease. 'Myron Kemper,' he read.

'The coat of arms belongs to the Fifteenth Regiment.' Glassy-eyed, Isherwood leaned forward, placing elbows on knees. 'Their lineage traces back to the Civil War – as indicated by the red acorns. The Chinese dragon reflects service in China during the Boxer Rebellion. Before the Big One they trained in Virginia, where the First Battalion was commanded by none other than Dwight D. Eisenhower.'

Paging through the file, Spooner glanced up.

'They served in Sicily, Italy, North Africa, France, and Germany. I went straight to the personnel records for Company B – Hart's company – and then narrowed it down, through platoon level to squads. That gave me twelve names. Four live in Manhattan. Checked those against missing persons reports, but came up blank. But by then the workday was wrapping up, so I started knocking on doors. First man, I found home with his wife. Second man, no answer. Didn't want to take a chance on the super giving me trouble, so I let myself in.'

'And.'

'The apartment was a workshop, Chief – a gun shop. And there were bloodstains. Still tacky, although someone did a pretty good clean-up job.'

Spooner's eyes narrowed. Isherwood nodded. 'Myron Kemper was killed recently – within the past day, give or take. He was cut up and then sunk, just like the underchef in the country club. He served in the same squad as Richard Hart. And he was a gunsmith.'

GETTYSBURG

The rifle is an extension of your body.

Shivering in the cold, Karl Schnibbe guided her hands with his own. In his ice-blue eyes she saw the setting sun reflected as a line of molten lava. *And vice versa: your body, Liebchen, is an extension of the rifle. When taking aim, you feel no cold, discomfort, or pain. When taking aim, you are never hungry or thirsty. You think nothing of the past or the future. When taking aim, there is only target and gun. Target and gun.*

She lowered cheek to stock. One hundred yards away, a majestic buck nosed through frozen branches, oblivious to its impending doom. The world shrank to nothing except buck and rifle, target and gun.

Haste will be your downfall. Karl's face was so close that she could feel its warmth, smell its

255

cleanliness. *When you act, do so from a still quiet place.*

She nodded, holding her breath, and slowly tightened finger against trigger...

...and then woke with a start, sitting bolt upright in bed.

Her throat was dry. A gust of wind chased outside the house. Dunbarton's voice carried through the walls, sharp with irritation. Elisabeth sat in bed, listening. After a few minutes, she heard the front door bang open. Dunbarton's piercing voice receded, replaced by the usual murmurs of the herdsman's home: eaves creaking, radiators rattling, girls talking and laughing softly.

Elisabeth left the bed, quietly dressed. By the window, she spent a few seconds watching men work – pacing off security routes, tending livestock, mending a barn's gate. She searched in vain for a hint of Karl's high cheekbones and fine blond hair. For a time in Argentina, she had dreamed of him every night, and upon awakening would think she recognized him everywhere – lit by a kerosene lamp in a window across a dusty street, boarding a bus just behind her, fixing a roof on a decrepit cottage. He had survived Berlin after all, she would decide, and then followed her here. And now he wanted revenge. As if the *gottverdammt* blood-hungry Israelis were not enough to worry about...

But then she would see that the man in the window across the street was elderly, the one boarding the bus behind her just a boy, the one fixing the roof only a swarthy peasant. Only in

256

her dreams had Karl followed her to Argentina.

In a way, she had enjoyed the imagined glimpses, frightening though they had been. Seeing him again – even just for a moment, even only in her fancy – had gratified her. But scanning the agents and farmhands outside her window now, she found only dark hair, heavy overfed American faces. This, it seemed, was Karl's final revenge: he would not show himself to her again, even in her imagination. He did not appreciate the favor she had done him, rescuing him not only from his own dissolution but also from the humiliation of the hangman's noose at Nuremberg.

She took a deep breath. The past was the past, and there it must remain.

In the bathroom she conducted hasty ablutions. She showed her face only briefly in the kitchen, for coffee. By eight a.m. on November twenty-second she was walking down the long driveway, passing through the front gate, and turning east toward town.

ROUTE 30: NOVEMBER 22

Francis Isherwood drove west.

The morning was bright and clear and lovely, and might have passed for early spring instead of late fall. Shadowed mountainside steamed gently with evaporating snow. A foraging deer stood at the edge of the forest, turning its head to watch the Mayfair pass.

His foot leaned heavier on the gas. He would have been on this road sooner had Emil Spooner not waited until first light to make his executive decision. But years of black-tie dinners and political maneuvering had left the man over-cautious, unsure of his own instincts. At last, however, the Chief had pulled the trigger. Hart had murdered the gunsmith; now he would somehow smuggle a customized weapon onto the farm, attempting to finish what he had started eight weeks earlier at the Cherry Hills Country Club. But Isherwood would be waiting at the front gate. He would recognize Hart, no matter his subterfuge, and end this once and for all.

He passed the very ridge from which Richard Hart had taken his shot, six days before. A frown gathered between his eyes. His foot rode still heavier on the accelerator. The road before him descended into the steep pass; instead of slowing he downshifted, buying traction, and drove faster.

EIGHTEEN

GETTYSBURG

The young man answered the door on the second knock.

His breath smelled of eggs and onions. A rolled-up copy of *Photoplay* had been jammed carelessly into his hip pocket. He seemed eager to complete the transaction with a minimum of fuss; he must have learned from an appraiser that just one of the diamonds was worth as much as the car. By quarter past ten Elisabeth had traded the last of her gems for the pink slip and key to the Rocket 88. After bidding the young man good day, she slipped behind the walnut-finished steering wheel. When she started the engine the V8 thrummed beneath her, straining to be unleashed.

She smiled with satisfaction. She would murder their President, the vaunted architect of the *Fuehrer*'s defeat, right beneath their noses. Then she would flee the farm on foot; minutes later, having donned her disguise and been carried into town by motorized bicycle, she would slip behind the wheel of the Olds. And then an old woman would drive out of Gettysburg, gliding easily through any net they managed to cast. After crossing into the next state, she would change her identity again and find a new car. Then would come New York, and the passage overseas, and the numbered account ... and, sometime in the future, ballroom gowns and handsome dancing partners and luxurious Mitropa railroad cars.

But she was getting ahead of herself.

Driving into town, she chose an inconspicuous side street where she could leave the car safely parked for the next twenty-four hours. After locking up, she strolled toward Lincoln Square, smiling vacantly: a pretty, if not too bright, young girl enjoying the fine weather on her day off.

Sitting on a bench in Lincoln Square, waiting to

259

deliver a guitar to a girl he'd never even met, Buddy Buchanan thought: *Strange days.*

One hundred and fifty bucks, simply to pick up a guitar and then hand it off – but that was only the start of the strangeness. There was the suspicious way the gimp carried himself: shiftily, jumping at shadows. There was the shady way he had made his approach, and the oddly specific conditions to be met, and the stipulation that no one else could know anything. Strangest of all was the feeling the man conjured inside Buddy, that if something were to go wrong, blood would be spilled. It was the way Buddy felt whenever his dad unstrapped his belt, but magnified tenfold.

By the time Buddy thought twice about accepting the deal, however, it had been too late; he had already followed the man back to his motor court (strangely, all the way outside the edge of town) and accepted the instrument. Then he had been stuck. Still, he had considered stiffing the old duck, keeping the fifty and the guitar for himself. After losing the race at Table Rock – Buddy had jigged instead of jagged when he tried to shift into fourth, leaving the Bel Air's customized bent eight revving throatily but impotently – he had gone alone to the railroad tracks, where he had put down twelve of Milwaukee's Best without pausing for breath, pegging each empty can at a rat (and missing every time) in an effort to drown his sorrows. The indignity of losing the race was bad enough. Did he really want to top it off by being some weirdo flitty gimp's errand boy?

This morning, not wanting to show his face in town after the disgrace of losing the race, but not wanting to stay around his accursed keepers either, and *definitely* not wanting to go to school, he had caught the day's first show at the Odeon. Kicking up his legs inside their pegged jeans, inhaling the theater's stale scents of hot dogs and day-old popcorn, laughing nastily when an usher asked him to take his feet off the seat back, he had suffered through the newsreels (somewhat redeemed by a mention of President Eisenhower's successful ongoing recuperation outside the town of Gettysburg, which elicited a cheer laced with a few catcalls from the thin crowd), and tried to lose himself in the familiar story. By then, having drawn self-pity around himself as tightly as a rainslicker, he had decided to shaft the old gimp and take his chances. Nobody told Buddy Buchanan what to do. Buddy Buchanan made his own goddamned rules.

But during the third reel, he abruptly changed his mind. Right at the film's best moment, just as Natalie Wood raised her arms to start the race and James Dean revved the engine of his Mercury Coupe, Buddy realized that he was too distracted to enjoy the show, aces though it was. That feeling that the guy would kill him as soon as look at him was back, fresh as it had been the day before. If Buddy double-crossed the man, he would live to regret it ... or worse, he *wouldn't* live to regret it. Either way, he would start jumping at shadows, scared to turn every corner. It wasn't worth it. Beside, a deal was a deal – and a hundred extra bucks was nothing to sneeze at.

That was how Buddy found himself, at a few minutes before noon on Tuesday, seated on the bench in Lincoln Square, guitar in tweed case by his side, looking for a girl he'd never met.

Elisabeth's cool turquoise eyes ticked past a family of four, past a businessman chasing a hat caught in the wind, past a clutch of shop girls looking for a patch of sun in which to eat their lunch – and then backtracked to the greaser, sitting on the bench on the far side of Lincoln Square, unaware that he was being observed.

For a moment, her gaze lingered. Her contact was nowhere to be seen. The greaser was an unknown quantity. But he had the guitar at his feet and seemed to be waiting to make the trade-off. A trap?

After dallying briefly, her gaze slid back into motion. The lunchtime crowd was growing ever thicker. Workers from nearby shops and hotels mingled with tourists and newspapermen, all determined to enjoy what one might reasonably expect to be one of the last pleasant days of the year. She saw a pair of well-dressed journalists with press cards stuck in the brims of their hats, an elderly man sitting on a bench and whittling with a penknife, and a trio of young girls writing in notebooks. Brow knitted, she followed vehicles – a sea-blue Dodge Royal, a red Chieftain, a green Hudson Hornet, a white Pontiac – entering on the Chambersburg side of the square and being funneled around the one-way traffic circle. She registered patrons moving into and out of the Plaza Restaurant, and tourists stopping to read a burnished plaque near the door of the Hotel Gettysburg.

Checking back in with the greaser, she saw no change of note. Returning to the flow of traffic, she assimilated a new parade of cars ... beige Ford, yellow Mercury, brown Airflyte with white-walled tires ... but no sign of anyone else watching the bench. If it was a trap, she wasn't finding evidence.

The old clock ticked to twelve noon; distant church bells rang.

Either she took a chance and approached the bench now, or she risked missing the appointment.

Her weapon was right there in front of her, awaiting retrieval.

Raising her chin, she stood and walked boldly toward the bench, into plain view of the waiting greaser.

Seeing her coming, he reached down and picked up the guitar. She gestured for him to set down the case by the bench, where she could retrieve it and move on without exchanging a word ... but he not only ignored the gesture, he stood to meet her: a rank amateur.

'Aren't *you* a doll,' he said loudly. 'Nobody told me—'

She grabbed the case and walked past without a word of acknowledgement.

She could feel his amazement; but already she was moving away, swiftly, without a backward glance.

The road between Gettysburg and the Eisenhower farm ran straight – except for a single sharp curve around an immense, ancient oak.

For the past twenty-four hours Richard Hart had sat parked behind this oak, peering through a thick screen of branches. At first, he had stiffened every time a car drove past. At last he had accepted that behind his partition of branches, behind the wizened old trunk, the stolen Chevy was invisible. He was safe.

But the night had been cold. His leg ached; and early that morning, if it had not been his imagination, he had caught the overripe stink of decay coming from beneath the dressing on his right arm. Except for a single break to relieve his bladder, he had not left the car for a full day. Around midnight, he had finished the last of the food taken from Myron's apartment. The final cigarette had been smoked two hours later. More foresight, he realized now, might have helped matters. But every second spent out in the open seemed to be asking for trouble.

These thoughts came and went, subsumed beneath a larger truth:

Isherwood must die.

Far away, near the vanishing point, a silhouetted figure appeared on the road.

Hart squinted. He had been expecting this figure ever since sighting the girl walking into town, four hours before. Indeed, it was she, returning. And she carried the bulky black guitar case. The greaser had done his job. The youth would no doubt be disappointed, upon returning to the motor court, to find Hart and thus the rest of his payment gone; but by then it would be too late for him to interfere.

Hart watched the girl walk past. She looked calm, with her bell of blonde hair bouncing around slim shoulders in time with her stride. Then she was moving away, and he was alone again with birds and squirrels and pain and hunger and incongruously lovely late-autumn foliage opening overhead in a colorful canopy.

Minutes passed. Drowsily, he pinched a fold of skin inside his elbow between two fingers, startling himself awake again: an old trick from his war days. He wanted a cigarette. He wanted to piss. He wanted a drink of water. He wanted to impress the senator. He wanted to give the girl the chance she would need. He wanted clean hands, free of blood. He wanted to wind back the clock, one year, two, three, before any of this had happened ... but most of all, he wanted Isherwood dead.

The burr of an approaching engine. Again he squinted, peering owlishly through the screen of branches.

There: the Packard Mayfair.

His target, at last.

Steeling himself, he reached for the Chevy's starter button.

The road turned into a bend ahead.

Isherwood headed into the blind curve without slowing – and then jammed his foot against the brake, twisting the wheel, cursing hotly.

The Mayfair slammed into the Chevy at forty miles per hour.

Shuddering from grille to tailpipe, the car

bucked violently. Inside, Isherwood bounced commensurately, slamming his head against the roof hard enough to set off starbursts behind his eyes. His already-wounded shoulder jostled hard, bolting pain down his chest and back. The windshield buckled, sagging inward.

The world turned dark.

By degrees, light filtered back in.

Blinking, he reached up to rub his jaw. He couldn't remember where he was, or how he had gotten here, or what had happened to his face – had somehow slugged him? He was surrounded by steel and glass, and outside the steel and glass, steam hissed and dust settled. Bright-red paint had been splashed everywhere.

Presently, it dawned on him that the steel and glass and pumping steam around him belonged to a car. Working backward, putting the pieces together, he deduced that he had been in an accident. That made the red paint splashed everywhere not paint at all, but blood – *his* blood.

The radiator was mangled; hence the jetting steam. And his jaw was also mangled – and that was where the blood was coming from. Unless, of course, it was coming from the top of his head, which throbbed painfully. Shoulder, face, breastbone, ribs: throbbing, throbbing, throbbing. Keeping track of all the pain suddenly gave him a terrible headache. He decided to take a break from thinking and simply sat, looking dumbly at the blood dripping slowly down the inside of the craggy windshield, letting moments pass, trying to hold on to consciousness.

Ballooning dust seethed around him. Steam kept squirting. Blood trickled from his mouth and cheeks, off his chin. He looked to his left and saw a pretty autumn day, a forest quiet with shock. He looked, in slow motion, to his right; on the way, his gaze passed the wrecked Chevy into which he had plowed. The car had been accordioned by the blow and pushed a few feet down the road. Why had the goddamn asshole driver parked across the road like that? Right around the blind curve, too. Almost as if he had meant for this to happen—

Hart.

But where? Through the veil of dust and steam, Isherwood could see that the seat behind the Chevy's steering wheel was empty.

His gaze moved to the rear-view. *There* was Hart: materializing from the woods, shambling forward on one crutch. In his left hand the man held a gleaming revolver, aiming into the wrecked Mayfair.

Eyes widening, Isherwood threw himself down, grappling for his pistol in its holster.

Richard Hart lurched forward, crutch beneath right arm, Colt Python in left hand, blasting .357 Magnum shells mechanically into the stalled-out ruin of the Mayfair – *blam, blam, blam, blam, blam, blam* – until the six-round cylinder clicked empty.

Then he jammed the gun into his waistband, taking care to keep a layer of cotton between hot barrel and bare skin. He removed the scalloped blade, in case a *coup de grace* proved necessary.

267

He came up alongside the driver's side door, crumpled open. Agent Isherwood was slumped across the Mayfair's wheel, bleeding heavily from a wound to the temple and another to the shoulder, and another near the mouth and another by the ribs. The man's right hand rested in his lap.

Inside the hand, a gun barrel glimmered.

Without lifting his head, Isherwood fired a bullet into Hart's stomach from point-blank range.

Hart staggered back. Dropping the knife, he drew the Python again and tried to return fire – but the chamber was empty, and the hammer snapped ineffectively.

Clasping a hand over his bleeding belly, Hart looked down. Large pallid worms slithered between his fingers. After a moment, he realized that the worms were his intestines. He tried to hold them in, dropping the Python and bringing his other hand into play, but as he kept backing away, his intestines kept slithering out between his fingers, splattering against the unpaved road.

He lost the crutch. Swearing, he fell onto one knee. How had this happened? His plan had been simple and direct. He had made no mistakes.

Here came the pain in earnest: a terrible white-hot agony, which drew a sheer red film down over his eyes. Just one bullet against his six, but evidently it had hit something vital, opening his gut in the process like a can of soup. He waited for the red film to withdraw so that he could get back on his feet, finish Isherwood, and clean up after himself – the knife and gun and crutch and spent shells would need to be collected before he made his escape – and then get the fuck out of here. And perhaps this time he would not report back to Charlottesville. Perhaps the time had come to seek brighter horizons elsewhere, away from Senator Bolin.

He vomited a thin stream of gruel across the road's shoulder.

Steam and dust were everywhere. As he watched, squinting through an ever-thickening crimson curtain, a first lick of flame leapt behind the fog. The image was slanted sideways now, because Hart's head had lowered completely to the ground. Blinking, he opened his mouth. The only sound his parched lips could produce was a reedy whisper. *You know what they say about a boy who can't whistle...*

Listening to the venting steam and crackling fire, feeling the warmth of wintry sun against his cheeks, he let his eyes close.

A scraping sound made them open again.

Francis Isherwood was dragging himself from the burning Mayfair.

Hart felt a thump of admiration. Shot, butchered, bloodied – but the man was still going.

Watching Isherwood, he found within himself an untapped reserve of will. He tried again to stand, even though he felt a slippery release of intestine as his reward. His fury was so hot as to push back even the pain. Tottering, he tried to regain the knife. It was still not too late to correct his failures.

But his body refused to cooperate; he collapsed back to the road with a sigh. A new sound reached his ears, below the stealthy crackle of fire and the diminishing hiss of steam – the voice of the old gypsy fortune-teller, from the fairground in his native Ohio. Mingled with the stinks of spilled oil and burning fabric and peeled rubber wafted the slaughterhouse scents of blood and death. And entwined with them, forming a macabre confection, the enticing odors of corn dogs and cotton candy and popcorn and frying peppers, of youth and endless summers and illimitable promise...

You see here, how the ominous line crosses the lifeline – a short life, this one. A pity.

He gave another sigh. He let his eyes drift shut again. The fairground was waiting just ahead. The venting steam belonged not to a ruined engine, he realized then, but to an old-fashioned calliope, playing a merry old tune, beckoning him forward.

NINETEEN

The sky overhead remained a pristine chalky blue; but inside Elisabeth's mind, storm clouds were gathering.

Moving toward the front gate, she tried to swing the guitar case with a jaunty negligence – as if she was well-rested and calm and carefree, as if dark clouds were not filling her head. But she found herself unable, as she approached the gate, to look the guard directly in the eye. Instead, she concentrated on a large prominent nose beneath industrial spectacles.

Finding a smile that in reality probably came off more like a baring of teeth, she closed the distance. 'Hi.'

Stepping down from the booth, he searched her with slightly more than professional interest. Finishing, he turned his attention to the black case. 'Guitar?' he asked.

She shrugged lightly. 'Surprise Christmas gift for Josie. Don't spoil it by telling.'

'Let's take a look.'

She handed over the case. He set it on the gravel driveway and hit the catches. For a moment he admired the guitar in silence; then he nodded. 'Very nice.'

When he took out the instrument, her breath caught. But he seemed only approving, not suspicious. 'Nice,' he said again. 'Very nice. I play a little myself, you know...' To prove the point he straightened, leaning against the guard booth, and strummed a few chords. After adjusting the tuning of the highest two strings, he strummed again. Without warning he burst into song: 'Oh, some people say a man is a-made out of mud, a poor man's made out of muscle and blood; Muscle and blood and skin and bones, a mind that's a-weak and a back that's strong...'

She managed to keep smiling. 'What a lovely voice you've got!'

He blushed with surprising force, tucked the guitar back into the case. 'Great gift,' he said. His voice cracked on the last syllable, and

271

suddenly she realized that this man was sweet on her. If she had not been so distracted, she would have seen it earlier. 'Josie will love it. And our ears won't bleed after listening to her play. Hide it in your room and don't let anyone see it until Christmas Day! Don't worry – your secret's safe with me.'

Inside the herdsman's home, she climbed the stairs quickly.

Cursing the lack of a lock on the bedroom door – Dunbarton's insistence – she pushed the guitar under the bed until the case encountered the wall. Briefly, she considered using a pillow to block it from view; but that might attract attention. Better to trust the shadows. It would be a matter of small time anyway.

Sitting on the bedspread, she tried to shove back the encroaching mental thunderclouds and form a plan of action. Afternoon had not yet turned on its axis toward evening. Enough daylight remained for her to assemble the rifle and take the shot now. But the optimum time to fire would be morning, when the sun, due east to anyone standing on Farm One, would give her essential extra seconds of confusion.

Haste will be your downfall.

She bit her lip hard enough to draw salty blood.

A dainty knock on the door; then Josette allowed herself entrance without waiting for permission. 'Do you ever have the feeling,' she asked as she came in, 'that you've been waiting so long for something that you slept right through it?'

Elisabeth fixed a smile onto her face.

'That's how I feel today.' Josette plopped down beside her on the bed. 'In a way it's a marvelous feeling though, because I know it's not true. What did you find out from the travel agent?'

Elisabeth paused. She had forgotten her promise. 'Josie – they were closed.'

'What?'

'I meant to get back later in the day. But time just ran away with me.'

Josette gave her a black look. 'Time,' she repeated, 'just ran away with you.'

'I had errands to run.'

'Errands to run.'

Elisabeth shrugged.

'Libby,' said Josette after a moment, gravely. 'Sometimes I wonder about you.'

'Oh, don't make a big fuss. On your day off you can swing by and—'

Josette stood. The mattress sighed relief. 'I can read between the lines. I told you: I may be a lot of things, but I'm not stupid.'

'Josie—'

'If you really wanted to go with me, you would have done this. So I guess you don't. But that's all right.' She wiped an easy tear from one round cheek. 'Better to find out now, I suppose.'

'You're making too much out of this,' said Elisabeth.

Deep creases appeared on Josette's face. 'Well, that's good to know,' she said.

Turning, she let herself out.

Stonily, Elisabeth watched the door, waiting for the girl's return. Twenty seconds passed;

forty; a minute. At last she released a strained breath. This proved the point. During daylight, behind an unlocked door, there was insufficient privacy to assemble the rifle.

She changed into her Viyella robe and then went to draw a bath in the second floor's free-standing, claw-footed tub. When she eased into the scalding water, her back and legs unclenched gratefully. Pushing wet hair out of her face, she settled deeper. She soaked until her entire knotted body relaxed, releasing tension in a spasm. Then she toweled off, returned to her room, collapsed across the bedspread. Her muscles oozed; her breathing was rapid and shallow. She found her still, calm center and tapped into it.

One last bit of sangfroid, she told herself, would carry the day.

Her stomach was flipping. She was happy to skip dinner, lying motionless as the sun slowly crossed the blue sky outside her window. By the time the sky turned red, the evening chill was growing teeth.

FAYETTEVILLE, NORTH CAROLINA
Emmerich and Rudolf Wulff settled down around a crowded table.

Both men shared their father's piercing gray eyes, thick white hair, and stately profile. Emmerich, the elder, had the sharper wit and chin, and Rudolf the sharper nose and sartorial sense. Their guests were a high-ranking officer of the FBI, a congressman who had made his reputation chairing the House Committee on Un-American Activities, and a quartet of millionaire bankers who had earned their fortunes trading with German industrialists between the two wars. Despite widespread knowledge that their wealth had been made rearming the Fatherland on the backs of slave labor from concentration camps, these men had thrived during the past decade. As far back as 1924, the Teutonia Club of Chicago had begun an active campaign to make inroads into American business and politics, and now there was far too much money at stake for any capitalist worth his salt to stand for very long on principle.

Wives were present, and so conversation remained light. 'This Rauschenberg,' said one. A dismissive wave of her hand rattled pearls on a heavy bracelet. 'Pure tripe. An insult, is what it is.'

'Making art out of trash,' said another, and chuckled. 'Or is it trash out of art?'

'You know, he got his hands on a drawing by de Kooning – and then erased it. Then he called *that* art. He couldn't have chosen a better subject, if you ask me. That one, he got right!'

Husbands listened tolerantly, indulgently. Whenever talk veered toward the political – the back-door socialism of the Salk vaccine, or Wayne Morse's defection from the Republican Party, or the rise of the minimum wage from seventy-five cents to one dollar, or the sudden eruption of violence between the North and the South in distant Vietnam – the men exchanged fraught glances and gently steered the discourse back toward more inoffensive channels: Lucille Ball, Ed Sullivan, Martin Melcher, *The $64,000*

Question. Plates were cleared, fresh wine decanted, finger bowls served on doilies, cigarettes lighted.

At nine o'clock, the elder Wulff excused himself for a moment. In the parlor he switched on the radio, scanning through broadcasts of breaking news. Returning to the table seconds later, he caught his brother's eye and gave his head a small shake.

Another bottle of wine was opened. 'Have you been to Altman's in New York lately? They're offering a mink-handled can opener now. And the funny thing is, I *want* it...'

GETTYSBURG

After consulting with the receiving nurse, Chief Emil Spooner was directed to a corner of the ER.

He was met by a doctor who seemed to his weary eyes too young to be out of high school. 'In layman's terms,' said the doctor, 'one bullet punctured a lung, which collapsed and is sucking air. This is a potentially life-threatening trauma. But I can tell you: he's a fighter. I think he'll pull through.'

'Can I see him?'

'He's in surgery. Needle decompression, tube thoracotomy.' The young doctor's professional courtesy did little to disguise the density of his personal indifference. 'The endotrach is being performed now by Doctor Edmonds, the best we have.'

'When can I see him?'

'Once he's out of surgery, he'll need rest. I think it's safe to say not before morning.'

Inside the waiting room, Spooner lit a cigarette. Taking a seat, he scuffed vengefully with one toe at a glob of paint that had dried unevenly on the floor. He had just finished losing one old friend. He could not take losing another.

He exhaled a contribution to the blue fog hanging in the waiting area, checked his watch. Couldn't see Ish until morning. The immediate threat to the farm had been removed – Agent Zane, calling with the news about Isherwood, had reported Hart's body found on the back-country road.

Spooner stood. He wanted to see Richard Hart, or what was left of him, face-to-face.

Beneath the sodium glare of the Fleetwood's headlamps, the forest at night evinced little charm. Three miles from the hospital, four black-and-whites belonging to Gettysburg's finest served double duty as roadblocks and spotlights. Soaked with man-made illumination, the crime scene looked artificial and unreal: remnants of two automobiles, splintered and charred, on an unpaved road littered with bloodstains and shattered glass and twisted metal and spots of pumice powder.

Spooner's driver pulled onto the shoulder, killed the engine. The Chief of the Secret Service stepped from the car. As he approached the cordon, a chill moved from the rear of his neck, stiffening the hairs, down to the small of his back. When was the last time he'd visited an actual incident? Years ago ... no, decades.

He ran his eyes over the baker's dozen of men on the scene, trying to find the officer in charge.

He saw cops from two counties, investigators, a medical examiner from the State Police, and various technical experts from both township and borough. Noting a human-shaped chalk outline on the road, he felt a sour flash of disappointment. Unless he wanted to tramp down to the morgue and pull rank, it seemed the conquering hero would be cheated the sight of his vanquished foe, after all.

He sighted a man wearing a dun-colored sheriff's uniform and gleaming silver star: heavyset, friendly-looking, with flushed cheeks and a thick brown beard. When the man passed close by, Spooner chose his moment and stepped forward, unfolding his shield. 'Emil Spooner,' he announced. 'Chief of the Secret Service.'

Inspecting the credentials, the man did a slight double-take. Then he removed his hat, as if receiving a lady. 'Hell,' he said. 'It's an honor. Sheriff Howard Knox.'

'Lead me through the scene, Sheriff?'

Knox provided escort through the border of security. As a forensic photographer circled, snapping smoky photos with a blinding magnesium flash, the sheriff guided Spooner between the carcasses of the cars.

'Here,' said Knox, pointing out a row of ejected shell casings running unevenly toward a nearby fringe of forest. 'Now here,' he said, taking a knee.

Aping him, Spooner found the residue of muddy footprints pacing the shells – and wandering beside the footprints, small round marks, sometimes ground into bloody smears of viscera.

He looked away, retying a shoelace that didn't need it.

'Tread from the soles belongs to your perp. Circles are from his crutch.' Each word puffed heavenward on a fragile wisp of steam. 'Your man Isherwood gutshot this prick. You can see how he staggered away through his own intestines – and then, here, ended up crawling; these marks are knees and elbows. And he checked out' – as Knox directed Spooner's attention to the chalk outline – 'over here.'

Spooner nodded.

'Here's how I break it down. Perp parks his Chevy around the blind curve...' Knox's index finger followed the trail of shells and faint footprints toward the forest. 'Vehicle reported stolen, by the way, thirty-six hours ago in New York. You can see the tire prints where he pulls off here, and then where he pulls back into the road, when he sees your man coming, here. Hurries back to the forest, gun drawn. Your man comes around the corner, as indicated by tire marks here; and hits the automobile here. Dazed. Perp leaves his blind and comes forward, firing six shots from his Colt Python – which we find over here. And over *here*' – indicating a spot about two feet away – 'a knife. Vicious little number: twelve inches. Entry points into the Mayfair correspond with the perp walking forward as he fires – but your man has ducked down his head. Suffers multiple gunshot wounds, but gets lucky – nothing fatal. There's a lot of smoke and radiator steam and confusion going on. But he's already banged up pretty good by the crash. Still, he's enough on the ball to get his head down and pull his service pistol. Waits until the perp is right up beside the vehicle. At which point he gets off his shot. Makes it count. Perp has swapped gun for knife, by this point; drops the knife here, and goes for the gun again, which he drops here, along with the crutch. Hurt pretty bad. Evidently decides that discretion is the better part, *et cetera*.' The index finger followed a purplish series of stains back toward the treeline. 'Only, he's dripping his innards the whole way. Goes down for the count. Meanwhile, your man drags himself out and away from the burning car, onto the road here, which is where our patrolman finds him. That's how I read it.'

Spooner lit a Winston with a shaky hand. 'No sign of a rifle?'

'Rifle?' The sheriff frowned. 'No, sir.'

Spooner frowned back. 'The Python,' he said after a moment. 'Modified?'

'Yes, sir. Nifty work. Down at the office now.'

'Modified how?'

'Balance, grip, sight – custom job.'

'Made to look like something else?'

Knox ran fingers through his thick brown beard. 'Sir?'

'You know. Hidden inside something else, innocent looking? A lamp, a book, a length of pipe, like that?'

The sheriff looked at him closely. 'No, sir.'

'A harness,' Spooner suggested. 'To keep the weapon hidden under the clothing, evade a search...?'

'Nossir.'

'The clothing itself: some kind of uniform, some kind of disguise?'

'Nossir. Street clothes. Little bit ripe, too.'

'But how did he plan on...?'

'Sir?'

Spooner shook his head. A bracket had formed on either side of his mouth, a cross-hatching on his high forehead.

Elisabeth opened her eyes.

Enough moonlight came through the window to limn the bureau, the blanket and pillows, the JESUS LOVES YOU wall plaque. When she pulled the guitar case out from under the bed – inch by cautious inch, holding her breath – the clasps gleamed like precious metal.

Hitting the high and low catches, she removed the steel-string Gibson from its backing of red velvet. The gunsmith's work had been excellent; the guitar looked exactly as it had when she had purchased it at the pawn shop eight days before.

Setting the instrument on the bed, she explored from top to bottom, feeling for hidden seams or screws. After the initial examination, she loosened the tuning keys, relaxing the strings until they fell free. Setting the strings out of the way inside the case, she examined the guitar again. Removable screws held pick guard and bridge to body, and headstock to neck. From the dresser's bottom drawer she fetched a butter knife, palmed days earlier from the kitchen.

She labored for ten minutes before the pick guard came off. Beneath the nicked plate she found only pale wood. After five more minutes of work, the saddle bridge came loose. She immediately sensed that it was more tubular than strictly necessary. A moment's exploration revealed the reason: stuck against the back was a high-powered scope, cunningly concealed.

Two open clips would attach the scope to the rifle's stock. Two tiny grub screws, for adjusting the cross hairs, had been glued into place. She had made clear that she expected no chance to sight the rifle, and would need the weapon to fire true the first time.

Placing the scope inside the case beside the strings, she returned her attention to the guitar. Working the screws connecting headstock to neck took forever. But finally the stock had been emancipated. Inside, she found a magazine containing eight .30-06 cartridges. Removing the bullets, she inspected each individually before repacking the clip.

The magazine went into the tweed case, beside the scope.

Peering inside the neck she found the truss rod, traveling the length of the instrument, glinting mellowly in the moonlight. Usually the truss would have been attached to a nut on one end and held carefully in place by longitudinal bracing – a guitar was essentially an air pump – but this rod was thicker, unbraced, floating free except for loose padding. Still, the thing had played sweetly enough to get past the guard at the front gate – although he had needed to tune it, she remembered. It had also passed two other cursory inspections coming up the long driveway. Considering the loosey-goosey inner workings, however, a few good thumps would probably knock it out of pitch irrevocably. No matter; its days of making music were past.

She managed to work one end of the tube out of the headless neck and then upended the guitar, bringing the rod sliding out another few inches. Reaching in through the soundhole, she located the far extreme of the truss and nudged it down, watching as the instrument disgorged a perfect rifle barrel—

—then her forearm bumped against the guitar's body; a booming dull thud reverberated across the darkened room.

She froze. For the longest moment of her life she remained motionless, one hand inside the soundhole, the other teasing the truss rod out through the headless neck, wondering if she must return instrument to case and feign sleep, or if she could continue with her work.

Seconds pooled, formed a minute, and then repeated the trick.

At last, furrowing her brow, she returned to the task of shimmying the rod from the neck. The barrel was particularly thick and heavy: a so-called bull barrel, which would decrease vibration during shooting and hence increase accuracy. Once the piece was free she raised it to the moon-glowing window and peered through, pleased by the intricacy of the groove tracing the interior of the cylinder. Extra grooving meant extra spin stabilization, which in turn meant still-greater accuracy. In every respect, the workmanship was first-rate.

The missing piece was the stock, which would

hold all the rest together, which must be inside the body of the guitar itself, accessible only by cracking open the wood – hardly a silent proposition. She inspected the instrument's ribs, tapping gently with her knuckles, determining exactly which sections were hollow. Presently, she decided that anything hidden inside was beneath the soundhole. Therefore she concentrated on opening the section above the hole, so as not to risk damaging anything vital. First she tried the butter knife to pry off the guitar's side, and then her fingernails. When neither proved effective, she resorted to brute force: wrapping the guitar's body in a blanket, forming a vise of two pillows in an effort to further absorb the sound, and then using a swift sharp blow from one elbow to splinter the wood.

Unwrapping the instrument again, she discovered a long winding crevice wandering from fretboard down to missing pick guard. Inserting the knife into the crack, she widened the crevice and used her fingers to tear off a plank of wood. Peeling strips from the guitar's body, she deposited them in the empty case. Thus did she uncover, more than withdraw, the stock. Tucked within the last shards of the guitar's shell she found the rifle's butt and trigger mechanism. Fitting barrel to stock, she lined up grooves and smacked them together – the snap was louder than she might have liked, but time was short. The scope clipped neatly above the breech. The butt went onto the rear of the stock, helped home by another smack. That left the trigger mechanism: trickier than the rest, requiring careful insertion and adjustment.

But the rifle felt good – better than good. Keeping well away from the window, she socked the butt into her shoulder and placed wood against cheek. Her left hand steadied the barrel, her right closing over the trigger. She brought eye to scope. Perfect. *Pluperfect*, as Josette would have said. The thumb of her right hand extended seamlessly over the small of the stock, creating a spot weld between cheek, thumb, and gun. The rifle was an extension of her body. Her body was an extension of the rifle. If she kept the contact firm, she would not lose her aim between shots, if indeed more than one shot proved necessary.

She sighted on the wall plaque, the letters of which had been magnified by the scope to ridiculous proportions. Closing her eyes, she made herself relax, exhaling. When she opened her eyes again, the cross hairs remained dead on target: she read a giant E from the name JESUS.

Gently, she squeezed the trigger.

From within the breech came a soft answering snap.

Satisfied, she lowered the rifle.

A faint knock at the door. In the next heartbeat Josette stepped into the room, wearing a white nylon peignoir. 'I heard you moving around,' the younger girl stage-whispered. 'I'm sorry about before, Libby. I guess I can be...'

Trailing off, she took in the scene before her.

TWENTY

Isherwood dreamed.

Sometimes silhouettes blocked out the light above him, coming and going and then coming again. Sometimes the edges of the silhouettes took on a brush stroke of gold, making him think of Evy, her hair backlit as she read a book in bed at night. Sometimes the darkness intensified – an undertow, a sucking rip tide – and then the dreams surfaced, finely hewn, pressing away everything else.

He dreamed he was sitting with the Chief and Evy and the President in the parlor of a big, empty country house. On an upper floor, something larger than a man clumped around noisily. Outside, the wind lifted, rattling windows in their panes. But one window, facing east, stood open to a keening blade of freezing air. And the footsteps – or were they beating hooves? – from the house's second floor sounded ever louder...

Then he and Eisenhower sat together in a fancy hotel lobby, carried with nary a ripple from one setting to another by the fluid logic of dreams, facing each other in matching red-upholstered armchairs. They held dainty teacups filled with whiskey and tried to speak politely above the overwhelming bustle of bellhops and desk clerks and knocking machinery in the walls. But neither man could make himself heard. Nevertheless, it struck Isherwood as absolutely vital, in the dream, that he find and raise his voice – in fact, the very fate of the free world might depend upon it. But he had already sampled the whiskey, and a warm glow tangled his tongue. He found himself unable to speak, unable even to resist raising the teacup for another taste...

He stood in the backyard of the Anacostia house, holding a shovel. Cats watched through windows, arching and pressing against glass, as he heaved the shovel up and then down, biting the blade into frozen earth. He was digging a fallout shelter – and a good thing too, because sirens wailed in circles, air horns blasted, and it had finally happened; the fools had finally done it. The Bomb was on its way. But the shelter would not be finished in time. The lawn was littered with state-of-the-art equipment – chemical toilets and backup oxygen tanks and hermetically sealed food supplies – all of which would prove useless, because Isherwood had moved too slowly. Yet there was a dusky relief in failure, in giving up. Rocking back onto his heels, he dropped the shovel and watched hellfire rain from the sky. Pastels turned to primaries, crust to magma. Einstein and Truman and the warrior-poet Oppenheimer had spat in God's eye, and now God was spitting back...

Faces hovered above dark water, taunting him. There was Evy; and there was Eisenhower; and there was Richard Hart. And beside Hart was the Chief. *Last chance,* the Chief was saying. *Last chance to make things right.*

Elisabeth stepped forward.

The rifle came swinging up, catching Josette full-force on the left temple – Elisabeth could actually feel the girl's brain bounce inside her skull. But a thick skull it must have been, for although Josette teetered, with a look of pained amazement coming over her features, she did not fall.

Elisabeth swung again, aiming for the exact spot on which her previous strike had landed. This time Josette's eyes rolled back in her head like a cartoon character's, showing whites. Down she went. Elisabeth lurched forward, juggling the gun, and managed to catch the dead weight before it hit the floor.

Dragging Josette into the room, she softly closed the door. Her eyes moved to the window. A smear of stars, a diffuse rosy glow high in the sky. Dawn was not far off.

Clinically, she looked back at her friend. Even through closed lids, Josette seemed to gaze at her reproachfully. The girl was breathing so shallowly that one might have thought her already dead. Her head skewed at a strange angle atop her neck, emphasizing her double chins.

For several moments Elisabeth considered, a fine crease appearing on her pale brow. Then she gently set down the rifle. Strangulation would be fast and simple. She reached for the loose folds of flesh gathered beneath Josette's jaw...

...but the girl's eyelids were fluttering.

Confusion and hurt and anger registered on the round, unhappy face. For an instant Elisabeth paused, despite herself.

Harshly, she reminded herself: the fate of empires lay in the balance.

She closed her hands around the girl's throat.

Fingernails came up, raking across Elisabeth's brow. *Good*, she thought icily. So long as the pig fought back, pangs of conscience would not interfere.

Without loosening her grip, she drove a knee into the girl's abdomen. Josette's lungs emptied like bellows. The sounds coming from the fat throat took on a gooey quality. Elisabeth adjusted her grasp, pressing harder. The girl grunted, gasped, wriggled and writhed, thrusting forward and back; to no avail. One foot beat a weak, jerky tattoo against the floor. Horrible, now, the sounds coming from her throat.

Suddenly, a wet stickiness was gumming Elisabeth's eyes. The wound on her forehead was suppurating blood. Grimacing, she shook her head. Tiny droplets scattered like dew. But she felt no pain. Again she flicked her head, scattering wet strands of hair from her eyes, and refocused on Josette, whose movements were slackening now, like a winding-down toy. Just a few more seconds, and it would be finished...

The sounds coming from Josette's mouth turned thin, and then cut off. Her struggles lessened, then ceased.

But Elisabeth kept up the pressure for another full minute, just to be sure.

GETTYSBURG HOSPITAL: NOVEMBER 23
Isherwood's eyes opened.

Reflexively, he took hold of a tube coming from his nose – the damned thing was interfering with his breathing – and started tugging. Two hands closed over his, restraining him. 'Hold on, Ish. Easy does it.'

Filtered through a warm screen of painkillers, the face hovered very close to Isherwood's own: hollow-cheeked, smelling of Winstons, eyes webbed red. The Chief.

Moments later a white-coated doctor passed the room, waylaid a passing nurse, and took over the job of detaining Isherwood's hands as the nurse inserted a syringe into a small canvas pouch coming off the tube. The pouch drained sibilantly. The tube was withdrawn, scratching painfully against a parched throat – a pheno-menon as distinctive as it was unpleasant. 'Breathe,' the young doctor commanded, and Isherwood thought, *No shit, asshole.*

He sucked in an aggrieved breath. Released it shuddering, and drew another. 'Breathing off the ventilator,' the doctor told the nurse.

But other tubes snaked out of Isherwood's body. He began to pull them free. Tendrils of the dream clung obstinately: the Bomb on its way, the window to the east standing open, the fate of the free world in his hands.

'Ish,' Spooner said. 'Slow down.'

'Take your friend's advice. That tube in your side is decompressing your lung. If you tug it out, you risk a collapse.' The doctor leaned for-ward, inspecting his patient dubiously. 'What we're going to do is take some X-rays, see how fully your lung has expanded, and then stitch you up if things look good. For the time being, you must not exert yourself. Just relax – lie back. If all goes well, we might have you out of here by the end of the day.'

Consulting a clipboard, the doctor and nurse left the room. The Chief watched them go. Then he turned back to Isherwood and communicated more with a wry lift of his brow than he could have with words.

Darkly, Isherwood laughed – and then winced.

'I'm getting you out of here.' The Chief spoke furtively, beneath his breath. 'With or without their by-your-leave. I need you back at the farm.' He described the night just passed: joining Sheriff Knox in a canvas of local motels, looking for evidence of a room rented by Richard Hart. At three a.m., they had found the motor court at which the man had registered under the name Robert Farrow. But inside was no sign of a disguise, rifle, or other concealable weapon ... which to Spooner's mind suggested trouble.

'A second triggerman,' he clarified. 'Hart was lying in wait for *you* – but another assassin is lying for Eisenhower.'

THE EISENHOWER FARM

Breathing hard, Elisabeth leaned away.

She took inventory of herself. Except for the wound on her forehead, she seemed unharmed. She listened, concentrating. Nobody seemed to be rushing toward the room to investigate. Tentatively, she explored her brow with her fingertips. Two deep, bloody furrows marred the fine skin. Otherwise she was all right.

She felt a whisper of self-recrimination. This could cause problems. She should have been prepared for the counter-attack.

She would manage.

Wetting her lips, she looked around the room. The instant the body was found, the farm would doubtless be locked down and every inhabitant thoroughly investigated ... but as long as there was no corpse, it would take time for worst-case conclusions to be reached.

Experimentally, she got her hands beneath Josette's arms. The girl weighed twelve stone if she weighed an ounce. Elisabeth lowered the body again. The best place to hide a cadaver would be inside the corn crib, underneath the recent harvest – but dragging the heavy body out there, beneath the paling sky, would be too dangerous. Josette would need to be stowed right here, inside this room.

Carefully, Elisabeth rolled the corpse beneath the bed. For a moment her friend's face was unfortunately close to her own: black tongue lolling out thickly, eyes rotated to white. Then Josette turned over and hit the wall with a soft thump.

Reaching for the tweed case, Elisabeth found that the assembled gun was slightly longer than the container, which was already half-filled with remnants of splintered guitar. Briefly, she considered partly disassembling the weapon – even just removal of the butt might do the trick – but decided against it. She needed to be ready to move at an instant's notice. Instead, she wrapped the rifle in her navy pea coat and then slid it beneath the bed, up against Josette, followed by the case. The knife went back into the bottom drawer.

Blood spots marred the floor. As she wiped them up with a stocking, she deliberated. Somehow she would need to deflect suspicion as news of Josette's disappearance swept the farm, until the sun had risen high enough in the sky. The gouges taken out of her forehead would not help matters – but she had come too far to quit now.

Outside, a rooster crowed gutturally; chickens clucked, coming awake.

Positioning herself before the mirror, she went to work on the gouges, applying a light concealer, blending it in, and then moving on to a darker shade. Then powder, using a compact pad, dabbing evenly and gently. Then foundation, again light before dark. Then blush, taking care to match her pale skin tone. A quick touchup, and she was satisfied.

A last pass over the floor; the bloody stocking went inside the dresser drawer beside the butter knife. She lay back down. The creak of bed springs sounded cataclysmic. She braced herself to make contact with Josette through the thin mattress, but thankfully did not.

Even a few minutes of rest would have been welcome. But only seconds passed, it seemed, before the house matron moved down the hallway, knocking on doors.

As Dunbarton let herself in, Elisabeth prepared for the woman to notice something awry. The matron would bend over to peer beneath the bed. Elisabeth would move silently to the dresser. The

293

knife, dull but adequate, would fit into her hand like an old friend. The back of the harridan's neck would be exposed; she could envision the pale hairs, the slim tough muscles, the single ugly mole which would serve as a bullseye...

But Dunbarton hardly glanced into the room. 'Get dressed,' she said crisply. 'Your day off was yesterday.' Then she closed the door and moved off down the hall, rapping smartly as she went.

GETTYSBURG HOSPITAL
Spooner tried the supply closet's knob.

The door slipped open. Refraining from looking down the corridor, he stepped purposefully inside. Closing the door behind himself, he felt an illicit thrill plait down his spine. Against all expectations, he had become again the boy he once had been: shoplifting from Woolworths with Max, emulating Pretty Boy Floyd.

He found a light switch. The closet was filled with cleaning supplies, rubber gloves, boxed sutures, wrapped syringes, rubber tubing. Hanging on a hook he found a doctor's white coat, fraying at the collar; pressed against the rear wall he found two folding wheelchairs.

Five minutes later, head lowered, white coat flapping, he wheeled Isherwood through the waiting room, right past the young doctor, who was engaged in conversation with a pretty nurse. Outside, he manhandled the wheelchair roughly forward, across an oval-shaped pavilion and curving turnaround, toward the Cadillac Fleetwood parked by the curb.

THE EISENHOWER FARM

The house matron appeared in the kitchen doorway. 'Where's Josette?' she demanded.

None of the half-dozen girls in the room answered. Frowning, Dunbarton put hands on hips and cast her gaze penetratingly back and forth. 'Speak up. Someone must know.'

Silence.

With visible effort, Dunbarton restrained herself. Carefully, she fixed a flyaway strand of hair. 'Miss Grant – my office, if you please.'

Elisabeth followed the house matron into her first-floor office. Closing the door, Dunbarton took a seat behind her glossy walnut desk. Before speaking again, she let her gaze drill into her young charge. Then, with venomous restraint: 'Where ... is ... Josette?'

'Last time I saw her,' said Elisabeth meekly, 'she was on her way to bed.'

'So where is she?'

'I don't know, ma'am. But...'

'But?'

Elisabeth hesitated.

'Out with it, Miss Grant.'

'But she was always talking about leaving the farm, ma'am. Going to Hollywood, she said, and trying to get discovered at a soda fountain. Like Babs, she said.'

'Oh, for the love of God.' Dunbarton's nostrils flared. 'You girls and your stupid movie magazines. Your empty little heads get filled with all sorts of ideas.'

Elisabeth said nothing.

'Did she truly give the impression that she

planned on leaving last night, just like that?'

Elisabeth shrugged.

'And did you try to talk her out of this foolishness?'

'I told her it sounded risky.'

'Risky.' Again Dunbarton visibly checked herself. She shook her head in disgust. She started to open a drawer, and then thought better. After another moment, she sighed violently. 'You're dismissed, Miss Grant. Get yourself to work: post-haste.'

TWENTY-ONE

Turning into the driveway, the Cadillac Fleetwood jerked to a stop before the barricade.

Isherwood fought off the slip-sliding feeling of skating toward a lagoon of dreams. He watched blearily as Spooner exchanged a few words with Bob Skinnerton, inside the booth, who nodded and turned away to raise the barrier.

Isherwood sat up straighter. His side objected; he caught his lower lip in his teeth and bit down hard. *Hang in there*, he thought harshly. *Miles to go before you sleep.* The Chief would not have spirited him away from the hospital only to let him bleed to death here on the farm ... he hoped.

At the fork in the driveway, Spooner's driver turned west, toward the Secret Service office.

Isherwood raised a hand in protest. 'Silo,' he said thickly.

'Zane's watching it,' answered the Chief.

Elisabeth moved to the nearest window.

Visible beyond the partition of Norway spruce, Farm One sprawled in hillocks and furrows beneath the climbing sun. Changing her angle, she found the Georgian farmhouse with its screened-in porch.

The President was already standing behind his easel, in bathrobe and greatcoat. A Secret Service agent with a Superman curl hanging over a wide forehead stood motionless behind him. As Elisabeth watched, Mamie Eisenhower appeared on the porch between the two men. She offered something in her hands to her husband: a deck of cards. Words were exchanged; then they moved together to a small wicker table, pulling out chairs on either side.

From shadows thrown by the Norway spruce, Elisabeth judged the position of the sun in the sky. The time had come.

She looked down at her arms. They had broken out in gooseflesh.

'And I say, what are you afraid of?' Mamie Eisenhower threw a fan of cards onto the wicker table. 'Why must you act like such a child?'

The President rolled his eyes. 'Because I don't want to make trouble where there's no need. A little milk of magnesia will set me right.'

'That's what you said during the coronary. And so there you lay for twelve hours, suffering,

297

rather than get the help you needed. Because you're stubborn as a jackass and proud as a peacock.'

Agent Leo Wayne, standing near the back of the porch, had become very interested in the cuticles of his own right hand.

'Gas can be a sign,' insisted Mamie. 'Gas can indicate an obstruction. There's too much riding on your damned health for you be such a damned selfish fool all the time—'

'And that's why I've spent the past goddamned month living like a goddamned prisoner inside this goddamned pink house, for the love of Christ!'

'Just tell Howard. That's all I ask.' She looked around theatrically. 'Where *is* Howard?'

'Mamie,' said Ike. 'Take the hint; he doesn't want to hear about every fart and cough. Now sit down and quit being such a damned busybody. Do you want to play cards, or not?'

'Cards,' she grumbled. *'Bridge* is cards. *Canasta* is cards. This is kid's stuff – like those stupid western novels you're so fond of.'

Eisenhower forced air out between clenched teeth and reached for the stock pile.

In the kitchen, Caroline Dreyfus was telling Linda Larsen about a recipe she'd seen in *Good Housekeeping*.

'They call it a "grape chiffon pie" ... grape juice and marshmallows and gelatin and whipped cream, all in a pastry shell. You know me, I could burn water. But I think I might give it a try, it just looks so yummy ... Libby, where are you going?'

Elisabeth paused, turned to face the kitchen. With a sunny smile, she raised her goose-fleshed arm. 'Just getting a sweater.'

She climbed the stairs quickly, moved into her room, and reached beneath the bed. The skin on her forearms still crawled. Her hands themselves felt oddly cold.

We've watched our parents dress in rags and scavenge food unfit for a dog. We've listened to the promises of our teachers that things will get better. And we've seen with our own eyes that the elder generation is not truly willing – or able – to take the necessary steps. Karl's sculpted cheeks had caught the sunlight as he spoke, revealing his Aryan bone structure, glorious and strong. *We've come to understand that it falls to us, the chosen ones, the future, to step up and take our rightful place in history – as the authors of history.*

From the guitar case she transferred ammunition into a pocket of her afternoon maid's uniform. She withdrew the rifle, wrapped in her pea coat, and then pushed the case back beneath the bed, wincing slightly as it bumped against Josette's body. Catching sight of her reflection in the mirror, she adjusted her bundle until it was mostly hidden along the line of her body.

We are not bound by tradition, by old ways of thinking. We are pure and strong, and mastery over others is our birthright. We will do whatever is required to attain victory.

The indignities were over. The menial work, the suffering in silence beside swine who had humiliated her countrymen on the battlefield, the living in fear of a knock on the door – all in the past. One way or another, she would now be only herself.

She moved her head slightly, catching a ray of sunshine on her own sharp cheekbone. Drinking in the sight, she spent a long moment admiring her true face: unsmiling, beautiful, and pitiless.

Then she turned, positioning her bundle carefully, and left the room for the last time.

'Didn't Jim Hagerty tell you the same thing? "Ike," he said, "you can't be such a stubborn damned fool any more; there's too much riding on your shoulders for such obstinate behavior." I know he said it because I heard it, during his visit just two days ago, with my own ears.'

'You were eavesdropping?'

'I was *passing by*.' Angrily, Mamie reached for the stock pile of cards.

'Goddamnit, woman. Hard enough being cooped up in this goddamned place without you watching me like a—'

'We all know you're depressed, dear. But there's no reason to take it out on me.' She discarded. 'There's no shame in it. Feeling blue after a heart attack is the most natural thing in the world. Rest assured: soon enough you'll be downing salted peanuts and scotch and water like there's no tomorrow. But for now, you've got to show some patience.'

'So now I'm a glutton, eh?'

'Just a mule, dear.' A too-sweet smile. 'Have you taken this morning's Coumadin yet?'

'Hell with this,' muttered Eisenhower, throwing down his cards. 'Nag, nag, nag.'

Angrily, he pushed up from his chair and turned toward his easel, reaching for a brush. On the linen canvas, amateurishly rendered in oils, waited a half-finished facsimile of the grain silo he now faced, visible above the row of Norway spruce.

Inside the Secret Service headquarters, Spooner waved Isherwood into a chair. 'We need men we can trust,' he said, 'pronto.'

Settling himself gingerly, Isherwood nodded. After a moment's thought he said, 'Mitch Carter. Elmo Gordon. Frank Carlo...'

Spooner reached for the phone.

The door opened. Bill Brennan came into the office, leading a tall young farmhand with full round cheeks, a mop of curly hair, and a handlebar mustache. Brennan looked piqued, but, as always, immaculately groomed. 'Chief,' he said, tipping an imaginary hat.

Receiver in hand, Spooner paused.

'I know I'm AIC these days in name only, sir.' Brennan couldn't resist shooting a sidelong glance at Isherwood as he said it. 'But I think you might want to hear this.'

Spooner raised his eyebrows expectantly.

Elisabeth descended the stairs quickly and lightly, on the balls of her feet, favoring the sides of the risers, which were less likely to squeak.

At the foot of the staircase, she stepped into a shadowed telephone nook from which she could see the parlor's side door. Dunbarton's muffled voice emanated from her office – checking in with the guard at the gate, from the sound of it, to see if Josette had left the farm during the night. The rest of the girls on the first floor remained gossiping in the kitchen, with Caroline Dreyfus taking the lead.

Elisabeth focused on the north-facing window beside the door. After thirty seconds a guard appeared, heading clockwise around the house. When he had passed, she swiftly crossed the room. Before placing hand on knob, she briefly paused again. Breathe. Maintain control. She found the still, quiet place within herself.

Turning the knob, she stepped out of the herdsman's home, closed the door behind herself, and moved to the familiar oak. If caught, she would claim need of a cigarette and fear of Miss Dunbarton's bloodhound nose. If anyone asked to inspect the bundle inside the coat, she would kill him.

She sighted the perimeter patrol, up past the bullpen, walking away. From careful observation she knew that fifteen minutes would pass before the sentries came again into a position to see her. That left only the usual farm workers to worry about, and farmhands were not known, as a rule, for their vigilance.

Her eyes roamed: past the corn crib, the Maternity Barn, a few strutting chickens pecking at cold mud, and an outdoor pen in which a handful of cattle enjoyed the fine, cool day. A man wheeled a barrow full of fertilizer, another lugged a bucket of feed, another carried a coarse sack and horse brush. They were focused on their work, and if she timed her movement carefully and walked with purpose, should pay her no attention.

Her heart had stopped beating. She urged it back into action. Then she stepped away from the oak, carrying the rifle bundled in the pea coat flush against one leg, and moved with a measured tread toward the pine.

She came to another stop inside a cone of dense needles. The unpleasant smells of manure and compost, half-deadened by frost, made her nose wrinkle. A steel gate clamped shut inside her mind. The corridor leading to victory lay shining before her; all she had to do was walk forward.

She left the shaded pine. Between her current position and the grain silo, a last bit of cover was offered by the shed. But there were no agents in sight, and the nearest farmhand was a long stone's throw away, paying no attention, so she forsook the cover. Instead, she headed directly for the silo, her movements swift but unhurried, as if she had every right in the world to be walking here in the midst of a sunny, late-autumn morning. In flashes between the Norway spruce she could see the sun porch, still occupied by Eisenhower.

Twenty yards remained until she reached the silo. Fifteen. Once it was done, her reward would be waiting in the numbered account. Ten. She would have enough to buy true security; she need never look over her shoulder again. Five. Nothing could stop her now. JESUS LOVED

HER, so there. The time of day was ideal, the sun hanging perfectly in the sky. The stars had aligned so faultlessly – in the case of the sun's position, literally – that she hardly dared breathe for risk of breaking the spell. Two yards.

She closed the distance.

Reaching the silo door, she felt for the handle – and at that moment heard a voice calling out, echoing off low hills:

'*Hey!*'

Breath snagging in her throat, she halted.

A frisson of panic moving down her vertebrae, she turned.

A short, slim agent was hastening across the property from the herdsman's home: hair slicked back with pomade, pique written across his narrow Semitic face.

'Go on,' urged Brennan. 'Tell them what you told me.'

The young farmhand shrugged muscular shoulders. Addressing both Spooner and Isherwood, he said, 'Well, sirs, I don't want to waste anyone's time. But in a nutshell: you know the girl that's run off – Josie Brown?'

Isherwood and Spooner traded a glance. 'Run off?' said Isherwood.

'Missing since last night, sir. They think she's gone to Hollywood, to get herself discovered.'

Isherwood frowned. 'What about her?'

'Well, sir ... nothing was written in stone, but we were ... we got a little cozy with each other.'

'Your name?'

'James Weaving. I work in the barn, mostly.'

304

'What have you got to tell us, Mister Weaving?'

'That's the devil of it, sir. Just a feeling. I tried to tell Agent Brennan here...'

'Spit it out,' said Brennan.

'Her running off just doesn't sit right. Anything's possible, of course. But Josie's got more talk than walk, if you know what I mean. And she grew up in this town. She's got family here. Plus she had a good, steady job. And as much as she liked to gripe, I think she was pretty happy here, sir. Plus...' He hesitated. 'At the risk of tooting my own horn: I think she liked me. And *I'm* here. Even though we had agreed to, uh, see other people.'

'Josie Brown,' repeated Isherwood. He tried to picture her. Concentration proved difficult; pain and painkillers danced a leisurely waltz through his head, and an endless kaleidoscopic lightshow seemed to play just outside of his field of vision.

'Works in the herdsman's home, sir. Pretty little thing. Wouldn't kill her to, uh, reduce a bit.' Weaving seemed about to add something else, and then stopped. With long fingers, he nervously stroked his mustache.

'Go on, Mister Weaving. Spill.'

'Sir ... well, it's awfully thin, sir.'

'Might be nothing,' put in Brennan. 'But – permission to speak freely – even though I don't seem to have your ear any more, Chief, I wanted to run it past you, just to be sure.'

'Go on, Mister Weaving,' said Spooner.

'I don't like to go around pointing fingers for

305

no reason, sir. When a man points at somebody, my mama told me, he should remember that four of his fingers are pointing back at himself.'

'We'll take that into account.'

Weaving paused to light a Parliament. 'Josie had gotten awfully chummy with the new girl – the senator's former housekeeper.'

A long moment passed as Agent Zane crossed the low hills, drawing to within five feet of Elisabeth before stopping.

The tension drew to a fine singing hum. Then he gestured at the rifle swathed in the coat, half-hidden behind her leg. 'What's that?'

She sifted through possible replies. None would guarantee her safety if he got it into his head to inspect the bundle; and how could he not?

Instead of answering, she took a step forward. Raising the gun slowly, unwrapping the pea coat, she revealed a glinting edge of metal barrel – which she then whipped up violently into his nose, even as he started to reach for his holster, sending an incongruous spurt of blood arcing into the sunshiny morning air.

Grasping the rifle in both hands, she dropped the coat and plunged the butt-end of the weapon into Zane's stomach, coaxing out a terrific *whuff* of breath. Fighting to regain his wind, he staggered backwards, dropping his pistol. She had all the time in the world to target the bridge of his nose and strike again, this time breaking the skin, sending him down to his knees.

But he came promptly back at her: bouncing

up like a coiled spring, eyes streaming with tears. Disoriented, he tried to land a punch. She easily stepped aside, jabbing with the rifle as she dodged – the urge to shoot him would, if indulged, bring agents swarming – aiming the jab at one red, watering eye. He turned his head, and as a result she missed the eye but connected with an ear, which caught against the leading edge of the metal barrel and tore half-free.

He staggered back again; she moved in for the kill, bringing the stock around in a whistling arc. This time she hit him just below the pulped remains of his ear, solidly, at the base of the skull. A slick of bloody spit spilled out across his chin. He stumbled sideways and then pitched forward, rapping his temple hard against the silo.

Breath raking out, Elisabeth raised the rifle again. She brought it down hard against the back of his head. The resulting sound was like a bursting pumpkin. Again she struck, and then again, splattering gore, even as some part of her insisted, *You can stop now; it's over; get inside, under cover.*

Finally, she moved away, leaning against the silo, breathing laboriously, sure she must have been seen; the encounter seemed to have taken forever. But as she kept breathing, and moments kept passing, slowly she came back to herself and realized that in fact it had taken very little time.

Her macabre handiwork lay splayed before her. Freckles of the man's blood and brains decorated the siding of the silo, the barrel of the gun, the bib and apron of her uniform.

Hurry.

Yes. The steel gate inside her mind had raised enough to let in cold light, but she slammed it back down.

She looked around. Nobody was looking back. For the second time in four hours she bent, slipped her hands beneath a corpse, and pulled.

TWENTY-TWO

'New girl,' repeated Isherwood, still frowning.

'Elisabeth Grant.' Weaving shrugged. 'She replaced Barbie Cameron, after Babs took off. I get a bad feeling about her. Now, I can see how that sounds. Like so much tittle-tattle – like working folks just chinwagging. Not exactly a hanging offense. But now Josie's all of a sudden gone, and I just got this feeling, sir—'

'What senator?' Isherwood interrupted.

'Sir?'

'You called her the senator's former housekeeper.'

'Libby used to work for ... I think Josie said Senator Bolin. He recommended her for the position after Babs—'

Moving as one, Isherwood and Spooner went for the door.

* * *

Elisabeth pushed into the silo.

With a creak, the door gave way. She stumbled into cobwebs, sacks of burlap, tubes of sealant. A ladder ran up the silo's interior. In the dome overhead, a tiny platform poked out from the wall, with an inverted silage fork hanging on a nearby hook.

After depositing the agent's body among the burlap, she went outside again and recovered the rifle and pea coat. Back inside, she strapped the rifle over her shoulder. Wetting her lips, she looked up, at shafts of sandy light coming in through the dome's ventilation slats.

With her left hand, she took hold of the ladder. It felt sturdy.

After a final moment to gird herself, she started to climb.

Her arms were tired, almost trembling, from the melee. She could not shoot well with trembling hands. And so she paused, after having ascended about a third of the silo's height, to rest for a moment. Breathing hard, heart hammering inside her chest. *Slow down*, she commanded furiously. *Do it right.*

At last the threat of trembling in her hand subsided. She reached for the next rung and resumed climbing.

The sun hung directly behind the silo, blazing.

In battle, thought Isherwood as he piled from the office, *high ground counts for everything*.

Chief Spooner followed his gaze. Judging from the clouds massing on the man's brow, his thoughts ran in a similar direction.

Their eyes met. With a jerk of his chin Isher-wood managed to communicate an order. *Get the President under cover.*

Spooner nodded. Isherwood struck off across uneven ground toward Farm Two, limping and swaying but moving with raw speed. Beyond his field of vision, the light show played on. Turn his head a few degrees past it and there would be only yawning, stretching, endless black. But despite the light show, the punctured lung, the fresh spotting on his bandage, the belated realiz-ation that his firearm was lost – back at the hospital, or the crash site – and the horrid crawl-ing sensation of blood pouring like water down his flank, he felt again that sense of strange euphoria. Under fire he was his best and worst self simultaneously. This was the only Francis Isherwood that didn't crave a goddamned drink.

The rasp of ladder letting go of silo wall filled her ears.

Adrenalin surged through her veins. Her feet kicked, propelling her up two more rungs. Then she was only four from the top – but the ladder kept groaning, starting to separate both from itself and from the wall.

She scrabbled up, eyes fixed on her goal. A hand seemed to push from below, lifting her. And then somehow she had made it: collapsing across the small wooden platform, praying that the shelf itself did not give way.

With her weight removed, the ladder ceased groaning. Looking down she saw wood hanging out from the wall with several exposed inches of nail showing, right and left side rungs spread apart like legs akimbo.

She repaired the ladder as best she could while hanging half upside-down off her roost, banging it back into the wall until only a centimeter of nail showed, trying to coax the side rungs into something resembling parallel lines. After doing her best to assure a clear escape route, she unstrapped the rifle from her shoulder and prepared to complete her mission. The still, quiet place inside her mind expanded, soaking up everything else like a sponge. She felt calm, able, focused.

Evidently, she was not the first to discover this unused perch – a few discarded cigarette butts littering the platform spoke of time wasted by idling employees. She faced west, toward the Eisenhower home, and from her pocket withdrew the magazine, which thumped solidly home inside the rifle's stock.

Biting her lip, ruffling her pale brow, she raised the rifle. Sticking the barrel through the ventilation slat facing the sun porch, she brought scope to eye.

Shielding his eyes against the glare as he crossed through the Norway spruce, Isherwood fought to make out the silo rising before a lustrous sun.

He could see only a dark silhouette. But in the next moment the sun dimmed, obscured by a tendril of cloud drifting across the sky, leaving an after-image imprinted on his retina. He raised his gaze to the highest extreme of the towering grain silo.

The barrel of a high-powered rifle poked out, like the snout of a steel wolf.

She sighted on the President.

Facing the silo, beside his easel, features set in an attitude of artistic contemplation, he could not have presented a better target had he actively tried. Socking the rifle butt into her shoulder, she moved the stock flush against her left cheek. One hand steadied the barrel. Her thumb formed a spot weld between face, hand, and gun. The rifle was an extension of her body, and vice versa. Beneath her, the platform jiggled threateningly; but it would remain secure for a few more instants, all she needed. The sponge in her mind had soaked away all thoughts of ruses and escape routes and numbered accounts. At this moment there was only target and gun. Target and gun. Target and gun.

From the corner of her eye she sensed a presence rushing toward the sun porch. An intruder; a problem. But too slow, too late.

In the cross hairs she lined up President Eisenhower's familiar face: balding, framed by a fringe of sandy gray hair, and yet boyish, ruddy-cheeked, with uncanny blue eyes focused intently at the moment on his painting.

She closed her own eyes and opened them again. The face hadn't wavered.

Deliberately, her finger tightened on the trigger.

Francis Isherwood pushed into the silo.

He tripped over the bloody, lifeless body of

Philip Zane. *Oh God, no.* If not for Isherwood's recommendation, the man would not have been here. *Later.*

He plundered Zane's body like any soldier plundering the dead, tearing open the dark jacket, ignoring his savage grief, finding the standard-issue Detective Colt still inside its holster, tearing the gun free. As he turned to look at the figure high above, the figure was also turning, at the sound of his entrance, to look down at him.

As Isherwood took aim, the shooter fired down the length of the silo. He steadied his right hand with his left, ignoring the warning flare from the incision in his side. Pain was gone; confusion was gone. He had ceased breathing.

The slug thudded an inch from his left foot, kicking up a plug of dust. He returned fire, squeezing the trigger three times, fanning the barrel from right to left.

A suspended, timeless instant. Then a slow tumble, as both figure and rifle plummeted end over end off the platform. Instinctively, Isherwood fell back against the wall of the silo, making himself small.

The girl and rifle landed atop him with a heavy, terrible thud.

She writhed with fury, trying to claw at his face. Her turquoise eyes, filled with hate, were just inches from his own. He fought back clumsily, batting her hands away while trying to bring the gun around.

In silence broken only by harsh breathing, they struggled. But she was strong – even wounded, as she must have been, she had incredible strength. And he was weak, more so every moment. The bottomless black pit still yawned open, and now he was slipping into it, powerless to stop his descent.

A fist pumped mercilessly into his side, into the already ruined lung. Air escaped with a weak tea-kettle hiss.

Shadows were folding in, closing around him. The black void just to one side yawned ever deeper, even blacker. He was sliding into it. He felt himself go limp. *Finished.* He could only hope that he had moved with speed enough to save Eisenhower – and that he would not find too many demons waiting in that darkness.

He found not demons but a pleasant vision of a fine young son, with Evy's coloring and frank challenging gaze. The boy took Isherwood's hand with small fingers. Francis Isherwood held the tiny hand with great pleasure, trying to keep up – the lad exhibited the boundless energy of the young – as the boy pulled, tugged, laughing musically, urging him forward, into the gentle dark.

The mission had failed; but she still lived.

Pushing away the agent sprawled atop her, she listened.

Voices spoke, but not from directly outside the silo. Through tiny cracks in the splintery wood, she managed to catch glimpses of the land immediately surrounding her. Agents moved in packs, like flocks of black birds – securing the front gate, searching the herdsman's home, bolstering the perimeter between Farm Two and Farm One. But the path due east, toward the patch of woods she had scoped out long before, where she had hidden the disguise and the bicycle, was empty. The sentries there had been summoned to reinforce the President's position, just as she had anticipated.

And so she recovered the pea coat, pried the Colt from the hand of the agent, and then slipped out into the sunshine, not running, which would attract attention, but certainly not dawdling either. All it would take to defeat her now was a man glancing over his shoulder at the wrong moment. Yet as the seconds passed, no calls rang out. JESUS LOVED HER, after all.

She stalked clumsily – more like her childhood self every moment – becoming aware as she moved of new wounds, fresh insults to her body. A gunshot in the shoulder – but the bullet had apparently passed through. Her leg, injured in the fall, had turned into a doll's leg, stiff and unwieldy.

Awkwardly, she moved past the corn crib, past the bullpen. Atop the section of fence she'd chosen to cross, barbed wire coiled like a sleeping snake. The fence was too high to jump. But a horizontal cross-beam five feet up provided a potential footrest; the fence had been designed to keep intruders out, not in.

She flung the pea coat into the air, watched bloodstained fabric billow and then tangle against barbed wire. Bracing her right hand against a vertical post, she levered herself up onto the cross-beam. Her wounded right side proved unable to support her weight, and she nearly tumbled back to the ground. Instead, using her left hand and her momentum, she grabbed one dangling sleeve of the tangled coat and managed to drag herself up onto the fence top.

Never look back, she thought.

And yet, before dropping down onto the far side, she did.

Bedlam was already giving way to military order: perimeters established, search parties fanning out. The silo, which marked the scene of her final ignominy, stood awash in brilliant sunshine. The distant porch was empty, offering no sign of Eisenhower. Of course he would have been hustled inside by now, under cover, and surrounded by a ring of armed men. She would have no prayer of reaching him.

She released the coat. Falling to the hard ground outside the property, she found the blighted chestnut she'd chosen as a landmark. The disguise and Huffy were waiting behind it, and in town, the Oldsmobile. But what, she wondered as she maneuvered her dead leg over the bicycle's saddle, came next? She had failed.

The important thing was to put some distance between herself and here. Find proper medical treatment. Change her identity, again and again.

Keep running.

TWENTY-THREE

FAYETTEVILLE: DECEMBER 1955
The entire table was laughing.

The man who had told the joke leaned forward, glowing with self-satisfaction and Cheval Blanc, and reached for the bottle. He refilled his wife's glass, and then extended himself across the table to refill the glasses of Emmerich and Rudolf Wulff.

'Believe it or not,' he said, setting down the bottle as the laughter died away, 'I heard that one from a professor at Harvard Law School, when we were working together in Shanghai.'

Emmerich gave a last chuckle. Plates were cleared; from the kitchen came the rich smell of brewing Arabica beans. 'Coffee,' a butler announced, 'will be served in the parlor.' Walking past the elder Wulff, then, he leaned down and added something in a whisper.

Emmerich and his brother made brief eye contact. As they left the dining room, Emmerich veered off toward the library. 'Rudolf,' he called, 'might you entertain our guests for a few moments without my assistance?'

'It would be my sincere pleasure,' said Rudolf solemnly.

Inside the library, Emmerich Wulff failed at

first to recognize his old friend; he thought the butler must have given him the wrong name. Then he realized that in fact he was indeed looking at Senator John Bolin. Although mere weeks had passed since their last encounter, the man was almost unrecognizable. He had lost weight. He needed a shave. His suit – a cheap linen ensemble, far less glamorous than his usual outfit of bone-colored silk – was grubby and frayed. His rimless spectacles were marred by a hairline crack. Even more profound was the change in his body language. He radiated pain and uncertainty. Even his cold blue eyes seemed different, two shades darker.

Closing the doors behind himself, Emmerich checked his own composure before speaking. 'John,' he said then, evenly. 'What a surprise.'

Bolin shook his head, sighed, and covered his eyes with one hand.

'Relax, my friend.' Emmerich took Bolin's elbow, leading him more fully into the room. 'Cognac?'

Bolin managed a stiff nod. His hand lowered; his tongue came out, scraping across dry lips. 'Yes,' he said. 'Thank you.'

Crossing beneath antique tapestries, ancient leather-bound tomes, and mounted heads of bucks and tigers, Emmerich reached for a sideboard by a humidor. Splashing brandy into two snifters he asked politely, 'Cigar?'

'Yes – yes.'

Equipped with brandy and cigars, they settled down on either side of a dark chessboard inlaid with pearl.

'I know I'm not supposed to be here,' started Bolin. 'I can see from the cars parked in the drive that you've got guests...'

Emmerich waved carelessly.

'...but our so-called friends in Buenos Aires double-crossed us, Emmerich. I had no other way of reaching you. They didn't hold up their end of the deal; so plans must change.'

Sanguine, Emmerich lit both cigars from a vintage brass-capped lighter.

'They put me in a hovel: a literal hovel. Cockroaches everywhere. Filth ... insects ... disease.'

Sympathetically, Emmerich nodded. But his eyes remained empty, dull.

'The problem,' continued Bolin, 'is that we chose the wrong friends. This two-bit dictator Aramburu – he's no good. He's crooked. He bites the hand that feeds him. And McCarthy – a drunken fool. His day is past. And that operative of yours ... everyone said she could do no wrong. But when push came to shove, she fumbled the job.'

'Unfortunately, I must agree.'

'Even my faith in my most trusted associate, my lieutenant, proved misplaced.' Bolin straightened, and for a moment a flash of the old hauteur was visible. 'But with time and patience, Emmerich, another chance will present itself. And if this time we have the right men in our corner—'

'Our dinner guest at this moment is a candidate for such an honor.'

The senator caught the hint of reprimand. 'I'm sorry to arrive this way,' he said after a moment;

'without warning, putting you at risk. I have agreed to be, and I shall remain if necessary, *persona non grata*. But you don't know what it's been like.'

Another nod.

'Just getting back into this country took everything I've got. They're all crooked down there, the swine. They'll cheat you as soon as look at you, and if they realize that you need them, then God help you. I'm penniless, Emmerich – absolutely without a penny. If not for some old friends who owed me favors, I never would have made it back over the border. They're looking for me, you know. I'm told there's a standing arrest order. One of my staff confessed that the girl never worked for me; the cover story is ruined. Now I'm an accomplice. A wanted man. My accounts frozen, my assets forfeited. Even John Hoover can't help me now.'

Emmerich smoked. 'Were you recognized, on your way here?'

'No. Of course not. I took care.' Bolin looked at the brandy in his hand, which he seemed to have forgotten. Raising the glass, he drained it in a draft.

'*Meinem Freunde*: take a deep breath. You're safe now.'

Bolin made a sound between a laugh and a scoff. 'Easy for you to say. You've lost nothing. But I—'

'As you say: another chance will present itself.' Coolly, hoping his example would lower the room's emotional temperature, Emmerich sipped his own brandy. 'Our operative came within a heartbeat of success. Consider this not a failure, my friend, but a lesson learned. We come out wiser than we started. Next time, we will have our day.'

Bolin regarded him through half-lidded eyes. 'I want to believe it,' he said slowly. 'I'm desperate to believe it. But...'

Emmerich waited.

'They've been put on high alert. They've doubtless reinforced security, and then reinforced the reinforcements. We'll never get so close to Eisenhower again.'

'So. Look at the long game, as they say. Time is on our side.'

A curl of the lip from Bolin. 'How do you figure?'

'Give the country four more years of Bolshevik policies – bleeding them dry with regulations and taxes, organized labor keeping them in a chokehold – and the American people themselves will succeed, where we have failed. They will correct their own course.'

'And what happens, Emmerich, if after four more years the country *likes* the way Eisenhower leads? The weak like to be coddled. They shirk from battle. Hold their hands, pay their way, and they respond like dogs thrown bones.'

Emmerich shrugged. 'As I said: we come out wiser than we started. We know now that this country can be helped, if necessary, despite itself.' He drank his cognac, puffed on his cigar. 'This time, we missed by a hair. Next time, if a next time is required, we will not.'

Bolin removed his spectacles, rubbed his eyes.

'If the Russkies have anything to say about it, we won't be around long enough for there to be a next time.'

'Say what you will about Eisenhower. He's a military man, and a fine bluffer. He'll keep the Soviets in check.'

'With Wilson, that glorified accountant, as Secretary of Defense? They say "unify" – but they mean "conciliate".'

'One thing at a time. You've traveled long and hard...'

'Good Lord, you don't know the half of it.'

'But you've done the right thing in coming here. We'll take good care of you.' Emmerich made a show of pondering. 'Why don't we tend to your needs – a decent meal, a decent bed – and take it up in the morning. In the meantime, I should return to my guests before they wonder what has drawn me away...'

'Of course.' Bolin upended his glass, draining the very last drop of brandy. 'You're the salt of the earth, Emmerich.'

'Of course,' said the elder Wulff absently, 'it is my humble pleasure.'

He left the man alone in the study and then paused, alone, in the corridor.

Bolin's sudden appearance presented problems. Emmerich could only hope nobody had recognized the former senator *en route*, or trouble might result down the road.

For now, he shelved the concern. The pressing issue was how to proceed tonight. Throughout everything, the Wulffs had managed to farm out the hiring to others – first and foremost, to Bolin himself – and thus avoid any chance of exposure. But as a result, they now lacked the necessary connections to make a man disappear. And it was hardly the kind of enterprise Emmerich Wulff felt comfortable taking on himself. Decades had passed since the last time...

But life sometimes took unexpected turns; and if not him, then who?

Stopping by the parlor, he offered his apologies, announcing that he would rejoin the party in a few minutes. He then visited the kitchen, ordering that a plate be prepared and a fresh bottle of wine opened. Then he climbed a spiral staircase and crossed through a bedroom to a spacious lavatory, handsomely appointed in marble and smelling faintly of lavender, which he shared with his younger brother. One advantage to reaching old age in modern times was the ready availability of a wide selection of nostrums ... browsing labels on glass vials, he made his selection.

Back in the kitchen, he dismissed the help, found a mortar and pestle in a drawer among burr mills and herb grinders, and crunched up half a dozen pills. After pulping them to a fine powder, he sifted the results into an empty wine glass. A dash from a freshly-opened bottle of Cheval Blanc dissolved the precipitate. He stirred until all traces had vanished, filled the glass nearly to the rim, and then sniffed for odor. He risked a tiny, cautious sip for taste. Satisfied, he set glass, silverware, and prepared plate of food on a tray. Calling the butler, he ordered the tray delivered to the library. He would check on

Bolin in an hour. If the man still lived he would doubtless be unconscious, and easily finished. An unfortunate turn of events ... but not, now that Emmerich found himself in this position, actually so difficult to accomplish.

He fixed his cuffs, preparing to rejoin his brother and their guests in the parlor. The young man awaiting him there, one Everett Howard Hunt, had served at length with the OSS and the CIA. Hunt had personally engineered the overthrow of the president of Guatemala, and acted as agency station chief in Uruguay and Mexico City. He was a man of many capabilities, many connections, and realistic values ... a valuable ally for the future.

A thin smile crossed Emmerich's face, and he went to rejoin the party.

DELPHOS, INDIANA

Ralph Jessup, MD, reached the front door just in time to see a slim figure limping away down his driveway.

He pulled the door open. 'Hey,' he called. 'You ringing my bell?'

For a moment, he thought his visitor – an attractive young lady who may have been representing 4-H or UNICEF or Grit, although an hour past sundown seemed an odd time for a visit – had moved out of earshot. Then she turned, just beyond the rim of light, so he could make out only general details: a lithe figure, with a shoulder-length bell of blonde hair, and a strange way of carrying herself that suggested stiffness, perhaps arthritis, although surely she was too young for that.

She came forward again, into range of the porch light. Older than he had first thought, she wore torn and stained second-hand clothing, no coat, and an expression of grim determination. 'Doctor Jessup?' she said.

'Yes'm, that's my name.'

'I'm sorry to bother you, sir.' A trace of a southern accent; another hesitant step forward. 'I saw your shingle out at the end of the driveway...'

'You need a doctor?' he asked.

'I'm not sure. But I got a bad pain.'

'Well, come on in and let's have a look.' She didn't move. 'Don't worry about some big old bill, now. When someone needs my help, I provide it. The Good Book says to do no less. Come on in.'

Still she dithered. Perhaps, he thought, her issue was less financial than ethical. During his years in Delphos, he had helped more than one young woman end an unwanted pregnancy. Word had gotten out, and now those in need of his services kept showing up.

'Come on in,' he said again, more gently. 'Whatever it is, ol' Ralph can set you right. And you don't need to tell me anything more than you want to. I promise.'

At last, as he held the front door, she came inside. She walked eccentrically, dragging one leg. 'You live here alone?' she asked.

'All by my lonesome, ever since my Lillian passed on. But don't you worry, darlin' – I'm one of the good guys.' He switched on a lamp and then faced her candidly. 'What seems to be the trouble?'

Inside the parlor, beneath the lamplight, her uncertainty had vanished. She was prettier than he had realized, if too thin. And in her right hand...

...she held a gun.

One hour later, he straightened from the makeshift operating table.

He wiped a strand of sweaty gray hair from his eyes. 'That's about all I can do for you,' he said groggily, 'unless you'll let me take you the hospital.'

For a long minute, his patient didn't respond. Ralph Jessup felt a flicker of hope, although the desire violated every tenet of the Hippocratic Oath he had sworn, that the girl had passed during the procedure. Then her right hand, still holding the .32 pistol, stirred. 'No hospitals,' she said thickly.

As she struggled to a sitting position, he backed away. Her resilience baffled and astounded him. She had categorically refused painkillers, turning away even a glass of Ripple; yet all during the operation she had stayed awake, watching him as he worked. He had patched a bullet wound, well on the way to infection despite a previous sloppy effort to repair it, and a broken leg, which evidently had been poorly set some days before, and had since started healing wrong.

Once she had drawn herself up, Jessup tried again. 'Listen: that's a patch-up job I did. We bought you some time. But you need a hospital, missy. They've got to look inside you, see the extent of the damage. I just plain don't have the equipment here.'

Her striking turquoise eyes found his face.

'Listen,' he said again. 'I don't know any other ways to say it. If you don't get to a hospital, you're dancing with the devil. All we've got to do is pile into my truck and I can have you—'

The gun barked, silencing him.

She searched the house.

In a cigar box beneath an upstairs bed she found sixty-five dollars and fifty-three cents, which she pocketed. In an adjoining bathroom she found iodine, Goody's Headache Powder, Neo-Aqua-Drin lozenges, Alka-Seltzer, Pepto Bismol ... except for the iodine, all worthless.

She vomited into the sink. Her belly churned; the bandage around her shoulder dotted red even through the gauze. Leaning against the edge of the porcelain, she fought to remain conscious. The old sawbones had spoken the truth: sooner or later, she would need a hospital.

But not yet. Not until she had made more distance.

She spent a few queasy seconds studying her reflection in the cabinet's mirror. At the moment, she was no longer Elisabeth Grant. But she not yet become someone else. She was between identities. Perhaps she had reverted to Elisabeth Hübener, of Wittlich, in the Rhineland – not the cool exquisite beauty molded to perfection by Karl Schnibbe, but the pale, sickly original

327

model, fussed over *ad nauseum* by her mother, shunned and despised by everybody else.

After a few seconds more, she moved on.

She kept searching, looking now less for things of value than for a comfortable place to spend the remainder of the night – traveling again without resting was out of the question. The back porch, with its cold fresh air and clear lines of sight, was tempting. But she would risk frostbite out here. Still: she could allow herself a moment.

Settling down onto an old-fashioned porch swing, she looked out across a pond scrummed with ice. Another mirror, she realized suddenly: this one reflecting a line of silhouetted black pines on the far bank. A distant loon called with enviable aplomb. The crisp smell of resin filled the night, summoning bitter-sweet memories of a long-ago Christmas.

After a few minutes a blustery wind picked up, creaking the hinges of the swing, coaxing a watery tear from one eye. She went back inside. Forsaking beds and couches, she chose a creaky old rocker from which she could easily slip out the back door if necessary. Pulling a hand-woven quilt across her lap, holding the gun with its two remaining bullets loosely in one hand, she closed her eyes.

The Blood Banner flapping, Karl Schnibbe uncompromising and uncompromised, ranks of soldiers goose-stepping in perfect unison down the Unter den Linden ... she could hear the rap-rap of their boots now. She smiled faintly. It was a sound filled with promise.

Libby, Josette had said, *sometimes I wonder*

about you.

She rubbed a hand over her face, pulling the features into a tragic mask. Then she forced her mind ahead. In the morning, she would keep moving. She would know her destination only when she reached it.

All paths, she thought, led somewhere.

She sat very still, wondering if that was really true, for a very long time.

EPILOGUE

ANACOSTIA

Trudy Zane wept.

Her father comforted her, patting her back as if burping a baby. The minister delivered a brief eulogy. Beneath a cold wind, Isherwood tried to balance on his cane while keeping hands jammed in coat pockets. A registrar and two gravediggers milled nearby, looking disinterested.

After the service, people lined up to toss dirt on the coffin. Philip Zane's infant son, passed back and forth between relatives, squalled and fretted. The turnout had been respectable but not tremendous. Isherwood could not help thinking that Zane deserved better.

Shortly thereafter, he found himself inside the nearest dark bar, telling himself he had come only to fill his growling belly. Funerals, his father had used to say, made a man want to eat and fuck. Neon signs blinked and buzzed in frosted windows. When the barkeep approached, Isherwood ordered a burger and a Moxie. Working down the soft drink in a few gulps, he ordered another and then staked out his territory: Zippo, crumpled prayer leaflet, cane, cigarettes, and baleful glare.

When his hamburger arrived, Isherwood pushed away the plate without touching it. Downing his second Moxie, he lit a cigarette instead. He looked at bottles lined behind the bar. They reminded him of glittering soldiers, preparing to mount an offensive. They would come in force, and his defenders, bristling in square, would successfully repel the first wave, and then the second ... but the enemy would keep coming. Without eternal vigilance, he risked being over-run.

Halfway through his next sickly-sweet pop, someone settled onto the bar stool beside him. Through a series of tacit clues, Isherwood endeavored to let the stranger know that he wasn't interested in conversation. But the man wouldn't take the hint. When the intruder ordered a vodka, Isherwood recognized the voice. Turning his head, he grunted acknowledgement.

The Chief took one of Isherwood's cigarettes. The travails of the previous weeks had left new grooves on the man's face ... but, of course, none of them had come through unscathed. 'Been trying to get in touch,' he said. 'You can be a hard man to track down.'

'Evy's back.'

'Making up for lost time, eh?'

'Something like that.'

'Glad to hear it.' Spooner picked a book of matches from a bowl on the bar, folded back the cover. 'I was hoping to ask you to swing by Treasury. We'll get the paperwork moving, strike that provisional from your status ... Consider yourself fully reinstated, Ish, whenever you're ready.'

Isherwood's response was slow. Four days since his last pill, and five weeks since his last drink, yet still he found himself stringing thoughts together listlessly. Dressing that morning for the funeral, he had lost himself in a dark valley, staring into space for ten full minutes in the midst of putting on a sock. 'Appreciate that,' he said at last.

'Well, hell; we can use you. Ike's on his way back to Washington.' Spooner's cigarette described a strained little circle, perhaps at the thought of all the protection Eisenhower might still require. 'He says Key West was as bad as Gettysburg. Now he needs a vacation from his vacation. I told him, be careful what you wish for; he'll have his hands full, gearing up for the convention.'

'He's decided?'

'Funny thing. Rumors aside, he was on the fence right up until the end ... but now he's committed. Won't give his enemies, he told me, the satisfaction of doing their job for them.'

Isherwood nodded. In the end, it had proved impossible to shield Eisenhower from the truth. Of course, the President had slammed a lid on the story. The chief executive had to maintain the illusion of invulnerability. Agents Zane and Whitman had officially died in the line of duty – their wives would get the pension – but files with details had been permanently misplaced.

A black-and-white television hanging in one ceiling corner played footage of Soviet trucks carrying missiles. Isherwood watched for a moment, and then looked away. 'The girl?' he

332

asked.

Spooner shook his head. 'No match from AFIS, and nothing else to work with. She's plain gone. Same with Bolin. Dead ends and blind alleys, whichever way we turn.' He ground out his cigarette and pushed the ashtray a symbolic inch away. 'Everything's self-contained; nothing leads out. The puppet masters covered their tracks well. Only thing we've turned up is the missing housemaid from the farm. Found her beneath a bed, once she started to go rotten.'

Isherwood smoked hard, exhaled a clock spring of smoke.

'But look at it this way, pal: the glass is more than half-full. The President's alive. That's what counts.' But the Chief sounded dubious, as if trying to convince himself, and the nuanced look on his face belied the simple confidence of his words. 'And the DA finessed that thing. You'll have to present before the grand jury, but it's just a formality – they'll go for necessary force.'

A few empty moments passed. The neon signs flickered and droned. Spooner pulled the ashtray closer again and helped himself to another cigarette. 'You know who the real winner is in all this? Dick Nixon. Ike's got cold feet, after all he's been through, so he'll stick with a known quantity – Nixon stays on the ticket after all.'

The bartender glided by, read the situation, and kept going. Spooner let the man get some distance and then, with sudden feeling, laughed. 'Hell, old buddy,' he said, 'that was a close one, huh?'

Isherwood closed his eyes briefly.

'Scared the hell out me, I don't mind telling you. When you can't trust your own ... That's how they got Caesar. It's the ones inside the wheelhouse you've got to look out for.'

'We dodged a bullet,' said Isherwood.

'Pun intended, I trust.' Spooner took out his wallet. 'Listen, I'm heading back to Treasury. You want to tag along?'

After a few seconds Isherwood slipped off the bar stool, collecting his talismans – leaflet, cigarettes, Zippo – and reaching for his cane.

'Heading home,' he said. 'Thanks anyway.'

Evelyn snored lightly beside him.

He smiled slightly in the darkness. The snoring would mortify her, had she been aware of it. And it would keep him awake, as would the lack of space in the bed – after so many nights spent alone, sharing a blanket again was taking some getting used to. But it was the kind of getting used to he didn't mind.

Plink.

His gaze traced a network of cracks in the ceiling. Restlessly, he conjured pictures from the mosaic of ragged lines: boiling oceans, cities of ash, expanding mushroom clouds; corkscrews, bottles, Martini glasses, whiskey tumblers, vials of pills; Zane's squalling wife and baby, the rifle sticking from the top of the silo like a steel snout, the slow tumble of girl and gun falling together off the platform. At length, he closed his eyes.

Plink.

Without whiskey, the wheels in his mind never stopped turning. When he did eventually lapse into sleep, dreams would be waiting – abstruse and perplexing skeins which left him feeling, upon waking, slightly unmoored from reality, one step to the left. But at least he could not recall the details of the dreams during the days. Small favors.

Plink.

He sighed, flipping over. That afternoon he had spent two hours wrestling with wrenches and washers and screwdrivers, but his victory had been short-lived. The bathroom faucet was leaking again. In the morning, he would redouble his efforts. There would be time to kill between morning and afternoon doctors' visits. Until then...

Plink.

...Well, he wasn't sleeping anyway. And Evelyn seemed somehow able to snore right through it.

His mind kept wheeling. He yawned: tired, beyond a doubt, but unable to switch off his troubled brain. Turning over again, he laid an arm across Evelyn's quiescent form. He remembered the Chief's words from what seemed like very long ago. *There's no lack of men in this country today sitting just where you are now – dying for a drink, and trying to get the hell past whatever happened over there. There's no shame in it.*

In fact, he thought, there must be more of us now than ever. Korea had produced a new crop of veterans, and thus a new groundswell of baffled wives and families back home. And fresh schisms had opened, in the so-called United States of America, along other fronts: between the big bands and a colored wildman from New Orleans named Little Richard; between the Supreme Court, declaring that state laws establishing separate schools for blacks and whites were unconstitutional, and a determined resistance led by Senator Harry F. Byrd; between the parents of countless new babies born after the war, and those who had to find schoolrooms and teachers to accommodate the sudden boom. At least there was comfort to be taken from the idea that, in passing his sleepless nights staring at cracks in the ceiling, he had company.

He yawned again. Eventually, he would need to figure out what to tell Spooner about the job offer. But for now, he still had time.

He sank farther – away from consciousness, away from Evelyn's snoring and the leaking faucet, away from thoughts of past and future – to a place where dreams and nightmares still churned but, upon waking, went unremembered.

* * *

From The *Anacostia News*. Wednesday,

September 12, 1956, Page 28:

Anacostia births:
ISHERWOOD – to the wife of Francis K.,
610 Good Hope Street; a son.